THE WILD BIRD

Trying to put an unhappy love affair behind
her, Elizabeth determines to throw all her
energies into running her new home, the
beautiful historic estate in Sussex bequeathed to
her by a rich lonely old man. It was his dying
wish that she should care for it and all the
possessions he had loved. But from all sides she
meets opposition and hostility. The local
people are unfriendly and give her a chilly
reception. The staff think her too young, too
brusque in her dealings. And Archer Hewitson,
who manages the estate, sees in her the end of
his supremacy and peace. He wonders how long
he can put up with her interfering ways. It is to
be a heartbreaking and lonely job for Elizabeth.

The Wild Bird

Denise Robins

CORONET BOOKS
Hodder Paperbacks Ltd., London

Printed and bound in Great Britain for Coronet Books,
Hodder Paperbacks Ltd,
St. Paul's House, Warwick Lane,
London, E.C.4
By Hunt Barnard Printing Ltd.,
Aylesbury, Bucks.

ISBN 0 340 15810 7

CHAPTER 1

THROUGH the casement windows of Elizabeth Rowe's studio in Chelsea the faint orange of the sunset struggled to illuminate the canvas on which Elizabeth was daubing an impossible vamp with enormous eyes, wickedly slanting, and a wicked red mouth.

Elizabeth, a slender figure in her blue smock, crouched on the stool before the easel. She smiled at the ludicrous woman she was creating in oils for sheer amusement. She was not seriously at work.

Soon the warm orange of the sunset faded. The long, charming studio with its low ceiling and corner chimney-place filled with pale, mauvish shadows. Elizabeth threw down her brush, yawned, and rose. From a large cushion on the floor a splendid Dalmatian also yawned.

'Grock,' said Elizabeth, 'I'm bored and so are you. Lilian's late for tea and Guy hasn't turned up for his quiet half-hour. I'm peeved!'

Grock sat down again and thumped a tail hard on the polished floor. He blinked with lazy golden eyes at his mistress. He would have liked to suggest a walk on this fine April afternoon, but he knew full well that Elizabeth would not leave the studio while there was a chance of Guy coming. Grock was aware that nowadays the man named Guy took first place in Elizabeth's heart. He was the only person in the world of whom Grock was jealous and with whom he refused to make friends.

Elizabeth walked to a mirror which hung against the wall opposite the window. She took a small comb from her pocket and ran it through her hair, then grimaced at herself.

'Ugly!' she said.

The reflected Elizabeth smiled back at her.

She was not ugly. She was small and perhaps too thin. But her eyes, darkly brown, were bright and beautiful. The softness of her lips was a contradiction to the hardness, the resolution of her pointed chin. She was twenty-two and looked about sixteen in her blue overall. Her dark, smooth hair was bobbed and cut in a straight fringe across her forehead.

'Ugly!' she repeated to the reflection in the mirror, and turned to the photograph of a girl; a misty, modern impression of a beautiful head and shoulders.

'There, Grock,' said Elizabeth, 'is true beauty. Why wasn't I born with a face like Lilian's? And why did Guy fall in love with me?'

Whereupon she smiled again, showing white, even little teeth. The smile made her face extraordinarily attractive. She stooped to caress the Dalmatian's absurd white head with its round black patches and soft, pinkish nose.

'You're the most beautiful thing in the world, Grock,' she whispered.

Grock sat on his haunches and blinked at her. The subject of beauty was less amusing to him than talks about walks or bones.

Elizabeth lit a cigarette. She strolled up and down the studio, humming. It was time that Guy was here. He had phoned to say he would be with her by tea-time. Lilian, who shared her studio, had just gone out to buy cream buns. She, too, ought to be here at any moment.

For over a year, Elizabeth and Lilian had shared this studio and tiny flat in Elbury Walk, Chelsea. Elizabeth had two hundred a year, which her father had left her, and the money which she made illustrating magazines and doing posters.

Lilian Maxwell had a hundred a year of her own and a 'flair' for clothes. She could design and make exquisite things. At the moment she was helping a cousin of hers to run a shop for hats and lingerie in Baker Street. She had been at school with Elizabeth, and, both of them having recently been left alone in the world, it had not taken them long to decide to run this little home together. They were the antithesis of one another, but were excellent friends, and enjoyed their Bohemian life. In funds one moment, 'broke' the next.

Guy Arlingham was a writer who had achieved some distinction with his pen. Elizabeth, until she had met him, had been inclined to scoff at romance and deny that she

6

was sentimental. She discovered from the hour that Guy fell in love with her and she with him that she was full of sentiment, even though she could not easily show it. She was passionately in love with him. She believed that he cared deeply for her. They had met at a Chelsea Arts Ball and known each other only a month before Guy asked her to marry him.

Lilian, in Elizabeth's opinion, had changed since the engagement. She was by nature an amiable, sweet-tempered creature. Lately she had become morose and silent – even sulky. Elizabeth supposed she was miserable because their jolly, intimate life together was soon to end – with her marriage. She was sorry. She loved Lilian. But she loved Guy much more.

It was a quarter to five and Elizabeth could not make out why she was not back; and why Guy, who had telephoned to say he would be here at four, had not arrived.

However, she did not worry. Having combed her sleek black head to her satisfaction, she put on the electric kettle. Lilian would be here at any moment. The gate-legged table by the fireplace was already laid for three.

Elizabeth dragged her easel and the vamp to one side and made some pretence to tidy up the studio. But she was not very tidy by nature, and loved the confusion of the room. The whole flat was beautiful and original. She hated the idea of leaving it even for Guy's much more magnificent flat in Victoria.

The two girls had saved for months to buy bits and pieces for the studio. There were two fine rugs on the floor; a low divan piled with cushions; an old oak dresser with pewter plates and some beautiful china. Some black and white sketches and two exquisite water-colours by a famous modern painter furnished the walls.

Elizabeth liked music. The portable gramophone and heap of records on the floor belonged to her. She avoided what she called 'high-brow stuff' and kept to light music. Most of the records were dance tunes. They often danced in the evening in the studio.

Lilian's uncle and guardian, who was a broker in Bombay, had sent her the lovely orange Bokhara silk which made the curtains framing the square-paned windows. And to Lilian belonged most of the decorative, multi-coloured cushions.

7

Elizabeth wandered to the windows and looked out at Elbury Walk. It was grey and misty in the April twilight. She loved Chelsea at this hour. It was mysterious and beautiful.

She wanted Guy to come. Hers was a complex nature. She appeared, on the surface, self-possessed and cool. She found it difficult to express herself or her feelings – but inwardly she was passionate, almost painfully sensitive, and full of sensibility.

She wanted Guy this evening more than she had ever wanted him. It seemed to her that the clasp of his arms and the warmth of his kisses were the most thrilling things in the world. Yet if he had been here beside her at the moment she could not have voiced these feelings. When she was most deeply moved she grew dumb.

Guy, who was excitable and showed it, often said:

'Why don't you tell me you love me? Go ahead. Tell me how much you care for me, little Lizbeth.'

'Little Lizbeth' was his name for her . . . that and 'Funny-one'. She supposed she was funny; must seem difficult to voluble, temperamental people like Guy. . . .

But she could only answer him by saying:

'I can't tell you. I just do care . . . that's all!'

The studio door opened. Elizabeth turned. It might be Guy . . . or Lilian. But it was a woman in hospital nurse's uniform who entered the room.

'Miss Rowe, could you slip upstairs to Sir James for a moment? He is asking for you,' she said. 'Your front door was open, so I took the liberty of creeping in.'

'That's all right,' said Elizabeth. 'I'll come. But I can't stay. I'm expecting Miss Maxwell back at any moment, and another visitor.'

'Well, even five minutes will do the poor old chap good,' said the nurse. 'You know how he loves you, Miss Rowe.'

Elizabeth nodded. She walked with the woman up to the flat above her studio. Sir James Willington was fond of her with the friendliness of a very old man . . . and he was dying. The doctors gave him a very few more days of life.

Elizabeth knew little of the old man's private affairs. He was a solitary eccentric being who had spent many years and much time and money on the poor in the East End of London. It was only since the summer that he had occupied the furnished flat upstairs. He seemed to prefer the seclusion and comparative poverty of it – for it was a mere attic, badly furnished by an impecunious artist – to his own home. The nurse said he was 'queer'. Elizabeth found him quite sane and liked his clear, broad outlook upon life. He had made no friends in the building or district other than herself. He seemed to like her. Every day he sent for her. He wanted her to sit by him, talk to him. She was touched by the pathos of his lonely philanthropic life and its still more pathetic close.

Today she found him a little more frail; more pathetic than usual. He was too ill to read. He seemed absorbed in his own thoughts. When Elizabeth in her blue smock, her face flushed from the exertion of running upstairs, appeared in the doorway of his bedroom a smile of pleasure spread over his face.

'How good of you, child,' he said. 'You are always kind to an old man.'

'It is not kindness. I thoroughly enjoy my talks with you, Sir James,' said Elizabeth. 'How are you?'

'Not too good,' he said. 'I haven't very much longer, Elizabeth. Sit down – just for a moment.'

She obeyed. He looked like some portrait she had seen of a Catholic Pope; frail and shrunken. His eyes were full of kindliness. She often wondered what history lay behind the old baronet; why he lived here alone and without the luxuries he might so easily afford; why he had never married; had no family and few friends to visit him. This afternoon, for the first time since their acquaintanceship, he enlightened her on this subject.

'Elizabeth,' he said. His voice was very tired. 'You have been the one, the only friend I have had for years. I like you, child. I admire your intelligence. I have found endless pleasure in talking to you – seeing through your young eyes. You are a modern. Well! Why not? I don't mind your short skirts, your cigarettes, your cocktails, your unconventionality. With it all you are a good child, a fine little woman, Elizabeth. Today I have been thinking a great deal of you. You are going to be married. I pray God this man, Guy Arlingham, will be worthy of you.'

'Too good for me,' she said instantly. 'Guy is wonderful, Sir James.'

'Even a good man can never be quite so wonderful as a good woman,' said the old baronet. 'You do not give love easily, Elizabeth. I know you. I have studied you, my child. Well, make sure you have given that fine heart of yours to the right man.'

'I am sure of it,' she said.

The old man sighed.

'Once I thought as you thought,' he said. 'Shall I tell you my story? I have never spoken of it to any living soul since . . . it happened. But now I am a dying man and you are my little friend. I would like to tell you.'

'Please do,' she said.

'Once,' he said, 'I was young . . . impulsive . . . spirited . . . like yourself. Does it seem possible? And I loved. I had never cared for any woman before. Her name was Gladys. She was a beautiful thing – fair – as fair as you are dark, Elizabeth. I believed in her, trusted her implicity. I swore to do great things for her. I gave her my whole heart and soul. Then, on the very night before our wedding, at a dance, I found her in the arms of a man whom I disliked and mistrusted. They were lovers. It was a bitter shock. Gladys had seemed a kind of angel to me. She married that man. I resolved from that hour to put my faith and love in no other living soul – to devote my riches to those who were poor and who suffered. That is my history in a nutshell. That is why I have been a recluse for such years. My home in Sussex is full of historic interest. A lovely Tudor house. It is called "Memories". But I have never lived in it for longer than a week or two at a time. It has been in the hands of my housekeeper and my estate-agent, Archer Hewitson. I had meant to take Gladys there as my wife. From the moment of my disillusionment I wanted to see a little of it as possible . . .'

He paused for breath, then continued:

'I have told you about Gladys only to prove to you, child, that the being one loves and trusts absolutely is apt to betray one's faith. Don't love your Guy too much. You might get hurt, dear.'

Elizabeth leaned forward and took one of the old man's hands in hers.

'Sir James, I am terribly sorry you had such a rotten experience,' she said. 'But honestly, don't worry. I mean,

Guy is devoted to me.'

'He ought to be,' said Sir James. 'God forgive him if he fails you. Until I met you, Elizabeth, I made no friends, save among the poor in the slums where I knew I could find sincerity. But you're sincere. You have fine truthful eyes. Yet Gladys had beautiful eyes . . . ' He broke off, sighing painfully. 'Who can tell . . . who can guarantee to pick the Jewel of truth from the rubbish-heap of lies and deceit. . . . '

Elizabeth kept silence. The poor old man was rambling a bit. Poor Sir James! So the disloyalty of the woman he had loved in his youth was responsible for his hermit's life. It was very sad.

His gloom seemed suddenly to communicate itself to her. She excused herself from his bedside. She felt sure that Guy would be down in her studio now. And she wanted him. This ache and need for his arms and lips had been strong upon her all day. She wanted him all the more in this hour. Her cheerful spirit had been damped by the old man's melancholy.

She promised to visit him in the morning.

As she left the dim bedroom she heard him muttering to himself.

'Hearts never break . . . no, so the poets say . . . they do not break . . . they only sting and ache . . . and the best song of all is the one that says, "Give crowns and pounds and guineas, but not your heart away".'

Elizabeth went down to her flat. The front door was still open. She walked into the tiny hall shivering a little with depression and the sudden chill of the April dusk. She wanted Guy and the cheery warmth of the studio.

She heard voices and her eyes brightened. Guy had come. Lilian, too. That was Lilian's rich voice. She was full of richness and colour, with her contralto voice and Titian hair and full tall figure.

The studio door was ajar. Elizabeth advanced with a smile and a gay word on her lips. But the smile and the welcoming word died. She stood still, hands in the pockets of her smock. Her face grew suddenly scarlet.

Guy and Lilian were in the studio obviously under the impression that they were alone and unobserved. The man stood with his back to the tall chimney-piece. He was leaning slightly against it. The girl was in his arms.

11

Just for one petrifying instant Elizabeth saw her fiancé and her best friend through a haze . . . a kind of red mist . . . red with primitive anger and jealousy . . . and the bottom was knocked from her world.

The haze passed. She saw the couple clearly. They were lovers.

Even in the bitterness of that moment she thought vaguely what a handsome couple they made. Guy Arlingham was a tall man of the Saxon type; fair, ruddy, blue-eyed. He was always debonair and carefully groomed. An electric light had been turned on just behind him, and threw up the gold tints in his hair. Elizabeth had loved that gold head of Guy's with the artist's pride as well as the woman's passion.

Lilian was a match for him . . . lovely Lilian with her flame-coloured mass of hair which she had never bobbed and was plaited about her head. Her long white throat was tilted backwards, her lips raised with abandon to his. And now Elizabeth knew why her friend had changed, had sulked, had avoided her. She loved Guy. Guy loved her. He was saying so.

'It's the very dickens, darling. I don't know what to do. I know I made a mistake about Elizabeth. But she's such a dear I don't want to hurt her – let her down – yet I do love you – with a most terrible love, Lilian. It's driving me mad.'

'And I love you, Guy,' said Lilian in her deep voice. 'And it's driving me mad.'

For an agonising moment Elizabeth watched and listened and then was afraid that Guy was going to kiss Lilian. That was more than she could bear.

She rushed into the studio noisily, like an awkward school-boy anxious to avert a disaster, and said:

'Oh, don't . . . don't either of you go mad. There's no need . . . no need at all, you know!'

12

CHAPTER II

Guy and Lilian drew apart. They were startled by Elizabeth's sudden noisy entrance into the studio. Lilian, her face
scarlet, moved to the other side of the mantelpiece. She
gripped it with her hand, and leaned her head on the curve
of her arm.

The man put a hand up to his neck, straightened his tie,
coughed, and glanced at Elizabeth uneasily.

It was very painful to Elizabeth, who loved candour
beyond all things. Guy's look was so furtive. The fact that
these two for whom she had cared so deeply, and whom she
had trusted, had been lovers behind her back, hurt her as
much as the loss of Guy. It humiliated her. She had given
him her whole affection, believing that he wanted it. And
all the time he had wanted Lilian. Yet only a day ago he had
asked the same old question: 'How much do you love me,
little Lizabeth?' She supposed that he had asked it out of
guilt or curiosity, but not tenderness. It was horrible.

She dug her hands in the pockets of her smock and looked
at the floor. She heard her own voice as from a distance; a
strange, thin voice:

'Don't let's go off the deep end about this. Let's talk it all
over quietly – please.'

Arlingham cleared his throat.

'Elizabeth – good God – I – look here – '

'Oh, Elizabeth, what can I say to you?' broke in Lilian,
turning to her friend. 'You must think me an absolute
rotter. I'm so sorry. I couldn't help loving Guy. I tried to
fight it – we both did – '

Elizabeth clenched her hands until the nails hurt her
palms. She was quite white. She was suffering horribly. It
would have made it so much easier if she could have burst
into tears and said a lot of words like these two could say;
'Oh, God,' and 'Oh, my God,' and make a great show of
grief; of regret. But she wasn't built like that. She had never

13

been like that. The more she was hurt the more reticent she became. It was as though pain drove from her the faculty of speech – of demonstration. Always, from a child, she had been incapable of showing what she felt. That touch of the boy in her made her set her teeth and refuse to 'squeal'. But it made things harder. She could scarcely bear to stay here in the studio and talk to the man who had been her lover and the girl who had been her friend.

When she spoke it was quite quietly:

'Please don't – apologise – either of you. After all, these things happen. It's only right I should know. It would have been terrible to find out – afterwards.'

'Yes, of course,' said Lilian, biting her lips.

Guy glanced at her quickly, then looked away again and tapped his foot on the ground. Elizabeth's heart ached while she listened to that tap, tap of Guy's foot on the polished floor. Such a silly, familiar little thing to make one's heart ache. But it was so typical of Guy. Whenever he was irritated or worried he tapped his foot.

Arlingham did not like being worried. He was a spoiled darling of the gods. He was used to admiration. Men liked him; found him witty and clever. Many women fell in love with him. He shone in a crowd; always the centre of it; the chief attraction. He enjoyed playing to the gallery. He was an egotist, but to amuse and attract people he would go to limitless trouble. A form of egotism, because he relished the admiration he received in return for his trouble. He liked people to be happy. But still more he liked to feel they were grateful. One of the chief attractions in Elizabeth at the commencement of their engagement had been her absorption in him, her heart-whole devotion; the way those bright dark eyes of hers dwelt on him in passionate appreciation.

But later, as her love, her passion for him increased, the outward signs of it seemed to dimnish. She seemed to grow inarticulate. She worshipped in silence. That bored Guy. He preferred a demonstrative woman. The irritation caused by Elizabeth's reticence gradually affected his whole feeling for her.

And then he turned his attention to Lilian. Lilian, who was not only beautiful, but voluble – capable of telling him frequently that she adored him. All of which was gratifying

14

to Guy. She was, perhaps, a little stupid and unimaginative in comparison with Elizabeth, who had a quick wit and real intelligence. But she was truly charming to look at; adorable to make love to; and there it was.

He would never admit that any disaster in which he was concerned was his own fault. He was even now silently blaming Elizabeth for what had happened. He stared down at her and scowled. He looked like a handsome schoolboy glowering at a smaller boy with whom he is about to have a fight, aware that the contest is unfair.

'Oh, look here!' he broke out. 'We can't have a three-handed discussion. Elizabeth – I must speak to you alone.'

Lilian moved away from the fireplace toward the door.

'Yes, please – I'll go,' she said.

'No, don't!' said Elizabeth.

She felt sudden panic. She dreaded being left alone with Guy. She shrank from an intimate talk with him. She knew him so well. He would be emotional. That would make things harder for her. She would want to throw herself into his arms and cry and cry. And she couldn't. She would much rather have run away and hidden herself like an animal that creeps into a corner to die. She had loved him so much. She still loved him much too much. One couldn't change in a moment; an hour. Sometimes one never changed. She was horrified at the prospect of continuing all her life to love Guy – Guy, who would be married to Lilian.

Lilian left the studio. As soon as the door closed Arlingham recovered himself. He had been embarrassed by the presence of the two women. With Elizabeth alone he could deal. He walked to her side.

'My dear, what the devil can I say?' he began.

Elizabeth looked up at him. How very blue his eyes were. They were full of remorse. He was genuinely sorry about this. But it didn't make things any easier for her to bear.

'Give me a cigarette, Guy,' she said with difficulty.

He drew one out of his case and handed it to her. He took out his lighter and she lit the cigarette. He said in a slightly colder voice

'Perhaps you don't mind very much, after all.'

That was like a fresh blow on a raw place. The colour flamed into her cheeks. She took a swift breath of her cigarette and turned her head away so that he could not see

15

how her under-lip trembled.

'You – can't think that, Guy.'

Compunction smote him. She did care, of course. She was a queer little thing. He had always found her hard to understand. That was why he had turned to Lilian – Lilian, who was passionate and showed her passion. More human than Elizabeth. Elizabeth much too reserved – too controlled.

'Forgive me, my dear,' he said, all resentment gone from his voice. 'Damn it, I ought to be at your feet, begging your pardon.'

'I don't want you to be at my feet.'

'Elizabeth, look at me – come here – talk to me.'

She turned, but she did not go near him.

'Guy,' she said, 'there isn't much to be said. I release you from our engagement – of course.'

He saw her look down at her left hand. A small, square hand with thin, boyish fingers. The sort of hand that is vigorously scrubbed rather than manicured. On the engagement finger a beautiful opal flashed from milky rose to peacock blue; a wonderful changing stone in an old setting. She had chosen the ring. Guy had wanted to give her a more expensive jewel. But she had set her heart on an opal. She was not superstitious. Guy had said that opals were unlucky. But Elizabeth even now thought only of the immense happiness she had felt when he had given her that ring. The studio was blotted out in a mist for a moment. Then she blinked her eyes, took the ring from her hand, and gave it to him.

'Oh, don't do that keep it – please,' he said hastily.

'But I'd rather not, Guy. It doesn't mean anything any more.'

'Well, my dear, I can't take it – I simply can't.'

She put the ring in the pocket of her smock.

'Very well.' (Oh, if only her lips would stop quivering, she thought.)

He balanced himself on the arm of a chair opposite her. It was his turn to light a cigarette.

'Elizabeth, I feel I must just explain . . . I . . . my dear, I was terribly fond of you when we got engaged – I still am. But I think it would be rather a mistake for us to marry.'

'I expect you're right, Guy. I'm sure you are.'

He gave her a quick, shamed look. He felt suddenly

16

humble. There are times when the egotist likes to humble himself, so long as he is still in the limelight.

'I don't think I'm good enough for you, anyhow. You're such a little brick – I do admire you tremendously.'

'That's scarcely a compliment to Lilian.'

'Of course, she's wonderful. And she – she understands me better than you do.'

'You don't want a lot of understanding, Guy.'

That worried him. It was a slightly contemptuous remark. And from Elizabeth . . . who he thought had adored him. He coughed and frowned.

'Well, you've got very high ideals, haven't you, my dear?'

'Guy, must we discuss my ideals or plunge into an analysis of the affair?'

'Oh, you are so difficult to talk to!' he groaned.

'I'm not, Guy. But I can't stand being dissected, and I don't want to lay you and Lilian on the operating-table either. Let's just accept plain truths. Facts, if you prefer it. Lilian is more suited to be your wife than I am. I realise that. I quite understand it – honestly, Guy, I think she must be much, much more attractive to men than I am. I'm very fond of her, myself. And I think she's beautiful. I hope you'll be awfully happy.'

The generosity of this speech moved him. He was not a sincere person. He was governed largely by emotions. He enjoyed a sensational moment. He acted most of the time without being conscious that he was playing to the gallery. But before the candour and generosity of Elizabeth he lost all inclination to act and became sincere.

'My dear, you *are* a brick,' he said.

She smoked without speaking again for a moment. She could not help looking at that handsome head of his. Guy had such nice hair. And it came upon her with a devastating sense of loss that she would never touch that bright gold hair again; never again snuggle into his arms and be content.

He had said: 'Perhaps it doesn't matter much to you . . . ' He took it for granted that she did not feel the passion and grief of her loss because she preferred not to fling herself into his arms and beg him not to leave her.

She could not bear another moment in the studio alone with him. She pitched her cigarette-end into the fireplace

17

and tried to smile. She was afraid that if she stayed the tears would come.

'I don't think there's anything else to be discussed, Guy. If you'll excuse me, I'll go out. I want a walk. You stay and have tea with Lilian.'

He stood up and came toward her.

'Wait, Elizabeth. Say you forgive me.'

She dug her teeth into her lower lip. Why must he insist on drama? Why did he want to hurt her even more badly than she was already hurt by making her cry?

'Of course I do.' Her voice broke. 'Be happy, Guy. So long.'

'Lizbeth, I – '

He broke off abruptly, shrugged his shoulders, and turned back to the fire. He was baffled. He could not penetrate her reserve, and it was impossible to show her, in his own way, how sorry he was. He would have liked to have taken the forlorn little figure in his arms and kissed and comforted her. He could deal with a woman who wept in his arms. But Elizabeth and her reserve passed his comprehension.

She walked out of the room and quietly closed the door.

'Damn!' said Guy, and sat down on the arm of the chair and waited for Lilian to come back.

CHAPTER III

Elizabeth walked into Lilian's bedroom. She found her lying face downwards on the bed, sobbing passionately.

Now, why Lilian should sob, Elizabeth could not understand. She had won Guy, not lost him. Why spoil her beauty by crying? It exasperated Elizabeth. Her own nerves were on edge, and these people did not help her to fight her battle. They showed such a lack of self-control.

She walked to the bed.

'Lil dear, please stop crying and go to Guy. He's waiting for you.'

Lilian sat up, a handkerchief pressed to her nose, the tears gushing from her eyes. Her hair was a tangled mass.

'Oh – Elizabeth . . . I'm so m-miserable!' she said in an anguished voice.

'But why, my dear? You ought to be frightfully happy. Guy and I have discovered our mistake and he's going to marry you. What's the trouble now?'

'You only s-say that,' sobbed Lilian. 'You love him – you said the other night how terribly you were in love with him.'

Elizabeth's face grew more than ever elfin under the straight fringe of her hair. She was glad the bedroom was dark and that Lilian could not see her plainly. She was shivering.

'Please,' she said. 'Don't remind me of that.'

'But it's true,' said Lilian. 'And I feel a beast – I've taken him from you.'

'My dear old thing, don't be dramatic about it. You and Guy are bent on making a scene. I don't want to make one. You couldn't help taking him from me, could you? One doesn't deliberately do these things. It's quite all right, I assure you.'

Lilian stood up, wiped her eyes, and walked to the electric light. She switched it on. Immediately Elizabeth averted her face. But Lilian walked up to her and put an

19

arm around her small, erect figure.

'Elizabeth – darling – forgive me. You've been such a brick to me since we took this flat together. And I haven't paid you back very decently, have I?'

Elizabeth set her teeth.

'She can't help it any more than Guy,' she thought. 'They must be frightfully emotional. They are lucky in a way. I just can't, that's all. . . . But I want to lie down and die.'

Aloud she said wearily:

'It's all right, my dear. I've enjoyed sharing the studio with you very much. We've had some good times. So far as Guy is concerned, it would have been a hundred times worse for me if I'd found out after we were married that he preferred you.'

'I know,' said Lilian. 'But it's heart-breaking enough as it is. I feel a swine. Oh, life is damned unfair, Elizabeth.'

Elizabeth wriggled out of Lilian's embrace. She positively shrank from being touched or kissed by anybody at the moment. She never did care for demonstrations of affection from her women friends. Tonight she could not bear it. She wanted to be left alone.

'Hearts do not break . . . they sting and ache . . . ' She remembered old Sir James Willington's quotation. Suddenly she laughed.

'The breaking hearts theory is all rot, Lilian,' she said. 'Now, my dear, *do* wash your face and go to Guy.'

'What are you going to do? Won't you have tea with us? Oh, Elizabeth – '

'I really couldn't sit down and chew a bun with you both, although I assure you I'm feeling quite friendly toward the pair of you,' said Elizabeth, deliberately flippant. 'I'm going out for a walk with Grock.'

Lilian stared at her dismally. She did not quite know what to make of Elizabeth.

'You are funny,' she said.

'So Guy says, but I don't feel at all funny,' said Elizabeth. 'So long, Lil. See you later. I'll enjoy a walk with Grock.'

She walked out of Lilian's bedroom into her own. She took off her blue smock and put on a tweed coat and felt hat. While she dressed she hummed to herself . . . no particular tune . . . just a little droning noise. She felt she must do something. She did not want to think . . . think about Guy and Lilian. She refused to break down and cry.

When she was dressed she had to pass the studio in order to go to the front door. She whistled for Grock, who was in the kitchen, where he slept. The Dalmatian padded out to her, wagging his tail and blinking at her with eager eyes. Hat and coat on mistress meant walk. Good!

'Come on, old boy,' said Elizabeth.

The studio door was ajar and somehow Elizabeth's gaze dragged toward it. The instant she looked she regretted it. White-hot pain jabbed at her. Guy was there, standing by the fire, and Lilian was in his arms, crying (happily now, Elizabeth supposed). Her head was on his shoulder.

'Oh, Guy,' said Elizabeth to herself. 'Oh, *Guy*!'

She must not think of him as her lover again. He would never again ask her in his teasing way if she loved him. Nor would she hear him call her 'Little Lizbeth'. 'Little Lizbeth' was dead. A new Elizabeth survived who would never give her heart away again.

She stopped to pat Grock's head. He licked her hand furiously with his warm tongue. And then she shed her first tears — tears that forced themselves between the lids and pelted hotly down her cheeks.

She said in a strangled voice:

'Grock . . . Grock, you won't ever be fonder of anyone else than you are of me, will you? Oh, *damn*, Grock . . . I can't *bear* crying . . . !'

She marched out of the flat with the Dalmatian trotting beside her, his ears cocked. When the front door closed behind them he bounded forward into the road barking at nothing just for the sheer joy of being out.

The April night was dark and misty. There were no stars in the sky. Elizabeth lit a cigarette. She smoked fiercely as she walked; hands in the pockets of her coat. And while she walked and smoked the tears kept on chasing down her cheeks and her lips trembled so that the cigarette nearly dropped out of her mouth.

But she did not stop. She walked on doggedly, down to the Embankment where the lamps looked like great soft yellowish blobs of light in the spring mist and the river moved slowly.

After she had walked for half a mile she stopped to throw away her second cigarette-end and took the packet of

21

Players from her pocket. Grock trotted at her heels more circumspectly. His first exuberance of spirits had died down.

'I'm smoking too much,' thought Elizabeth. 'And I must get some more cigarettes on the way home.'

She no longer cried. The tears dried on her face. Her throat was dry. But her lips were firm again.

'I think we've gone far enough, Grock,' she said to the dog. 'We'll cut along home now.'

She turned her steps toward the part of Chelsea which was home. She felt better for the brisk walk. And the Embankment soothed her. She liked it. She loved old London. In her most restless moods she felt in tune with the hum and throb of the great city. The lights, the buildings, the traffic, the crowds that surged through the streets, were all familiar and friendly. She had been born and bred in the town. But sometimes she felt a desire for the country. . . . She had even contemplated living in the country. She would not mind the loneliness. Until she had met and fallen in love with Guy Arlingham she had never depended on anybody for her happiness. It had seemed to her a mistake. A contented nature from childhood, she had made her own happiness. She told herself now that she had grown too dependent on Guy for the delights of life. In consequence, he had been taken from her. And the loss of him hurt horribly.

As she walked homeward she decided that she would never care for any living soul, man or woman, as she had cared for Guy. It was too precarious; too agonising – this thing called love.

'Give crowns and pounds and guineas, but not your heart away – '

Those lines came from one of Housman's poems. How right he was! It was advice worth taking, she decided in the bitterness of this hour.

She remembered the serenity of the days before she had met Guy. She had 'jogged along' on her £200 a year, sharing the studio with Lilian happily; taking the ups and downs of life without worrying much about anything. She had met various men whom she liked, but none had roused passion in her until Guy had come along with his attractive personality; his handsome face. During her engagement to him she had learned the raptures of love; of loving. At times she had been almost afraid of the emotion that his hands and lips roused in her. But the difficulties and anxieties attached to love – to any love affair – had not escaped Elizabeth. To love a man, to be engaged to be married to him, meant an end of freedom and of spiritual as well as physical independence. So Elizabeth had found it. Guy, the typical male, had wanted to possess her utterly . . . her thoughts as well as herself. And she had found it hard to surrender quite so completely as he desired. She had loved him. But something within her had always held back . . . refused to submit.

That reserve . . . that holding back of something both in mind and body . . . what was it?

'Just something that belongs to myself,' she thought. 'I'm not a bit surprised, now I come to think it over, that Guy fell in love with Lilian. She can just take herself in both hands and throw herself at him. That's what he wants. I wanted to do it. But I couldn't. Perhaps I never shall be able to do it with anybody on earth.'

When she reached the flat in Elbury walk she felt very little better. There was nothing to look forward to now that Guy had deserted her. Nothing. But nobody must know the horrid pain of hurt love and hurt pride which niggled inside her all the time.

She was relieved to find that Guy and Lilian had finished tea and gone out. Lilian had left a note for her friend on the mantelpiece.

'Guy wanted to take me out to dinner and we were sure you would not mind. I'll be back at eleven. Leave the key under the mat. Oh, darling, we're frightfully happy. Try to forgive us.
'Lil.'

Elizabeth read this twice, then twisted it into a lighter and with it lit her fifth cigarette. She crouched back on a hassock in front of the studio fire. She hugged her knees with her arms. Grock, tired after his walk, stretched himself on the rug beside her, head upon his paws.

'I'm glad they're frightfully happy,' she thought, 'And I wish they wouldn't keep asking to be forgiven.'

She sat like that without moving for a long, long while, staring into the heart of the fire. Then she began to feel hungry, and she remembered she had missed her tea. It was time she thought about supper. She and Lilian usually had

23

eggs or sardines or a cold pie, which they got for themselves, and Mrs. Harridge, the daily 'char' who cleaned the flat, washed the dishes up in the morning.

Elizabeth stood up. She put her hands on her hips and stared round the studio. It was very quiet and very lonely. She swallowed very hard. There was such a lump in her throat.

'I really don't want any food – yet I must eat, Grock,' she said to the dog. 'And you do, I'm sure. Come on, old fellow, let's have our bone. What's the use of sitting here moping?'

While Guy Arlingham and Lilian drank to a new love and a new engagement at Taglioni's, Elizabeth and Grock shared their evening meal in the tiny kitchen of the flat.

CHAPTER IV

ELIZABETH was up early that next morning and in the studio working on a new poster before Lilian had even opened her eyes.

Soon after she started to paint, Sir James Willington's nurse came down for her.

'The old gentleman wants you, Miss Rowe,' she said. 'He's had a very restless night.'

Elizabeth laid down her brush, rose, and wiped her hands with a rag.

'Oh, I'm so sorry, nurse. Is he worse?'

'A good deal weaker,' said the nurse. 'I honestly don't expect he'll last more than a day or two now, you know. His heart is giving out.'

'Poor old dear,' said Elizabeth. 'What a lot of people in the slums will miss him . . . to say nothing of myself. I'm awfully fond of him.'

'He thinks the world of you, Miss Rowe.'

Elizabeth went upstairs with the nurse and took a chair beside the old man. He smiled and gave her one of his hands.

'My dear. Good of you to come.'

His voice was very feeble. Elizabeth could see that he was worse. She felt heavy-hearted. She did not want to lose this very good friend. She had lost so much . . . since yesterday.

Sir James said:

'Child, I was thinking so much about you through the night. Somehow I had a feeling all was not well with you.'

She did not want to sadden his last hours by telling him her troubles, but her cheeks flushed painfully.

'I – I'm all right,' she said.

The old man's eyes studied her. He shook his head.

'No, Elizabeth. What is it? What has happened?'

'Why do you think – '

'I know,' he interrupted. 'I've had a presentiment. Is it your lover, child?'

She braced herself to answer.

'If you must know, dear Sir James, my engagement is – over.'

'Ah!' he said. 'I knew it. And why?'

'Guy and Lilian Maxwell, who lives with me, have found out that they care for each other. But I assure you it's all right,' she added hastily, as she saw the look of distress that puckered the old man's face. 'I'm not – unhappy about it. They are really very well suited . . . more suited than Guy and I would have been.'

'Bravo, my dear,' said Sir James. He squeezed her hand. 'You've a lot of pluck. I'm very, very sorry. I know you loved that man. But I was half afraid something like this would happen. You were too good – too good for that fellow. Didn't I say so yesterday when you were up here? I said, "Make sure you are giving your fine little heart to the right fellow".'

'Don't – please,' she begged. 'I've fought it all out with myself, Sir James, and I don't want to be pitied.'

'Don't be afraid, my dear. I won't offer too much pity. In a way I'm glad. I like to think of you like a wild bird, Elizabeth – free – and yet – '

'What?' she said, smiling with an effort.

'When there's nothing to look forward to . . . nothing very much . . . it does hurt,' he muttered. 'When I found that my lovely Gladys didn't want me any more . . . ah me, how it hurt! But you're not going to break your heart, Elizabeth, because hearts do not break, do they?'

'Of course not,' she said. 'And now don't let's talk about me. Tell me how you feel.'

'My thoughts are all of you, Elizabeth. I'm forming a wonderful plan in my head.'

She thought he was rambling.

'What about, Sir James?'

'Now you are alone, Elizabeth – quite alone, aren't you? You haven't got marriage to think about, and Miss Maxwell will be leaving you to go to this man, won't she?'

'In time – of course.' Elizabeth was tight-lipped, but she felt the tears near to the surface when she was forced like this into thinking intimately about Guy and Lilian.

'What are you going to do?'

'I don't know in the least, Sir James.'

'You couldn't stay on in the flat alone.'

'I might.'

'Have you no relations in the world?'

'None. I am absolutely alone – have been since my father died.'

'H'm,' said the old man. He whispered to himself for a few seconds. Then he said to the girl, 'Would you like to live in the country, child?'

'I really don't know. I imagine I should like it.'

'You shall,' he said. The frail hand lying in her strong young fingers trembled. 'Elizabeth, you shall have a country home and everything you want in the world.'

'Sir James – what do you mean?'

'I mean I shall not die peacefully thinking of you fighting your battles alone downstairs – deserted by these two. I'm going to ensure the fact that you have a big interest in life. The interest of your own home. Elizabeth, would you like to own my home, "Memories"?'

Elizabeth flushed.

'Sir James!'

'Yes,' said the old man, obviously thrilled by the plans which were forming in his head. 'I would like to think of you there in my old home . . . mistress of "Memories" . . . of all my possessions.'

Elizabeth was embarrassed and frightened. What did the poor old man mean to do? Hastily she bent over him. She patted his hand.

'Try and rest, Sir James,' she said.

'I think I shall be able to rest when I have made my will,' he said. 'Elizabeth, child, I am going to leave all that I have in the world to you.'

'Oh, don't please!' she cried.

'Yes – everything. Will you be happy in my old home, Elizabeth? Will you promise to look after my house, my garden – all the things I loved and cared for when I was a little boy?'

Her cheeks were hot.

'Sir James – please – I couldn't accept any such offer – Sir James – please – '

'Little Elizabeth, don't refuse to grant my dying wish,' he broke in. 'I want you to have my possessions. I want you to love my people down there in Sussex. The windows of

"Memories" look over a wood and a lake. You will love it.'

'Yes, Sir James, but –'

'Listen to me, child,' broke in his weak, eager voice. 'Don't refuse me. I shall, I am sure, rest happily in my grave if I know that you are there in Sussex, looking after my home. I have no heir. I had intended leaving most of my money to charities.'

'Please do – ' she said in an agony of embarrassment.

'No – to you, Elizabeth. You shall have an interest in life – you shall be mistress of my home, and care for it and love my people. My housekeeper, Mrs. Martlet, has been with me twenty-five years. Keep her with you. And Archer Hewitson – my agent and secretary – keep him. He will look after your interest.'

'Sir James –' began Elizabeth again.

The old man closed his eyes. He fought for breath. She was afraid that he was dying and called for the nurse.

Sir James rallied sufficiently to send for his solicitor and make his last will and testament. . . .

And it was made in favour of Elizabeth Mary Rowe, of Elbury Walk, Chelsea.

The old man died on the following day. Elizabeth, to her horror, found herself with £10,000 a year and a magnificent estate in Sussex.

She received the news from Mr. Parnell, Sir James's solicitor, with a great deal more distress than pleasure. She was not a mercenary, and she had never wanted a great deal of money. And here she was plunged into unknown responsibilities. The possession of a huge house, money, property. She saw, of course, that this was what the dear, kind old man had wanted, that she should have something to think about, care for, now that her engagement with Guy was broken.

But Lilian, of course, had very different ideas about Elizabeth's good fortune.

'My dear, it's the most marvellous thing that's ever happened!' she declared when Elizabeth gloomily told her about Sir James's will. 'Ten thousand a year and this place "Memories", and a staff of servants waiting to receive you. My *dear*, what more could you want?'

'I didn't want nearly so much,' said Elizabeth with a sigh. 'I assure you, Lilian, I am dazed at the thought of it.'

Lilian eyed her enviously.

'I wouldn't be dazed, unless it was with joy. Any normal ordinary woman wants tons of money. Think what you'll be able to do . . . travel . . . see the world –'

'No,' interrupted Elizabeth. Her eyes were thoughtful. 'I shall have much too much to do at "Memories". It was Sir James's wish that I should look after his home and love his possessions. I shall stay there for the summer, anyhow, and paint.'

'All alone?'

'Probably,' said Elizabeth. 'And oh, lord, that reminds me, I've got an agent to tackle now. Mr. Archer Hewitson.'

'Archer Hewitson,' echoed Lilian. 'What will he be like, I wonder. What an unusual name – Archer.'

'No doubt Mr. Hewitson will be exceedingly angry that "Memories" is to have a new mistress who has really no right to her inheritance. I expect he'll depart at once.'

'Is he young or old?'

'Young, I believe. Mr. Parnell says he is very able and clever and was at Oxford. I understand that he is a gentleman . . . that he was getting all sorts of honours and distinctions at his college; then at the end of the war his father died bankrupt and the boy found himself facing the world without a penny and never having been taught a trade. Some time later, Sir James came across him accidentally and gave him a cottage on the estate and the agent's job. Jolly nice for Mr. Hewitson.'

'I shouldn't think he'll desert his post just because you're going to live there,' said Lilian.

'We shall see. And now, my dear, if you don't mind, I must go away for a few days . . . down to Sussex. I've been left all this money and these things, and I must pull myself together and face my responsibilities. I must interview all the good folk down there and see how the land lies. I'd better wire to Mr. Hewitson to meet my train and take me over the estate.'

While Elizabeth was at the post-office, Guy Arlingham called to take Lilian out. He stood in the studio with her a few moments, smoking a cigarette and with one hand caressed her beautiful head. He inquired after the health of Elizabeth.

'Elizabeth, my dear,' said Lilian, 'is mad. She is bewailing the fact that the eccentric old soul upstairs has died and

29

left her his fortune.'

Guy raised his eyebrows.

'Indeed!'

Lilian told him the details, whereupon Guy whistled softly.

'Ye gods, what a windfall. Ten thousand a year and an estate in Sussex!'

'Yet she doesn't seem to appreciate it.'

'She's an amazing child.'

'I do hope she isn't going to be terribly unhappy and lose interest in life because she's lost you,' said Lilian.

She leaned against him and he held her close for a moment and kissed her. Her lips were warm and responsive. She appealed to all the warm sensuousness of his own nature. But while he caressed her his eyes looked over her head and saw Elizabeth – a new Elizabeth with the added attraction of £10,000 a year. It was the deuce of a lot of money. And money appealed to Guy Arlingham's nature. He liked the luxuries, the amusements which it could provide. He made a moderate income out of his books and his short stories. But he lived beyond his means. He was never without an overdraft. And it meant he must go on writing, writing; working perpetually to keep up his position. He had a service flat in the West End; a sports car; and expensive taste in clothes. His tailor's bill was huge. And when he married his wife would be an additional luxury. Marriage with Lilian would call for pecuniary sacrifices.

If he had waited twenty-four hours; controlled his passion for lovely Lilian; would he have given Elizabeth up? Elizabeth, the wealthy young woman with possessions.

Guy squirmed a little. He felt avaricious. Despicable. He wanted to kick himself. But he could not control his thoughts any more than he could control his emotions. Yesterday his new engagement had afforded him a great deal of pleasure. He felt angry and depressed because today the pleasure was spoiled – by the knowledge that Elizabeth had come into a fortune.

Lovely, stupid Lilian, who had very little mentality but plenty of charm and sweetness and a positive genius for looking exquisite, was much too passionately in love with Guy to credit him with such unworthy and mercenary reflections. She curved an arm about his neck and whispered:

'Darling! It's wonderful having you. But I can't help being sorry for Elizabeth.'

'I don't suppose she minds much,' he said.

Lilian failed to realise the cause of the gloom in those blue eyes of his. She clung to him happily and shut her eyes.

'There's a young man from Oxford, named Archer Hewitson, who is old Willington's estate-agent and protégé,' she murmured. 'Let's pray that poor, darling Elizabeth finds him very attractive and *vice versa,* and that a romance will develop so that they finally manage the estate hand in hand.'

Guy had nothing to say to that. But he suddenly felt that he would like to commit a murder. And Archer Hewitson seemed a probable victim for the crime.

Elizabeth, at the local post-office, sent a telegram to Mr. Archer Hewitson, c/o 'Memories', Maplefield, Sussex. She had had no idea where Maplefield was until she was informed at the post-office that it was close to Ashdown Forest and that the nearest station was Crowborough.

She made up her mind to go down to Maplefield tomorrow. Far from connecting Mr. Archer Hewitson with romance, she felt something akin to hostility when she thought of him. She was sure he would be hateful and that he would resent her sudden invasion of Sir James's place. He would look upon her as a designing young woman who had inveigled herself into the affections of an old, dying man.

'Grock,' she said to the Dalmatian who was her inevitable companion, 'I feel we shall have a fight with Mr. Archer Hewitson. Well, that adds to the excitement. I like a fight.'

Grock thumped his tail on the dusty floor of the post-office. He, too, liked a fight.

Elizabeth returned to her flat. She tried hard to concentrate on the thought of her new possessions and to feel that she was lucky because she had come into all this money. She could have a sports car, which she had always wanted, beautiful clothes to wear. She didn't care as much for clothes as Lilian did. But she was feminine enough to love really good silk undies. And she was very partial to well-made shoes and nice gloves and a well-tailored coat. She could have all those things now.

She was worth £10,000 a year and a Tudor house in Sussex.

Yet she could not summon up more than the faintest thrill about the whole business. It meant so little – without Guy. It would have been so glorious – to rush out and buy pretty clothes for him. So really thrilling to drive down to 'Memories' tomorrow with him and say:

'This is mine – and what is mine is yours!'

Poor old Sir James had left everything to her in order to give her a new interest in life; to make her forget her pain. But she could not forget. She wanted to fling aside these new riches and possessions and have her lover back again.

She walked into her studio with an aching heart and braced herself to face Guy.

CHAPTER V

GUY was walking up and down the studio, smoking, when Elizabeth came back from the post-office. Lilian was playing the gramophone. Elizabeth listened to the record – one Lilian had bought a few days ago. A sentimental song with a charming melody by Ivor Novello. The two girls had first heard it, together, when they went to a matinée of the *Symphony in Two Flats*. Elizabeth remembered saying:

'What a lovely bit of slop, Lil. . . . '

Slop . . . yes. She had laughed at it. Funny, but she couldn't laugh at it today. The words – no matter how stupid they might seem – hurt her somewhere inside.

> Give me back all the kisses that I gave,
> Give me back the life that you enchanted

The melody *was* haunting . . . Elizabeth had to bite rather hard on her lower lip when she walked into the studio and looked at Guy. He stubbed his cigarette end in an ashtray and stared back at her. She could hardly bear that look. It was so remorseful. She didn't want him to feel or show remorse. It made things so much more difficult for her.

> Give me back my heart.
> You won't be wanting it again

The 'lovely bit of slop' ended. Lilian took it off. Elizabeth smiled and said in an off-hand way

'Hello, you two. . . . '

And inwardly she was thinking:

'Give me back my heart . . . oh, yes, he won't be wanting it again. But it isn't so easy to get one's heart back. If only I could despise him and dislike him!'

But she didn't. She looked at Guy's fair, handsome head

and that amazingly good-looking face of his and felt that she loved him with a passion and yearning that were now quite shameful. He belonged to Lilian.

'Hullo, Elizabeth,' said Guy, breaking the ice. 'Lilian's just told me about your wonderful stroke of luck. I must congratulate you.'

'Thanks awfully,' she said, removing her gaze from him. 'I must go and make tea. . . . '

'No, it's my turn to make it, darling,' said Lilian, who felt that it would be a graceful thing to do. She was in a much more amiable frame of mind now that she had got the man she wanted.

She hastened from the studio. Elizabeth took off her hat, smoothed back a stray lock of hair, and balanced herself on the arm of a chair. Guy came forward with an open cigarette-case.

'No, thanks,' she said. 'I'm smoking too much. I'm going to try and cut it out . . . try acid drops or chewing-gum or something,' she laughed.

'She's as cold as ice,' thought Guy Arlingham.

But her coldness did not annoy him today. He was much too intrigued by the new glamour that surrounded this quaint, undemonstrative girl with whom he had once been so much in love – the glamour of a fortune.

'What a marvellous thing for you – this old josser leaving you all this money,' he said.

Elizabeth regarded the tip of her toe and thought how shabby it was. But of course she could afford to go out and buy a dozen pairs of expensive shoes now. How curious and unreal it seemed to be rich after one had been so hard up.

'I suppose it is marvellous, Guy,' she said. 'I'm not very thrilled.'

'My dear, you aren't human.'

'Yes, I am, but . . . '

She bit her lip and stopped herself. Her cheeks burned. No, she couldn't finish that sentence. How *could* she? She had almost said;

'But nothing seems to matter much now . . . money doesn't matter. It was you . . . *you,* my lover, who mattered.'

She said nothing. She was cross with herself because she would keep thinking of that silly song.

34

'*Give me back the life that you enchanted* . . .'

Yes, it is love, not money, that enchants one's existence.

'Well?' said Guy.

She looked up at him now . . . rather defiantly.

'Of course, it is a very great thing to have a lot of money. But it's a huge responsibility for me.'

'Ten thousand a year,' said Guy almost reverently.

'M'm.'

'Had you any idea the old man . . .'

'No, none. He was a great friend of mine. An absolute dear. He always took a great interest in me and I loved him. But I had no idea he would leave all his money to me.'

'And big estates, too, I gather from what Lilian has told me.'

'Yes, a house in Sussex . . . acres . . . half the cottages in Maplefield, I believe.'

'Maplefield . . . that's where?'

'Crowborough direction.'

'Lovely country,' said Guy absently.

He was thinking:

'Ye gods . . . and I might have managed it all with her . . .'

After which he chided himself for being a beast, and a disloyal one into the bargain, and tried not to concentrate too much on the thought of Elizabeth's newly acquired wealth.

'Lilian tells me you're off there tomorrow.'

'Yes. I don't know about permanently, but I shall take a look round and then possibly settle down there for the summer.'

'It will be very lonely . . . a little thing like you in a great big place. . . .'

Elizabeth refused to meet his gaze. She wished he would not use that charming tone of regret when he spoke to her. He knew he had hurt her, but he need not make things harder for her by being too charming. 'A little thing like you' – that careless intimacy from Guy was typical.

'Oh, I shan't mind being alone,' she said. 'And there will be plenty to do. Sir James used to tell me about his animals . . . I understand the stables are full. I shall be able to hunt. I love riding. . . .'

'It's all in the charge of an estate-agent, isn't it?'

'Yes, a Mr. Hewitson . . . a young Oxford man who was

35

a sort of protégé of Sir James's. He's been there some time. He's kept the place up for Sir James. The poor old man was away a great deal . . . the place had sad memories for him. Curiously enough, it is called "Memories".'

'Rather a nice name,' said Guy.

'Yes, I like it,' said Elizabeth, and then, suddenly, to cover what seemed an awkward moment, she said: 'I'm afraid I must break my resolution and have a cigarette.'

'Look here, Elizabeth,' said Guy, as he flicked his lighter into flame and held it to her cigarette, 'as you say, this is a big responsibility for you. You haven't anyone working in your interest, have you?'

'What do you mean?' She looked at him now, quickly.

'I mean – you have no relations – men to help you with business affairs.'

'No. Only Mr. Parnell, Sir James's solicitor. And the agent.'

'Will you keep this agent on? Possibly, if he has had sole charge during Sir James's lifetime and been left a lot to himself, he'll be full of bumptious ideas and want to manage you as well as the place.'

Guy knew quite well that he could not have said anything more calculated to put Elizabeth's independent young back up against the wretched agent.

'He won't manage me!' she said swiftly. 'I can look after myself and my own interests.'

'Why not engage a new agent now?'

'I promised Sir James I'd keep Mr. Hewitson in the post. I can't break that promise, no matter how much Mr. Hewitson and I disagree.'

'Which you probably will do.'

'It's likely,' said Elizabeth. 'But, of course, he may be very nice.'

'I hope so, my dear. I feel rather anxious about a little thing like you going down there alone and taking over all these big worries.'

Elizabeth gave him a sudden, twisted smile.

'Thanks, Guy, but don't worry about me. You needn't. You and Lilian must . . . must come and stay some time. I shan't want fifteen bedrooms to myself!'

Guy frowned. He fingered his tie thoughtfully. He did not know quite what it cost Elizabeth to make that casual invitation. So he said what he had been leading up to:

'Well, look here, will you promise me something?'

'What?'

'That if you need any help and advice, apart from Parnell or this agent fellow, you'll let me know?'

'That's very nice of you.'

'It isn't nice.' He reddened and cleared his throat. 'But I do want you to feel you've still got me as a pal.'

'Thank you,' she said steadily.

'You've got a big thing to run,' he continued. 'You know I'd do anything I could. And this agent feller'll want watching. He may try to do you right and left. You're only a girl and . . . well, there it is.'

There it was. Elizabeth nodded. She felt that Guy was quite right. She knew nothing about this Archer Hewitson, and he might be difficult to deal with. Sir James was not the sort of man to inquire too closely into details, and possibly Mr. Hewitson did what he liked with the estate. Guy's attitude helped to increase the vague hostility that she, herself, felt when she thought about Mr. Hewitson. And it would be nice to know that Guy was ready to give her friendship . . . help that she might, indeed, need.

'I *am* grateful, Guy,' she said. 'You're quite right. I don't know what this agent is like, and I might need a man's support.'

'Then promise you'll call on me?' he said eagerly.

'Yes – thank you very much. I promise.'

Arlingham gave a little sigh. He felt more satisfied now that she had given that promise. It meant that she would keep in touch with him. The old, intimate tie was severed. He was going to marry Lilian – much more suited to his temperament, of course – but he would not be altogether disassociated from Elizabeth – Elizabeth, who was now a young woman of wealth and property. There was some satisfaction for Guy in that thought

Elizabeth herself, honest and genuine, did not dream of attributing Guy's offer to help to any ulterior motive. She thought that he had made it out of sheer kindheartedness and friendship. Close though she had been to him, she had never really plumbed the depths of his character, never guessed that he was mercenary and a little mean. She would have been shocked and horrified to know how he

37

regretted his break with her now, because she had inherited £10,000 a year.

Elizabeth thought of him only as the attractive and charming lover that she had lost. One invariably idealises the person one loses. Since Guy had turned from her to Lilian, he seemed more attractive than ever. Only in the first sharp pain of discovery that he was in love with Lilian had Elizabeth condemned him as disloyal. He had been disloyal. So had Lilian, her friend. But Elizabeth understood human nature. She knew that it played queer tricks with people. She was also possessed of that rare virtue – humility. She was quite sure that she was dull and unattractive compared with beautiful, red-haired Lilian. How could she blame Guy for being attracted by her? How could she blame Lilian for loving Guy?

They had hurt her, but she had forgiven them for that. All she wanted now was the courage to put Guy and her passion for him behind her. It was so much more difficult to achieve that than to forgive them. She could feel sympathy and even friendship for these two who were instruments of her pain. It was the pain that was so intolerable; so hard to bear.

Arlingham, meanwhile, deceived himself into thinking that he was a fine fellow – full of honest desire to help little Elizabeth and make sure she was not 'done down' by this estate agent. He could make himself believe anything. If anybody had told him that he was avaricious, and that in offering Elizabeth his help he had an eye to the main chance, he would have hotly denied it and felt very misjudged.

'You must send me a line and tell me how you get on, Elizabeth,' he said. 'I expect you'll write to Lilian, won't you?'

'Yes, of course. I would have taken her with me – if – if things hadn't happened as they are. But, of course, now – you will want her up here. I don't mind leaving her in the flat, because you'll – you'll be looking after her.'

Arlingham fingered his tie and frowned a little.

'Yes, of course.'

'You'll be – getting married quite soon?' she asked, deliberately hurting herself by the question. In a funny sort of way she felt that she must know. Must know the worst. It would be a black day . . . an unbearable day . . . the day when Guy married Lilian. She wondered how she could sit here in the studio and comtemplate it. And only a few days ago . . . it seemed years . . . she had considered the fact that she would become Guy Arlingham's wife this Spring.

Guy did not answer Elizabeth's question for a moment. He was remembering last night . . . a passionate moment when he had held lovely Lilian in his arms in the car, coming home . . . and had said: 'I shall get a special licence. I don't want another long engagement. Marry me soon – next week – will you, dearest?'

Lilian had agreed to marry him when he wished.

Guy thrust his hands into his trousers pockets and walked up and down the studio.

'Damn!' he thought.

If he married Lilian next week, it would be a bit difficult for him to really enjoy his marriage. There wasn't enough cash. He might have thought about that before. But, then, Elizabeth hadn't had this wonderful stroke of luck. He was irritated because he felt that his pleasure in having won Lilian was spoiled. The fine edge of the thrill was indisputably blunted.

Grock, the Dalmatian, lying in a corner of the studio with his head on his paws, looked up as Arlingham approached and growled softly in his throat.

'Grocky! How dare you!' said Elizabeth reproachfully.

'He never liked me,' said Guy. He was a very conceited man, and he had always felt aggravated because he had been unable to secure the trust or affection of Elizabeth's dog.

'He doesn't really like anybody but me,' said Elizabeth. And her eyes softened as they rested on the Dalmatian.

Guy kicked the floor moodily with one toe.

'Well, he certainly hates me, and I've never heard him growl at anybody else. I expect he's glad he won't have to live with me.'

Elizabeth reflected that that was just the sort of remark that Guy would make to hurt her. What a spoiled child he was! He had always been a bit childish about Grock, because Grock wouldn't make friends with him.

Lilian came in with the tea. She was a perfect picture – a study in grey. A grey velvet dress with a soft grey chiffon bertha over her lovely sloping shoulders – grey shoes

39

and stockings. The one bit of colour about her was her glorious red hair.

'How could any man help falling in love with her,' thought Elizabeth, a little bitterly. Yes, try as she would she could not altogether eradicate bitterness. Lilian had gained all that she had lost; all that had made life so enthralling.

It was an impossible position here . . . a difficult and hopeless triangle, now. Under the circumstances, the sooner she left London and these two, the better.

She drank her tea; ate nothing; lit the inevitable cigarette and then excused herself.

'I'm going to throw a few things into a trunk. I shall be going down to Maplefield early in the morning. You'll forgive me, won't you?'

'Can I help you, darling?' said Lilian.

Lilian was, at heart, without guile. She was genuinely troubled because she had stolen the affections of Elizabeth's lover. If Elizabeth had appeared terribly upset and made a great fuss and scene, Lilian would, quite voluntarily, have walked out and left her to Guy. But funny Elizabeth hadn't seemed to mind so much. Guy thought that too. And she had this inheritance to interest her now. Lilian tried not to feel conscience-stricken.

'I don't want any help,' said Elizabeth.

She glanced at Guy. He was looking at her.

'So long, Guy,' she said. 'I may not see you again before I go.'

'Au revoir,' he said meaningly. 'You're not going to forget that if you need help down at Maplefield, I'm your pal?'

'I won't forget,' said Elizabeth.

Guy looked at Lilian.

'I'm sure you'll agree. She may need a man pal down at this place, Lil. She's got a lot to tackle – this Hewitson, the agent, may be an awful bounder, and out to do her right and left.'

'Oh, *of course,* she must rely on your help, Guy!' said Lilian warmly. 'I do so want to feel that we three can still be friends.'

Elizabeth paused in the doorway of the studio. She looked back at her friend and at the man who had once been her avowed lover.

'Go on,' she said to herself. 'Go on – face it! Grin and

40

tell them you'll be delighted. Make things pleasant for them – for everybody. It won't be very pleasant for you to stand by and watch the romance thrive. But go on – grin and bear it!'

Aloud she said quietly:

'Thanks – both of you. I don't see any reason why we shouldn't all be pals. One day, anyhow . . . and I'll be glad to let you know, Guy, if I need a man's advice and support.'

She walked out and shut the door. She thought:

'One day I suppose it *will* be possible for me to meet them – see them as husband and wife – and not care. But I do care now – frightfully. Oh, Guy . . . *Guy*!'

In the studio Lilian walked to her lover and looked up at him. Her white lids half closed in passionate expectation. He took her in his arms. He was thinking

'What a little sport Elizabeth is, really . . . not to make a fuss. Some women would have been very nasty in a situation like this. . . .'

And he was also thinking that he had been a fool to succumb to an infatuation for Lilian. He had been rash. He had acted in too much of a hurry. If he had waited – just twenty-four hours – he would not have broken with Elizabeth. He would have considered it his duty to stick to her – help her look after this place down in Sussex.

'Guy,' whispered the girl in his arms. 'Guy – darling – *darling*! I adore you. It's wonderful – to think we don't have to hide it from Elizabeth any more. Kiss me!'

He kissed her – with a passion that satisfied her. But there was something almost rough and angry about the way he held and caressed her – something desperate. As though, through sheer passion, he would shut out the irritating memory of that other girl who had never once said to him: 'I adore you' . . . . and whom he had regretted as soon as he had given her up. Yes, he knew it this afternoon quite definitely, and did not deny it to himself. Now that he had broken his engagement with Elizabeth, and the way to marriage with Lilian was cleared, the flame of his passion for her was flickering out. He wanted Elizabeth back again. Ironical – and perverse. The only person who was happy and content was Lilian.

Elizabeth moved about her bedroom sorting and folding clothes; placing what she needed in a big leather suitcase.

41

She liked that old suitcase. It had belonged to her father. He had travelled a lot in his life, and there were many old coloured labels of hotels out in the East still adhering to the case.

'I think, now I've got some money, I shall travel a bit – go abroad and see the world, shall I, Grocky?' Elizabeth addressed her dog.

The Dalmatian thumped his tail on the ground but eyed her anxiously. He seemed to say:

'It sounds all right – but can I go, too?'

Elizabeth stooped to stroke his head.

'No, my beautiful,' she said. 'I shan't go abroad and leave you. You wouldn't be allowed to come back with me again, and that would be dreadful. You are the only one in the wide world who really loves me!'

She hummed to herself; no particular tune; just a droning sound. Her lips were set. She folded a red georgette dinner frock, and the lips tightened still more. That had been Guy's favourite dress. He liked her in red. She could go and buy as many nice red frocks as she wanted, now, and he wouldn't even notice them. He would be choosing frocks for Lilian. She had auburn hair and couldn't wear red. Guy would hate *her* in red. That was something!

The small compressed mouth quivered slightly as the dress which had been Guy's favourite was folded and placed in the suitcase.

'Oh, damn!' said Elizabeth to herself.

She thought how frightfully lonely one could be when one was left alone after having had a dear and constant companion; a lover; for any length of time. She had never been really lonely before Guy came into her life. But he had taught her to appreciate the delights of intimacy and close companionship. It was so pleasant to share things . . . little, silly things . . . little likes and dislikes and fads and fancies. One could be great pals with a person of one's own sex. Yes, she had been good friends with Lilian . . . they had never quarrelled during the time they had shared this flat. But that sort of companionship was different. When one had a lover one shared that deep delight, that fine thrill, born of sex.

Elizabeth realised that for a long time now she had been living solely for Guy. She had dressed to please him; done a hundred trivial things to please him. Things that had assumed importance because of him. The way she had had her hair cut, for instance. In a fringe because he liked it . . . and the polish she put on her nails . . . slightly pinker than she, personally, liked . . . because *he* liked them very pink. A certain green jumper-suit – she had given it away to Mrs. Harridge, the char, because Guy disliked it. And all the dreams of the future had been built up around him – for him.

That was all over. Life seemed hideously blank; there wasn't much to look forward to. Nobody would care what colour she wore; what dress; or how she did her hair; or what book she had read and enjoyed.

She had lost her lover. She had lost all the thrill out of life. And dear old Sir James had thought his money, his house, his estates, would in a measure help to cheer her; be her recompense.

Elizabeth looked down into the suitcase at the red georgette dress. It was becoming strangely blurred from her sight. From the studio came the strains of the gramophone again. Lilian and Guy had been silent for a bit. Now there was music.

'Oh, *hang*!' said Elizabeth, listening. 'It's that wretched, sloppy song again.'

> Give me back all the kisses that I gave
> Give me back the life that you enchanted

Elizabeth walked to her bedroom door and turned the key in the lock. She went back to the bed and pushed the suitcase to one side. She jabbed her cigarette end fiercely in an ashtray. Then she lay down on the bed and hid her face on the pillow.

The voice from the gramophone penetrated through the thin walls . . . mocking her . . .

> Give me back my heart.
> You won't be wanting it again!

Elizabeth put her fingers in her ears. Her whole body was shaking. Grock came up to the bed and licked her arm. He had never seen her cry before. He did not understand it. But he offered what comfort lay within his power. He went

43

on licking her furiously . . . until she became aware of the warm caressing tongue. Then she roused herself and fought down the red-hot feeling of anguish that had suddenly come upon her.

She put out a hand – wet with her tears – and laid it on the Dalmatian's head.

CHAPTER VI

ARCHER HEWITSON stood in the doorway of his cottage, pipe in his mouth, frowning at a letter which he was reading. The last paragraph seemed particularly to annoy him.

'Between us, my dear Mr. Hewitson, I must say I consider it a grave mistake on the part of my late client to have bequeathed his entire property to this young woman, about whom we know nothing. But it is a mistake which cannot now be rectified. I can only express the hope that you will carry out Sir James's wishes and remain in charge of the estate. It would seem sad to see the old place pass into a stranger's hands and be entirely altered and spoiled. . . .'

Archer Hewitson looked up from the letter. It was from the late Sir James Willington's solicitor – Mr. Parnell. And Archer Hewitson agreed with every word of it. It was, in his opinion, nothing less than a tragedy that the old man should have made a will at the eleventh hour leaving the whole of his estates and his money to this girl – Elizabeth Rowe.

Who was Elizabeth Rowe? Nobody knew. Mr. Parnell had met her at Sir James's funeral. Archer had been unable to attend because of an attack of 'flu. Parnell said she was very young – not more than twenty-two – and called herself an artist. One of the 'Chelsea art crowd,' which Archer Hewitson despised and deplored. Parnell said she 'seemed quite nice and amiable.' No doubt. It was a very agreeable thing for her to come into £10,000 a year and 'Memories', which in Hewitson's estimation was the most beautiful property in Sussex.

He had made up his mind that Elizabeth Rowe was a 'vamp'. Yes – she must have 'vamped' the poor old man. Pathetic, the old fellow living in that lonely way of his in

45

Chelsea, working amongst the poor. Always so generous, so kind. Then to get caught by a little gold-digger who called herself an artist. It infuriated Arther Hewitson.

During this last week, since Parnell had sent him the news that Sir James had died and left everything to Elizabeth Rowe, Archer had made up his mind several times to pack up and clear out.

For the last five years he had lived here looking after the estate while Sir James was away. The old man had been a great deal away. Archer managed everything. And because he loved the place, and was intensely grateful to the old man for giving him the job, he had done his best here. He had Sir James's interests at heart.

How could one help getting fond of the place? Hewitson stared moodily across the tiny garden of his cottage; across a meadow, yellow with buttercups, to the perfectly kept grounds of 'Memories'. One could just glimpse the grey timbered walls of the old Elizabethan house through the trees. It stood on a little hill. The front garden sloped to a big pond, which glimmered like a sheet of glass in the May sunlight. Lovely, that pond, thought Archer. On one side of it, clipped lawns, a rose walk, and a few slim poplars. On the other, a beech wood. The trees were just bursting into the fresh, exquisite green of the spring.

Archer Hewitson knocked his pipe on the heel of his shoe and turned back into his cottage.

'Damn!' he muttered.

He could have repeated the word when he glanced at his desk under the diamond-paned casements. A flimsy pink oblong sheet of paper lay there. It had come yesterday. It was signed 'Rowe,' and it informed him that Miss Elizabeth Rowe was coming down to Maplefield this morning, the first day of May, on the ten o'clock train. That meant he must order the car and meet her. Yes, he supposed he must meet her. He must be polite. He had decided to stay here – for the time being, anyhow. Sir James had been his friend and benefactor, and it was up to him to stick to his job now that the old man was dead.

Archer had heard from a pal in Burma yesterday. The fellow wanted him to go out East and join him in an oil company out there. Archer had a few hundreds saved up – a little that he had saved during the last eleven years. He might have joined old Grierson in Burma. On the other hand, the doctors had warned him not to go out East. Soon after the Armistice, at the age of nineteen, when his father had died bankrupt and he had been forced to terminate his career at Oxford, he had gone out to the West Coast of Africa. There he had contracted very severe fever which had affected his general health.

Even now he had recurrent attacks – torturing headaches and fits of depression. He had to chuck the job after a year. He had no home. His mother was dead. He was very much alone. But his quick brain and personality made friends quickly for him. He managed to fight his illness and go abroad again – this time to a more gentle climate in Ceylon. But a few years of that made a wreck of him again. He was warned to remain in England and lead an open-air life.

It was at that perid, five years ago, that he had met old Sir James Willington. Something in the melancholy of the young man's eyes and the courage with which he faced ill health and the difficulties of securing suitable work at home appealed to the old philanthropist. He took Archer Hewitson down to Sussex – installed him in this cottage, gave him entire charge of the estate, and a generous salary.

Today, Archer Hewitson was as fit as any man of thirty could wish to be. He had led a life in the open air. Exercising the hunters; walking with the dogs; out most of the day, keeping in personal touch with the stablemen, the gardeners, the villagers of Maplefield, most of whom lived on land belonging to Sir James. He had almost forgotten what it was to have those agonising headaches which were a form of the peculiar malaria from which he had suffered in West Africa.

He certainly did not want to leave 'Memories' and his comfortable cottage and the pleasant existence which he led here. It had never bored him. He was not easily bored. He was too fond of the country and interested in the estate. And he had made one or two good friends. A bachelor in a place like Maplefield was an asset. Archer Hewitson was in demand at most of the houses round the district. He played good tennis and bridge. He belonged to the golf club at Crowborough. He hadn't much time to be bored.

Now, however, faced with the prospect of managing the estate for a young and unknown girl, Archer was more than bored. He was thoroughly nettled. This was an end to his supremacy – to his peace. When Sir James had come down to 'Memories' it had been a pleasure to take his orders; to make this alteration, to draw up that plan at the old man's request. But it was going to be a very different thing to obey commands issued by a stranger. A slip of a girl, too.

Archer Hewitson was wrathful. Why the old man had allowed himself to be 'vamped' he could not think. Archer avoided young girls. He was afraid of them. He did not want to get married. He enjoyed his peaceful existence as a bachelor. He was content here at Quince-Tree cottage, with Dukes, the ex-service man who was his general servant, and Micky, his Cairn terrier, who was his devoted companion. There were one or two women he liked with whom he constantly played bridge and dined. Mrs. Kilwarne, for instance, who lived in the White House, between Maplefield and Crowborough. A very charming woman, Delia Kilwarne. But then she wasn't what Archer called a 'girl'. It was the very 'young things' who terrified him. He never knew what to say to them or how to deal with them. He was old-fashioned in a way, and considered the modern girl an atrocity. He disliked her precocity; her insolence; her knowing and cynical attitude toward men.

Delia Kilwarne was married and sensible. He liked Kilwarne, too. A good chap; on the Stock Exchange; went up to town every day. They were very friendly, and sometimes Archer met Delia Kilwarne at Crowborough Links for a game of golf. She played well. She was intelligent at bridge and quite amusing to talk to. He admired her.

If Sir James had left his estate to a married woman – or even a single woman of mature years – Archer Hewitson would have faced it more hopefully. But this twenty-two-year-old girl business defeated him. He felt thoroughly out of humour this morning as he sat eating the breakfast which Dukes placed before him.

'Dukes,' he said to the manservant who brought him in the morning paper, 'ring through to the garage and tell Bingham to fetch me in the Daimler at eleven-fifteen. I want to meet a train at Crowborough.'

'Very good, sir,' said Dukes, who was a thin little man

48

with a cadaverous face, a bald head, a hopeless lack of humour and a loyal devotion to his master. He stood looking down at Mr. Hewitson, fingering a corner of the green baize apron which he wore over an ancient khaki service suit. 'If I might be so bold, sir,' he added.

'Yes?'

'Is it possible that you'll be leaving the estate now this this – young lady is coming down to take over "Memories"?'

Archer looked at him sharply.

'Certainly not, Dukes. Who put that idea into your head?'

'Begging your pardon, sir, I was speaking to the 'ead-gardener last night, and he said he thought as he wouldn't take no orders from a strange young person, and he didn't think you would either, as – '

'That'll do, Dukes,' said Archer, more sharply than he had ever spoken to the man. 'You can tell Brownrigg from me that he can keep his thoughts to himself in the future. Brownrigg takes his orders from me as usual. And kindly remember that the "strange young person" – Miss Rowe – was a friend of Sir James's.'

'Yes, sir,' said Dukes meekly, and departed.

Archer scowled at his paper. Hang it all, he didn't want to defend Miss Elizabeth Rowe. He cordially agreed with the head-gardener. He didn't want to take orders from a 'strange young person.' But it wouldn't do to let the servants chatter and start insubordination of this kind.

It seemed to Archer only the beginning of discord and trouble. To the devil with Elizabeth Rowe! Things had been peaceful enough down here before her innovation.

'The very mention of her before she comes – brews trouble,' he thought.

He put down the paper. He felt disgruntled. He filled his pipe and looked round the living-room with an appreciative eye. He had grown very fond of Quince-Tree Cottage. It had taken its name from the old quince-tree which grew in the tiny front garden and bore fruit copiously. Dukes made very good quince jam in the season. The little place was as old as the big house, 'Memories'. This room had two magnificent old oak beams. It was charming, with its white-washed walls; diamond-paned casements; its uneven oak floor which was polished until it shone.

It had been already furnished by Sir James when Archer came here. But Archer had added bits and pieces during the last few years. That old dresser, with its pewter plates and row of Toby jugs of all shapes and sizes, belonged to him. So did the gate-legged table and the old Chippendale armchair by the fireplace – his pet chair.

An uneasy sensation stole over Archer Hewitson as he regarded his treasures. He stuck his pipe in his mouth; screwed up his eyes, and looked out at the garden, which was a mass of flowering bulbs. The tall Dutch tulips – flaunting scarlet – delicate mauve – golden yellow – were a picture this year. He and Dukes had planted them last winter.

Supposing this girl, this new mistress of 'Memories', took a dislike to him and told him he could go? Yes, that thought made him uneasy. He wouldn't like to quit this little cottage which had been his home for the last five years, or to lose his job and have to go out East. There wasn't any hope of work in England at the moment for a man with no knowledge of anything but trading in West Africa or tea planting; and the experience he had gained here as an estate-agent. He didn't particularly want to go abroad and get back that infernal fever, either.

Altogether the coming of Miss Elizabeth Rowe depressed him. He felt, too, that he would be 'cussed' when she came. He wouldn't make himself agreeable, just because he was afraid of losing his job and loth to say goodbye to a place which held his affection. He would be civil, of course – and do his best not to let her see that he was frankly hostile to the terms of Sir James's will. But he was not going to bow and scrape to this young 'vamp'.

Dukes opened the door. A small wheaten-cream Cairn, with little dark upstanding ears and beautiful brown eyes, dashed into the room.

Archer Hewitson smiled.

'Hello, Micky. Where've you been, old man? Chasing the rabbits?'

Micky – the most privileged person in Quince-Tree Cottage – wagged his short tail – showed a pink, curling tongue and very white teeth in what might have been a smile – and sat down in his usual place on the rug before the fireplace. He licked his paws succulently for a moment.

'This won't do, Micky,' said Archer. 'We've got to go to

the infernal station in half an hour, and there's work to be done first. Come along. . . . '

Last night Archer had received the information that the roof of the gamekeeper's cottage was leaking. He meant to stroll over the fields to the place and have a look at the roof before he went to the station.

'I suppose,' he thought gloomily, 'I shall have to ask Miss Rowe's permission, now, before I have the darned roof mended. The whole thing's a bore.'

What a pity Sir James hadn't carried out his original idea of leaving his money to blind children and turning 'Memories' into a home for them. It would have pleased Archer to carry on the place for such a decent sort of charity as that. Why on earth did the old man let this gold-digger from Chelsea get him in her clutches?

A blue two-seater drove up to the gates of Quince-Tree Cottage, raising a cloud of dust as four-wheel brakes were applied somewhat violently.

Archer looked out of the windows.

'Lord help the tyres,' he thought. 'That's Delia Kilwarne. She drives much too fast.'

A tall, slim, fair-haired young woman climbed out of the car. She came up the garden path, carrying a couple of books in her hands. Hewitson went to meet her. She was very good-looking, he thought, not for the first time. She carried herself well; looked nice in that tweed suit and brown Heath hat.

He went to the door to meet her.

'Morning, Delia . . . this is an early visit.'

'Good morning, Archie. How goes the world?'

Mrs. Kilwarne entered the cottage, smiling up at the man as she passed him. It was an eager and provocative smile. Archer Hewitson, not a very subtle man, not at all experienced with women and never aware of danger until he was flung into direct contact with it, was blind to the provocation. He was quite pleased to see Delia. They were good friends . . . she and Kilwarne and himself. Called each other by their Christian names and saw a fair bit of one another. Certainly he liked and admired her. But it never occurred to him to fall in love with her. Neither would he have dreamed of imagining she might fall in love with him. So far as he knew, she was fond of her husband. Charlie Kilwarne was a bit older than Delia; bit on the stolid side, perhaps; thoroughly engrossed in business; but he was what Archer called a good fellow. Good-humoured. Easy-going. He looked upon the Kilwarnes as a happy couple. They had been married five years; had no children; but shared many tastes in common.

Why should it enter his head that Delia Kilwarne's feeling for him was anything but platonic? He saw no guile in the blue, long-lashed eyes which she raised to his. But he thought, as he had thought many times, that she spoiled herself by using too much lip-stick. Her lips – she had rather a wide, full mouth – were too vivid a red.

She placed the books on his desk.

'Those are the Dornford Yates I promised you.'

'Thanks so much, Delia. I like Yates. he writes a good yarn. He amuses me.'

Delia Kilwarne took off her soft felt hat and ran a comb speedily through her fair, shingled head. A very sleek head; the colour of ripe corn. She was altogether sleek; smooth, pale skin; well-manicured hands; well-cut clothes. What Archer called a well-groomed woman. Delia always looked as though she had stepped straight out of a bath. But, certainly, her lips were too scarlet. When she smiled she was very attractive. In repose she had rather a discontented face; a selfish one. She was always extremely nice to Archer Hewitson.

'Archie,' she said, 'I came along to drop the books on you and also to have a chat – have you time?'

He glanced at the grandmother clock in a corner of the room.

'Not much, I'm afraid. I've got to go over to Hawkson's cottage – then to Crowborough station.'

'Why the station?'

'I've got to meet this Miss Rowe.'

'Oh!'

Delia Kilwarne's narrow brows – she spent a lot of time on the painful process of plucking them to make them so narrow – drew together in a frown.

'Nuisance, isn't it?' said Archer, sitting on the edge of the table and thrusting his hands into his trousers pockets. 'But there it is. The good lady arrives today and takes possession.'

'I think it's the most disgraceful thing!' Delia Kilwarne burst forth angrily. 'To have a chit of a girl taking over "Memories" and becoming your employer!'

'H'm,' said Archer. 'I don't much like it. A good many times I've thought of packing up and leaving Maplefield.'

'Don't do that!' said Delia hastily.

'I won't, simply out of cussedness. I won't let this girl think I'm scared off by her advent. And besides, I'm so damned fond of "Memories" and this little place.'

'Of course. You mustn't dream of going. What would we do without you?'

Delia Kilwarne looked at him hungrily now. But he only took her remark casually. He did not see the hunger in her eyes.

'That's nice of you. Well, unless I'm chucked out by my new employer, I don't suppose I shall go.'

She continued to look at him. He attracted her vitally – much too vitally, considering that she was a married woman. But she thought, this morning, not for the first time, how extraordinarily good Archer Hewitson was to look upon. Tall; thin; lithe; beautifully built. Well-shaped, well-bred hands. Well-shaped head. Darkish brown hair with a kink in it that no amount of vigorous brushing could destroy. The thin face, with the bronzed skin and very bright hazel eyes, bore traces of the East; of the illnesses he had been through. There were lines round the eyes and the firm thin lips. One might almost call it a haggard face for one so young. But he was undeniably handsome and had rather an abrupt, reticent manner which women found attractive. Delia Kilwarne had found him dangerously attractive, ever since she had known him. Now that she had broken through his reserve so far that they were acknowledged friends, she wanted something more. She was – under a mask of frank *camaraderie* and sportsmanship – a greedy, sensual woman, eager for admiration. She was tired of her husband and she wanted a flirtation. Her one thought, day and night, now, was how to make Archer Hewitson flirt with her.

It wasn't going to be easy. She knew it. She knew him well enough now to be aware that he had a strict sense of honour. He was not a prig, but he had a definite distaste for the somewhat loose maxims and morals of today.

If he hadn't known Charlie, her husband – hadn't liked

him – things might have been easier.

Archer, with no notion that this woman was in love with him, gave her a cigarette, lit it for her, and talked to her with a friendliness he did not show to everybody.

'It's a pity – the whole show, isn't it?' he said. 'I'm dreading the next few days. I can just imagine what the girl will be like. Parnell says she's an artist, living in a Chelsea studio, and alone in the world. She'll be full of bright ideas which I shall hate. She'll probably be domineering and impossible to work with, and she'll fill "Memories" with that ghastly "arty" crowd from Chelsea. Imagine it! The poor old boy must have been crazy to leave her everything.'

'Can't the will be disputed?' said Delia. 'On the grounds of insanity?'

'Oh, no, he was quite sane,' said Archer. 'Parnell saw him just before he died.'

'Has Mr. Parnell seen this dreadful girl?'

'Yes – as a matter of fact, he says she isn't too bad.'

'A lady?'

'Yes.'

'Pretty?'

'Parnell didn't say that,' Archer replied with a brief laugh.

Delia Kilwarne's large blue eyes were full of jealousy – a new sensation for her. She hated this Elizabeth Rowe . . . hated the thought that Archer would be constantly in touch with her because of the estate. However, she echoed his laugh.

'I shall have to come and protect you from the clutches of this vamp, my dear,' she said.

'I'll rush to you for protection if I need it,' he laughed again, and put his pipe in his mouth.

'Will you come along to the White House and dine to-night?'

'Thanks awfully – but I can't very well. It's Miss Rowe's first night here.'

Delia's cheeks crimsoned. She loathed the very thought of Miss Rowe. Even before she was actually here she felt that she was an enemy. Delia's competitive spirit was roused. She had had nobody in the district to compete with until now. Except for herself, there wasn't another young and pretty woman on Archer Hewitson's visiting-list. She felt panic at the thought that Elizabeth Rowe might be pretty and alluring and that she would see little of him in the future.

'For all you know, Miss Rowe may be so "vampish" that she'll vamp you,' Delia suggested.

This brought the heated answer she had hoped for.

'Not this lad! Miss Rowe may be an old man's darling, but she won't do anything but annoy me, I'm certain.'

'Good,' thought Delia. Aloud she said: 'Well, don't desert me, will you, Archie?'

'Of course not,' he said.

She drew nearer him.

'Will you dine with us tomorrow and have some bridge?'

'I'd like to very much.'

'And don't let this horrid girl drive you away from Maplefield.'

She was so close to him now that he could smell the faint perfume of lilac that clung to her. She always used that lilac scent. It was quite sweet. She looked charming, with the sunlight on her sleek, blonde head. Archer Hewitson – strict though his morals were and confirmed bachelor though he might be – was human. He felt his pulses suddenly stir at the sight of Delia Kilwarne so near to him. Alarmed at the sensation, he stood up and moved away from her. Heavens, what would she think of him!

'Well, if you'll forgive me, Delia, I just be off,' he said.

She followed his tall, loose-limbed figure with a gaze that had both passion and jealousy in it.

'Right you are, Archie. See you tomorrow. So long.'

He saw her into her car. She drove away, waving a hand as she turned the corner of the road. Archer realised that he had no time to walk over the fields to Hawkson's cottage now. He must see about the leakage in the roof after lunch. Bingham would be here with the car in a quarter of an hour.

Once again Archer's thoughts turned to Elizabeth Rowe.

'Hang the girl!' he muttered.

Later, in none too amiable a mood, he drove to Crowborough station to meet the new owner of 'Memories'.

And it was into this atmosphere of hostility, of resentment, that poor Elizabeth came when she stepped out of the London train – trying to be enthusiastic about her introduction to her new and future home.

55

CHAPTER VII

ELIZABETH, with Grock at her heels and a porter carrying her luggage, walked out of Crowborough station and stood a moment in the sunlight, looking around her. She had wired to Mr. Hewitson, but did not know whether or not she would be met.

Archer Hewitson recognised the future mistress of 'Memories' only by the Dalmatian. Parnell had told him that the girl had one of these spotted dogs, which never left her. He gave her a quick look and hesitated. Was this Elizabeth Rowe? She didn't look at all like the vamp of his imagination. There was nothing of the painted, fluffy baby type such as he had imagined had lured poor old Sir James into leaving her his money. This was a grave-eyed, rather sober little person, quietly dressed in a tailor-made and a green felt hat. She turned her head toward him, and he caught the inquiring gaze of a pair of very dark brown eyes set wide apart in a pale, pointed little face. Was this Elizabeth Rowe?

Archer took another look at the Dalmatian and marched up to the girl.

'Pardon me,' he said, raising his hat, 'but are you Miss Rowe?'

'I am,' said Elizabeth.

'I am Hewitson – Sir James's estate agent,' he said.

'Oh, yes,' said Elizabeth.

'I – er – have brough the car to meet you.'

'Thank you very much.'

Archer beckoned to the chauffeur.

'Bingham – Miss Rowe's luggage.'

Elizabeth followed him to the Daimler. Her car, she presumed. How peculiar it was . . . to have had so little a few days ago. To find herself today in possession of so much. *Her* car . . . that large, important-looking saloon. How absurd!

She scrutinised Archer Hewitson. Quite good looking, this tall, hazel-eyed young man with his athletic figure and thin, sunburned face. Perhaps she need not be afraid that he was going to 'do her down,' as Guy had suggested. Still, one couldn't go by looks, and Elizabeth was not going to be misled by them. With the quick, shrewd eye of the painter as well as the woman, she noticed one thing immediately. This man Archer Hewitson, had a hard, stubborn mouth and chin. He would not be easy to deal with.

She found herself seated beside him, driving away from the station, out of the town and down the hill on the Uckfield road. Her soul rejoiced in the beauty of the countryside this fresh May morning. Little white clouds scudded across a blue sky, driven by a pleasant breeze. Hedges were gaily green – bursting into bloom. Meadows starred with daisies; gilded with buttercups. The distant sweep of open country was brown and green and purple with shadows.

'I like this,' Elizabeth sighed. 'I've never seen this part of Sussex before.'

'It's very attractive country,' said Archer.

'Is Maplefield far from Crowborough?'

'A mile or two. We turn off the Uckfield road in a moment. The village lies between Nutley and Maresfield. It's all very open, close to Ashdown Forest.'

'It's real moorland,' said Elizabeth when they turned off the main road. 'Oh, look at the gorse – how splendid! And the hawthorn bloom – like snow! Why does anybody live in London in the spring?'

'Why, indeed,' murmured Archer.

His thoughts were not on the beauty of the countryside. He was trying to size up this girl – to make up his mind whether she was genuine, sincere, or full of affectation. She was not as bad as she might have been, anyhow, he decided. She obviously had breeding. That was something. But he could not eradicate the feeling of hostility, of resentment, because this girl was now his employer. Hang it all, she looked so young. She was only a child. She appeared to be wrapped up in admiring the scenery.

'This is the artistic stunt, of course,' Archer told himself gloomily. 'She won't have any business capabilities.'

But he was to come up against those business capabilities

57

in Elizabeth at a later date.

When they were almost at Maplefield, Elizabeth turned her attentions to the young man who had been sitting silently at her side.

'You have been with Sir James a long time, haven't you, Mr. Hewitson?'

'Five years,' he said stiffly.

'You – like looking after "Memories"?'

'Yes, I am very attached to the place.'

'Sir James thought a great deal of the way you managed everything.'

'I am glad,' he said in the same stiff voice. Elizabeth was trying to be amiable, but he took it for granted she was patronising him. When one's back is up against a person, one instinctively places a wrong construction on the most innocent speech.

'I shall be very grateful if you will show me round and tell me about everything,' she said.

'I shall be delighted.'

There was a coldness, a frigid courtesy in his manner which speedily froze Elizabeth. Never at any time did she, with her natural reserve and shyness, find it easy to establish friendliness with a stranger. As the moment went by and this conversation with Mr. Hewitson progressed, she found that the ice remained unbroken – in fact, it became more solid. The position was a difficult one, and the estate agent's chilly politeness made it more difficult. She withdrew into her shell and became curt – which was what generally happened to Elizabeth when she was embarrassed. She decided that he was a very difficult young man with a much too superior manner. He decided that she was abrupt. Rather a rude young woman.

Neither of them were speaking a word when the car turned in through the gates of 'Memories'. And if Elizabeth was enraptured by her first glimpse of the lovely old Tudor house; the gardens, so full of the fresh green of spring and the gay colours of the early flowers; she kept her raptures to herself. When she saw the shining pond, purple fringed with irises, sentinelled by tall poplars, and the adjoining beech woods, she thought:

'How very beautiful! What an enchanting place! And it's mine – all mine! Dear Sir James . . . what a heavenly

58

gift! I 'm going to love it as much as you did.'

Archer Hewitson interested himself in the 'plum-pudding' dog crouched at Elizabeth's feet. He had no particular love of Dalmatians. Big, clumsy brutes, he thought. He preferred small sporting animals – like terriers.

'There'll be trouble if Mick sees this spotted hound,' he thought grimly. Aloud he ventured to say: 'What's this fellow's name?'

'Grock,' said Elizabeth, and her eyes grew surprisingly soft and warm when she looked at her loyalest friend.

'Is he intelligent?'

'Much more than many human beings,' said Elizabeth. 'So many Dalmatians are rather stupid.'

'Well, Grock is not, as you'll find out,' said Elizabeth, indignantly.

'I've got a Cairn terrier,' said Archer.

'Terriers yap a lot, don't they?'

'One up to you,' thought Hewitson, and his lips suddenly twisted into a grim smile. 'Oh, Micky isn't the yapping kind.' he said. 'But he's a very good ratter, and there's scarcely a day he doesn't kill a rabbit. Most useful.'

'Grock wouldn't hurt a fly,' said Elizabeth.

'She's not a sportsman,' was Archer's immediate mental reaction to that remark. 'I knew that spotted dog was a sloppy sort of tripe-hound. Give me Mickey – he's got guts!'

The car drew up before the house. Elizabeth stepped out and stood a moment looking appreciatively at the grey timbered walls; the lovely old projecting porch; the mellowed bricks and tiles. 'Memories.' Yes, a host of lovely memories might well be stored within those ancient, historic walls. She was going to like her new home.

'I wonder,' – she addressed Hewitson – 'if you would tell me a little about the staff – who is here – what I am to expect. It's rather awkward – coming straight into someone else's home like this.'

'Quite so,' said Archer.

'Sir James didn't live here much, did he?'

'No. He came down at intervals. There is an excellent cook-housekeeper, Mrs. Martlet – she's been here twenty years. She was a young maid in the time of old Lady Willington – Sir James's mother. I suppose she must be getting on for sixty now. But she's hard to beat as a housekeeper –

absolutely honest and reliable. . . . I mean, you wouldn't find anyone better. . . . '

Elizabeth could see that Mr. Hewitson was trying to boost the said Mrs. Marlet.

'I shouldn't dream of supplanting those of Sir James's servants who satisfy me,' she said coldly.

Archer Hewitson came up against the independent young woman in Elizabeth. So she was not such a child after all. He felt suddenly that he would detest his subordinate position now that she was here.

'Who else is there? 'she asked.

'Only a youngish maid – Annie Judd – from the villlage. Nobody else at the moment. Sir James was so rarely here, and never entertained. He didn't need to keep a big staff. Of course, you will want more maids, no doubt.'

'I shall have to see,' said Elizabeth.

'Outside there are four men,' added Hewitson. 'Brownrigg – head-gardener; Tom, the under-gardener; Sandler, the stable-lad; and Bingham, this chauffeur who has driven us this morning and who is also groom for the moment. Oh, and there's Hawkson – the gamekeeper.'

'It seems to me a huge wage-bill – when nobody lives here.'

Archer pursed his lips. There she was – beginning to criticise already.

'Sir James liked the place to be run as though he lived here, and to find it in perfect running order when he came down. It might appear eccentric of him – but those were his wishes.'

'I see,' said Elizabeth. 'And where do you live, Mr. Hewitson?'

'In Quince-Tree Cottage – over there.' He took his pipe from his pocket and pointed with it across the fields. Elizabeth could just discern a small building in the distance; a spiral of smoke curling up into the blue.

'You have your own servant there?'

'Yes, a man cook-general. Dukes. Very decent fellow. Ex-service man.'

The big oaken door, studded with nails, swung open. A white-haired woman wearing a black dress and white apron appeared on the threshold. This, thought Elizabeth, was Mrs. Martlet. She had a sharp, rather forbidding face and unfriendly eyes behind steel-rimmed spectacles.

'She should be called "martinet",' thought Elizabeth.

'Good morning, Mrs. Marlet,' said Archer, stepping forward.

'Good morning, sir,' said the woman, her harsh features relaxing into what might have been termed a smile.

'This is Miss Rowe, who has come to live at "Memories",' said Archer, hating every word of the introduction.

Mrs. Martlet appeared to hate every word of it too. Her face resumed its forbidding look, and she greeted Elizabeth with the minimum of respect.

'Good morning, miss.'

Elizabeth saw that this was foe rather than friend. Of course – all these people resented her coming. In a way she did not blame them. But she felt chilled by her cold reception. It was so depressing. After all, this *was* her future home. Guy and Lilian would shortly be married and in a home of their own. She had promised Sir James that she would come here and look after his things. She would make an effort to do as he wished. But she foresaw trouble and some unpleasantness. It would be rather a lonely job.

She walked into the house. Despite the May sunlight slanting through the long, square-paned windows, the house struck chill. The atmosphere was gloomy. It had the rigid austerity of a place that is rarely inhabited. Everything was painfully ordered; meticulously clean. With the artist's eye, Elizabeth at once saw all the beauty, the possibility in old, walnut furniture . . . dark, golden with the polish of centuries. Everything was good and the type of antique stuff she would herself have chosen. But the draperies were old and out of date. The curtains, rich material, now faded, were too heavy for modern taste.

In the big drawing-room, from which Mrs. Martlet had unwillingly stripped the dust-sheets, there were hideous Victorian flowered satin chair-covers; ornate brocade curtains; antimacassars; waxen flowers in glass cases; stuffed birds; an atmosphere of the eighties. A spirit of the stiff, heavy ornamentation brought into the country by Victoria's German spouse.

'This I couldn't stand,' was Elizabeth's immediate feeling. 'It would be such a charming room, too, if a lot of the stuff was cleared out.'

61

Archer, believing it to be his courteous duty, conducted Elizabeth over the house. He paused discreetly in the upper landing whilst Mrs. Martlet showed her her bedroom.

'I have prepared the best bedroom for you, Miss,' she said primly. 'Sir James's old room.'

'Thank you,' said Elizabeth.

But she cast one look at the big room with its four-poster bed; its damask hangings; its ugly Victorian crockery and many pictures, and decided that this would not be her room. She would find a smaller one; one which she could strip ruthlessly; just have unadorned whitewashed walls and those delicous beams and panels and perhaps that lovely old tallboy and serpentine chest-of-drawers.

She said nothing to the housekeeper at the moment. She rejoined Hewitson on the landing. She had taken off her hat and coat. He looked at the slim, rather boyish figure in the silk shirt-blouse and skirt. That collar and her tie and her page's head, with its straight dark fringe, made her look ridiculously young. Archer looked quickly away again. What was this little creature going to do with all these possions? He would have liked her to appeal to him to help her – to tell him to carry on as usual. But she said nothng like that. She was very quiet. Deep, of course. The dangerous kind. Probably she was making up her mind to alter everything. There was a lot of will-power in that small pointed chin of hers. He wouldn't put it past her to order him about, in a moment.

They descended the wide staircase with its lovely polished oak banisters. A rosy-cheeked girl in cap and apron, whom Elizabeth presumed to be Annie Judd, was in the lounge helping Bingham with her luggage.

'If you'll come this way, Miss Rowe,' said Archer, 'We might have a chat in the study. The room Sir James used more than any in the house.'

Elizabeth eyed the tall figure in grey flannels.

'He isn't much more than an overgrown schoolboy who has got too big for his boots,' she thought. 'I wonder if he has an eye to the main chance – as Guy thinks.'

If only Guy were here! Her heart ached. It would have all been so different, so wonderful, if he had been here – her lover. Here, at her side, the future master of the house; of these possessions; one with her. How glorious everything would have been – then. Never had she felt the loss of him more keenly. But she kept a stiff upper lip as she followed Archer into the study. She liked the study. The walls were lined with beautifully bound books. Here was a feast of literature for her. There were comfortable saddlebag chairs and chintz curtains – faded, but more bearable than the rich velvet and brocade in other parts of the house.

'Won't you sit down?' said Archer.

'Thanks – I'll stand,' she said, and drew a packet of cigarettes from her bag. 'Have one?'

'No, thank you. I've got a pipe. Do you mind?'

'Go ahead,' she said.

He lit her cigarette for her. She noticed that he had nice, brown fingers which looked hard and capable.

Her hands were too square and boyish to please Archer. There was something altogether unfeminine about Elizabeth Rowe which annoyed Archer. He liked women to be thoroughly feminine. Here was the blunt, direct modern girl whom he detested. Now Delia Kilwarne, as a type, was much more attractive – soft, appealing. He couldn't imagine Elizabeth Rowe being appealing. What on earth was it that had attracted the old man into leaving her his fortune?

Gloomily he stuck his pipe between his teeth and puffed at it, his brows drawn together in a scowl.

Elizabeth walked up and down the room.

'Now, Mr. Hewitson, I suppose we must talk business.'

'Yes.'

'I've come into this money – this property – quite unexpectedly. I have no idea, beyond what Mr. Parnell has told me, what I really do possess. And certainly no notion what to do down here. I'd be awfully glad if you'd get out a statement of the expenditure – what it costs to run the place – as it is, with these outdoor men and the maids and the general upkeep of the estates. Then I can study it and know a bit where I am.'

Archer inclined his head.

'I'll get that done tonight,' he said.

'The property is fairly extensive, isn't it?'

'Yes. Sir James – I should say *you*' – he corrected himself stiffly – 'own most of the village. Several of the farmers rent their land from you. There are a good many rents collected from the surrounding cottages and small shops. The game that is killed has been sent up to the London hospitals by order of Sir James. The products from the vegetable garden and orchard have also been sent to charities. All the grapes – there's a very fine vine here – go to the children's hospital.'

'I see,' said Elizabeth. 'Yes, Sir James was a wonderful philanthropist.'

'Of course, you may wish to cancel those orders as you are going to live here.'

'I don't know yet how long I intend to stay,' said Elizabeth. 'For the summer, anyhow, yes. But I shall be alone except for friends that I may have down. I shall not be able to consume all that garden produce. Let it go up to the hospitals as usual.'

'Thanks,' said Archer.

He took a small diary from his pocket and made one or two notes about nothing in particular. Lord how he hated this business. Having to do what he was told by this child. Dictatorial little creature, too.

'Well, perhaps we might walk round the place this afternoon,' said Elizabeth. 'And you would tell me more about everything.'

'Certainly,' he said.

'And you'll get out the statement of expenditure and the receipts of the estate?'

'I will.' Archer bit his lip. Here were signs of business capabilities in Miss Elizabeth. Too much of it. She was going to interfere in the running of the estate.

'There's just one point I must ask you about – if you'll forgive me.' Elizabeth spoke awkwardly now, and her face flushed a little. 'Your . . . your own cottage . . . your salary . . . do I have to . . . to see to that . . . ? I mean, I suppose Sir James – ' She broke off.

Archer's own cheeks grew hot. He avoided her gaze.

'Sir James arranged with his bank to pay me my salary quarterly,' he said. 'The cottage I have rent free. My man-servant's wages are, of course, my own affair. Up till now I've had fruit and vegetables from "Memories", and fire-wood from the estate. But of course you may not consider – '

'Oh please,' she broke in. 'I have no wish to alter anything in that way.'

'Thank you,' he said coldly.

This was being made to feel his position as an em-

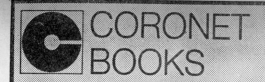

2

BUSINESS REPLY SERVICE
LICENCE NO. KE 2450

CORONET ROMANCE CLUB

St. Paul's House

Warwick Lane

LONDON

EC4B 4HB

ployee with a vengeance, he thought. Not very pleasant, after years of freedom; of being practically his own master down here. Yet he could not altogether blame Miss Rowe. She had to inquire into things – to see where she stood – what was to be done. And she was not being intolerable about it . . . quite nice, in fact. But he wondered how long he would stick this job now she had come. He wished heartily that he had not given the old man his word to stay on and look after the place.

Elizabeth felt thoroughly miserable. She could feel herself up against a stone wall of hostility with the young estate-agent. There was no breaking through it. She was not the type to attempt to break through it, anyhow; unless she was met half-way. But she would have given a lot for Archer Hewitson to say: 'Let's pull together – not fight – when we do start work.'

Archer, however, said nothing of the sort. He had only just met Elizabeth. He did not know her. He would have been amazed had somebody told him that she was just a lonely, miserable girl trying to get over an unhappy love-affair and aching for affection and friendship. She did not show her feelings, and he took it for granted that she was a cold, rather hard young woman possessed of a domineering spirit.

He put his diary back in his pocket.

'I don't think there's anything else at the moment, Miss Rowe, so if you'll excuse me – I want to get over to the game-keeper's cottage and see about a leak in the roof. If you . . . '

He stopped abruptly. The peace and serenity of the May morning was broken by the sudden frantic barking of dogs. A shrill yap; a deeper bark; ominous snarling and snapping of teeth.

Elizabeth rushed to the window.

'That's Grock!' she said. 'Oh, dear, what's happened?'

Archer knew what had happened. It was Micky, his Cairn terrier, out there, beside himself with rage and fury because the big, spotted interloper had appeared on the scene. Micky had followed his master over the fields from Quince-Tree Cottage. Used to being the canine lord and master of the estate, he resented the presence of a strange Dalmatian.

'It *is* Grock,' said Elizabeth, turning to Archer. 'He's

fighting a wretched little terrier. We must go and rescue it.'

Archer marched from the library, through the french windows, and out into the garden.

'The "wretched little terrier" is my dog, Micky and if that big brute kills him, there'll be blue murder,' he said between his teeth.

'I'm sure he started the fight!' exclaimed Elizabeth. 'Grocky's most peaceful. He never fights anyone.'

Archer bore down on the scrapping, snarling animals. Grock, his lip drawn back from his teeth, was in the victorious position now, standing over the panting yelping body of his opponent. Micky, on his back, waving all four paws wildly in the air, was showing the whites of his eyes and snapping at the air with his teeth.

'Come here, Micky,' said Archer sternly. 'Mick – come here at once! Grock – get off – you brute!'

Elizabeth came forward and seized the Dalmatian's collar and dragged him off the Cairn. He stayed by her docilely, but growled in his throat and kept an eye on the terrier. Archer stooped and picked Micky up in his arms.

'Your dog's bitten him through the lip,' he said.

'I'm very sorry,' said Elizabeth coldly. 'I'm awfully sorry – but I'm afraid Micky started it.'

'I must apologise – but he regards this as his property. He's had the run of the place for two years.'

'Of course, *I'm* sorry if Grock bit him.'

'I'll have to keep him tied up and stop him coming to "Memories".'

'Oh, no – please don't do that. He'd hate it. He's rather a nice little dog,' said Elizabeth. 'Let him go about as usual, Mr. Hewitson. I daresay he and Grock will get over this and make friends.'

'Well, I'll get along now and take him with me,' said Archer. He put on his hat. 'If there's anything more I can tell you, Miss Rowe – '

'Not just now. But after lunch. By the way . . . you . . . would you care to lunch here?' She stumbled over the invitation. But she supposed she ought to make it.

'Thanks very much – it's kind of you. But my man will have my own meal ready at the cottage. I'll come up afterwards and we'll take a walk round.'

He raised his hat and moved away. Elizabeth, still holding on to Grock's collar, watched him put the little Cairn down, at the bottom of the garden. Micky shook himself furiously and followed his master.

Elizabeth looked at her pet.

'Oh, Grocky, you shouldn't have bitten the little dog,' she said reproachfully.

Grock wagged his tail proudly, to show that he was proud of having bitten the little dog.

Elizabeth thought:

'There'll be trouble between that young man and me. He's hatefully superior and he thoroughly dislikes me. Well, we're quits. I can't stand him.'

She walked thoughtfully into the house. How big and quiet and lonely it was.

She stood an instant in the lounge, looking round her forlornly. She felt like bursting into tears. She didn't want this big house and the money and the estates and all these difficulties which faced her. She felt an aching longing to be back in the little flat with Lilian . . . with Guy. Oh, if only Guy hadn't let her down so badly!

The words of Lilian's record came back to her in this moment:

> Give me back the life that you enchanted . . .
>   Give me back my heart . . .
> You won't be wanting it again . . .

She bit very hard indeed on her lower lip and lit another cigarette.

'Grocky,' she whispered to the dog, 'it isn't going to be all roses here, old man. It doesn't look as if it will be for you either. You've started off with a squabble – fighting that cocky, quarrelsome little terrier which our grand and superior estate agent considers a more sporting animal than you.'

Grock thumped his tail on the floor.

Mrs. Martlet appeared from nowhere.

'Please, miss,' she said, sniffing, 'is the dog to remain in the house?'

'Certainly, Mrs. Martlet,' said Elizabeth.

'It was orders of Sir James that no dogs was allowed in the

house. They spoil the carpets and covers and – '

'I'm sorry, Mrs. Martlet,' interrupted Elizabeth. 'But I am mistress here now, and Grock, my dog, is used to being with me in the house.'

'Mrs. Martlet bridled.

'D'you mean he sleeps in the house, too?'

'In my bedroom.'

'What – with those good rugs and – '

'Mrs. Martlet,' Elizabeth interrupted again, gently but firmly, 'you must get used to Grock. You'll find he's a very clean, quiet dog, and won't be any bother to you. And, by the way, I shall not sleep in that room with the four-poster bed. I'd be glad if you'd show me a much smaller room without so much stuff in it.'

The housekeeper grew red in the face. Her mouth, which Elizabeth described to herself as a rat-trap, opened as though she were about to protest against this, then she closed it again, raised her brows, and said:

'Very good, Miss.'

She turned on her heel.

'Mrs. Martlet,' said Elizabeth, 'perhaps we could have a little talk after lunch – you've been with Sir James a great number of years, and I'm sure you know a great deal about things here.'

'Yes, I do,' said the woman, turning back.

'Then we might discuss the future running of the place.'

'Do you intend getting new maids, please, miss?' asked Mrs Martlet, her eyes snapping behind the spectacles. 'Because if a lot of these new-fashioned, lazy 'ussies are coming, I shall not wish to stay.'

Elizabeth's heart sank. Opposition and hostility here, in the house as well as out of it.

'I don't think you need worry that I shall engage a lot of new servants, Mrs. Martlet. And I'm sure Sir James would have wished you to stay, after all these years,' she added good-humouredly. 'So we'll discuss things quite peacefully, shall we?'

'Very good, miss.' The woman fixed Grock with a baleful eye and departed, muttering to herself.

Elizabeth sat down on the arm of a chair. She smoked in silence for a moment. Staring through the windows, she saw the tall figure of the estate-agent walking across the fields, followed by his terrier.

'They all hate us, Grocky,' she said, with a wry smile. 'It's going to be pleasant, I can see!'

And if Guy had been here . . . the feeling might have been the same, but none of these people would have dared show it. They would have been more inclined to accept a master . . . which was what Guy would have been as her husband.

She pictured him – handsome, charming, clever Guy – looking after things here, at her side. He would have been wonderful. And she would have been so happy – so amazingly happy!

She realised that she could, if she wished, dismiss Archer Hewitson from her service; Mrs. Martlet, too; all her employees. But they had been Sir James's servants. She didn't want to dismiss them; to start off with making a general clearance. It looked so disrespectful to the dead man who had been a philanthropist; who was her benefactor. And he had particularly named the estate-agent and the old house-keeper – asked her to keep them on.

She would have to put up with their secret opposition; their thinly veiled antagonism. But she told herself that she would remember Guy's offer to help her, she would have him down here with Lilian – as soon as she could.

She looked desolately around her. She had not felt so lonely, so miserable, since she was a kid; on her first night at boarding-school. But even as a kid, at school, she had not 'squealed'. She had not shed a tear. She was dry-eyed now, but as she walked upstairs to hunt for a suitable bedroom she felt that she would have liked to shed a good many tears, and nothing would induce her to. She held her head high and told herself to 'stick it' and not be a silly ass.

Down in the kitchen, Mrs. Martlet assailed Annie, who was aged eighteen and open to influence.

'*I* shan't stay here to be told what I'm to do and what I'm not to do by that chit of a girl, I tell you! Hoiking that great brute of an animal round with her – with his muddy paws on my rugs and covers – I've never seen the like. What sort of creature is it, anyhow, with its great black spots? Sleeping in this house. Sakes alive, Sir James would be horrified, and my lady'd turn in her grave if she knew, and I daresay she does. Mark my words, Annie – any trouble from upstairs and out I goes, and you go with me.'

'Yes, Mrs. Martlet,' said Annie, round-eyed and scared.

'I can see Mr. Hewitson don't like her here,' added the housekeeper with relish. 'As nice a gentleman as I ever met, too. But that Miss Rowe – stuck up – nosin' round – doesn't think poor Sir James's bedroom good enough for her.'

A bell pealed through the big stone kitchen, a charming room, with its red stone floor and rows of shining copper utensils hanging on the walls.

'There you are,' said Mrs. Martlet. 'That's her! Beginning already. I'm not going to answer it. Off you go, Annie!'

Annie went.

CHAPTER VIII

THE inspection tour of the estate was not a success. After lunch, Archer dutifully called at 'Memories' for Elizabeth She had not enjoyed her lonely meal, and she was feeling miserable – therefore inaccessible – when Archer came. He himself was out of sorts, and did not look for the good qualities in his new and youthful employer. He found her difficult to talk to, and told himself that she was rather a sullen sort of girl. True, she did ask after his dog.

'I hope the little terrier is all right?' she said, when they started out from the house together on the 'round'.

'Thanks, yes,' said Archer. 'His lip is a bit uncomfortable and swollen, but I've left him with my man this afternoon.'

Elizabeth gave Grock a somewhat guilty look. He was walking sedately behind her.

'It was most unfortunate,' she murmured. 'I've never known Grock attack a small dog like that before.'

'Oh, I daresay Micky began it – he *is* a fighter,' said Archer with some pride.

Elizabeth cast a quick glance at the young man. All she could see was a very excellent profile and rather set lips.

'I know I shan't like him,' she reflected.

She therefore turned her attention from Mr. Hewitson to the estate. For the moment she forgot the difficulties that beset her and lost herself in admiration of the beauty around her. They were walking down the drive which led from the house to the lodge at the gates of 'Memories'. Elizabeth found the wide straight road with the reddish dust on it most attractive. On either side, the clipped grass border flaunted masses of daffodils. There was a quarter of a mile of them – under the trees – on the banks – everywhere.

'What an amazing sight!' she could not help exclaiming.

Archer looked at the daffodils.

'Yes, they're nice, aren't they? Nearly over now. You'll find the roses are pretty good. Brownrigg's a conscientious

71

gardener. He's been in the habit of sending up some of his flowers to the Chelsea Flower Show. Got a second in the rose class last June.'

'He sounds a good man,' said Elizabeth. 'I must see him.'

'Yes, we'll call at his cottage now, shall we? He lives at the lodge.'

They neared the end of the drive. Here it was cool and dim. Two great chestnut-trees, their 'white candles' in bud, shaded the gateway from the sun-light. On the right stood a low-built, red-brick cottage with diamond-paned windows, in the shadow of two tall firs.

'A pretty little lodge,' said Elizabeth. 'I often like the lodges better than the big houses themselves.'

'I agree as a rule,' said Archer. 'But this particular lodge doesn't get enough sun for me.'

'No, it is dark.' Elizabeth frowned as she walked up to the cottage. 'It can't be very healthy, surely. Brownrigg's got a wife and children, I suppose?'

'Yes. Two little girls. One an infant.'

'Well, he ought to get more sun. It's those two firs just behind there that are barring the sun from the west. One of them, at least, ought to come down.'

Archer said quickly

'Sir James wouldn't have any of the trees cut down except those in the woods which are used for fire-logs. He liked all these trees in the drive.'

'But if it's a question of health – of sunlight for the people who live in the cottage?'

'Quite so – but those were his wishes,' said Archer stiffly. Elizabeth bit her lip.

'I don't expect Sir James thought of it from that point of view, or I'm sure he'd have allowed the firs to come down. I must speak to Brownrigg.'

Archer remained silent. But he thought:

'So we begin! I knew she'd want to make alterations. Brownrigg won't have it, anyhow.'

The head-gardener emerged from his cottage. A stockily built, reddish-faced man with gingery hair and a straggling, ginger moustache. He touched his cap and said:

'Af'ernoon, sir,' to Archer.

With suspicious and watery blue eyes he looked at the slim girl in the grey tailor-made. She had come out without

72

a hat. With that youthful bobbed hair she didn't look to him like a suitable mistress for 'Memories'. However, Mr. Hewitson told him it was Miss Rowe, so he said, somewhat sullenly:

'Af'ernoon, miss.'

'I've been looking at the gardens, Brownrigg,' said Elizabeth. 'They're beautifully kept. I expect you're always very busy.'

'Aye.'

'How lovely all the bulbs are just now.'

'Aye.'

'I'd like a talk with you about things later on, Brownrigg.'

The head-gardener eyed her askance.

'I haven't had time to go into things much yet,' added Elizabeth.'

His expression made her feel hopeless; incapable of dealing with a garden one yard square, let alone all these acres. And his monosyllabic replies gave her no opportunity for a lengthy discussion about flowers. Then Hewitson made some remark about some seeds that had come from Suttons, and Brownrigg became garrulous. He entered into a long, involved conversation about seeds and flowers, speeches punctuated by 'Yes, sir,' 'No, sir' . . . . showing every evidence that he liked Mr. Hewitson and would talk freely to him.

Elizabeth felt crushed.

'That's that,' she thought.

She made another attempt to establish the right footing.

'Is Mrs. Brownrigg in? I'd like to say a word to her,' she said, trying to be bright and cheerful.

The gardener sniffed and turned indoors.

'Al-ice – here, a moment!'

A thin, pale woman, with an anaemic-looking baby in her arms, appeared in the doorway.

'Miss Rowe wants to see you, Alice,' said Brownrigg.

Alice regarded Elizabeth with a pale blue eye as suspicious as her husband's. She had lived here in this lodge for twelve years and had had no mistress to contend with. She didn't relish any 'interference' from this new young lady from 'Memories'; as she had told Bert last night.

Elizabeth's heart sank as she sensed hostility here. But she walked up and touched the baby's cheek with her finger.

73

'What a little darling,' she murmured.

Mrs. Brownrigg melted very slightly.

'Yes, she is. Goin' on for ten weeks old now.'

The tiny creature's face had a bluish-white look and its hands were like claws. It seemed to Elizabeth, although she didn't know much about babies, that this one was in need of sunlight. Yes, at least one of those fir-trees must come down so that the little lodge could have some sunshine. But Elizabeth said nothing at the moment.

'What's the baby's name?' she asked.

'Gloria, miss.'

Gloria Brownrigg! What a priceless name, thought Elizabeth, and she caught Archer's eyes. Just for a fleeting instant a message of humour passed between them.

'After Gloria Swanson, 'oo we saw on the films in Crowborough,' added Mrs Brownrigg.

Elizabeth stayed chatting for a moment. But once the subject of Gloria Brownrigg was dropped Mrs. Brownrigg was inarticulate and on the defensive again. Elizabeth and Archer then moved off.

'I suppose, like most gardeners who have been a long while in one place, he has set ideas,' said Elizabeth. 'I mean he won't like to be asked to do anything unusual?'

'I don't suppose he will.'

'H'm,' said Elizabeth.

The next visit was to the stables. Here Elizabeth was more at home. She understood and loved horses, and she had been brought up to ride. The stables were good, clean, and well-managed. Bingham, who drove the car, was also groom here for the moment, with the help of a stable-lad. Elizabeth stood in one of the sweet-smelling boxes, her hand on the warm satin neck of a big chestnut mare.

'This a lovely creature. Who rides her?'

'I do, as a rule,' said Archer.

'You hunt?'

'Yes – I had Sir James's permission.'

She could feel the undercurrent of animosity. She said:

'Of course. I – I hope you'll continue to hunt. I see that all the mounts here are for men, too big for me to ride. Perhaps I could sell one of the others and buy a mount for myself.'

Bingham – a thin man of about forty, with a blue chin and a typical 'horsey' appearance – looked at his new employer with instant disapproval.

'Sir James was fond of all these mares, miss.'

'Yes,' said Elizabeth. 'I understand. But it's no good keeping up with an unnecessarily big stable. We'll keep this chestnut mare which Mr. Hewitson rides, and sell one of the others.'

Bingham tapped a thin, gaitered leg with the stick he was holding and looked aggrieved. Archer and Elizabeth moved away from the stone courtyard and through an archway into the gardens again.

Archer was silent, but he was thinking hard. He had to admit that the upkeep of three biggish horses was an extravagance, and that Elizabeth was quite right to sell one and get a smaller mount for herself. But somehow he disliked the idea of this girl making these alterations, and he could not get over the feeling.

'She has the right to do what she likes, and I'm being damned petty,' he reflected moodily. 'But I can't knuckle under it, somehow.'

By the time they had finished their tour of the estates Elizabeth felt deeply depressed. Nowhere had she received a welcoming smile or an encouraging word. The Brownriggs didn't want her. Bingham was sulky because she intended to sell one of the mares. And she was not at all a success when she inspected the kennels. There were two red setters there. One was a young dog – beautiful to look at, with its silky, golden-red coat. But the other – the mother – was an ancient animal, half blind, smelling badly, and with a running sore which Bingham said was incurable.

'We've 'ad a vet. to 'er recently and 'e says she's incurable, so we let 'er lie about,' he told Elizabeth.

Elizabeth felt quite sick when she regarded the pathetic old setter.

'I don't believe in allowing a dumb animal to exist in pain – she must suffer from that sore,' she said. 'I'd like you to have her painlessly destroyed, Bingham.'

Bingham nearly choked. He looked at Mr. Hewitson.

'But it was Sir James's favourite dog, miss, and – '

'Sir James had not been down here for many months and could not have seen the poor thing in this condition,' interrupted Elizabeth, 'otherwise he'd have agreed with me. Anyhow, those are my orders, Bingham.'

75

Bingham again silently appealed to Archer. Archer remained grimly silent. Once again he had to agree that Elizabeth was justified in what she did, but it annoyed him.

As they left the kennels, Elizabeth said, quite indignantly:

'No dog should be allowed to live in that condition. Good heavens, even if my Grock, who is my greatest pal, was like that poor brute, I'd have him destroyed – and gladly.'

'I suppose one would,' said Archer coldly.

Elizabeth knew quite well that she had put Bingham's back up, which was not a good beginning. But she was obdurate on that point. No animal in her possession should be allowed to exist sick and suffering and incurable.

She strolled into the village with Archer. He introduced her to one or two of her tenants. She found Maplefield a peculiarly old-fashioned little village, behind the times and indolent. There was only one dusty, wretched little general store in which she felt that paraffin became mixed up with the biscuits and butter. One tiny post-office and stationer's combined, in which glossy postcards of local views dated back forty years and showed the district as it was not today. One tiny draper's, with a grim display of woollen underwear and artificial silk hosiery in its window. One butcher's shop. Most of these tradesmen had rented their property from Sir James Willington for half a century. None of them appeared pleased that they were now beholden to this bobbed-haired, slender girl who was much too young and modern to please their dusty and conservative fancy.

'Ol' man must have been out o' 'is mind – leavin' everythink to a bit of a child like that,' was the opinion of the postmistress, Mrs. Cheeseley. And Maplefield in general agreed with Mrs. Cheeseley.

Elizabeth returned to 'Memories' at tea-time feeling that poor old Sir James had not altogether done her a service in burdening her with his possessions. Nobody in Maplefield wanted her. She felt that it would be a most difficult thing to make them like her or feel that she wished to be a friend to them as much as Sir James had been.

Everywhere they had gone Archer Hewitson had been warmly received. He was, apparently, very much liked. Elizabeth could see that. He must himself have noticed how cold and unfriendly her reception had been. But he did not remark upon it – and Elizabeth was too proud to let him know how much it had hurt her. In her usual fashion she said nothing – even made an attempt to treat the affair lightly. Up at the house she said:

'That was most interesting. I enjoyed seeing everything. Thank you very much, Mr. Hewitson. It has been a very instructive afternoon. I see a little bit more now what I do own and what I want to do.'

He regarded her somewhat dubiously.

'Doesn't seem to mind much,' he reflected. 'Ye gods, they all made it pretty plain they had no use for her. But she's not the sensitive sort, apparently....'

'I'll let you have those figures of general expenditure to-night,' he said.

'Oh, yes, thanks. What about tea?' She lit a cigarette to hide her embarrassment. She didn't want the surly young man to tea. 'Will you come in and have some?'

'Thanks very much,' he said, believing it to be the courteous thing to do.

They had tea in the library – a formal little meal with a stilted atmosphere. Neither thawed to the other. And, as soon as politeness allowed, Archer bade Elizabeth goodbye.

Then, despite his antagonism, he was suddenly struck by the thought that she was only a girl, and that she would be very much alone in this big house. Rather rotten for her. Archer was really a kind-hearted young man. He could not refrain from observing that he hoped she would not find it too lonely up here by herself.

Elizabeth coloured. The sensitive flush made him ask himself whether she was so lacking in sensibility after all. But she wasn't going to show him that she was 'down'. No doubt, if she whined, he would be sorry for her. But that was the last thing she wanted.

'I shall be perfectly happy, thanks very much, Mr. Hewitson,' she said brightly. 'I'm very fond of reading, and this room holds a store of treasure for me.'

Archer bade her goodbye and departed.

She stood at the open french windows and watched the tall figure striding across the fields toward his cottage. She then turned back into the library and was furious because her eyelids stung with tears. Lonely! Heavens, it was almost unbearably lonely. She wanted Guy. If only she could stop wanting Guy! Everything was hateful here. The house and the grounds and this delicious spring weather were beautiful. But Archer Hewitson – Mrs. Martlet – Brownrigg – Bingham – everybody in or about the place was hateful . . . unsociable . . . hostile.

Grock, who thought 'Memories' a heavenly spot – a hundred per cent better than London – because there were so many wonderful open spaces on which he could bound and caper, lay stretched on the hearth-rug in blissful slumber. Elizabeth smiled down at him.

'You're liking it, anyhow, Grocky.'

The sound of her voice roused him sufficiently to make him open one eye and thump a tail on the floor.Then he fell asleep again. Elizabeth swallowed very hard. She sat down at the desk and began to write a letter to Lilian, which she had promised faithfully to do.

Two miles away, at the Kilwarnes' house, Delia Kilwarne, in excellent spirits, talked to Archer Hewitson in her pretty, very feminine drawing-room, whilst her husband finished dressing.

'So you managed dinner after all, Archie. Marvellous!'

'Yes. I thought Miss Rowe might want me for something. But she doesn't. Only I can't stay for bridge, if you don't mind, Delia, as I've got to get out some figures she wants to see.'

Delia Kilwarne – blonde and quite lovely in a blue chiffon dress with a coat to match – looked anxiously at Archer.

'How did you get on? What's she like?'

Archer twisted his lips.

'Oh – quite nice.'

'Damned with faint praise,' said Delia happily.

Archer felt a bit mean.

'No, I wouldn't say that. I mean – she's quite nice, really. She only a kid – twenty-two. I mean, the thing's absurd. She isn't capable of managing a big estate.'

'But you'll do that for her.'

'Yes, but she's got ideas.'

'Oh, what a pity.'

'Yes. She wants to alter things. She's made up her mind to cut down one of those firs by Brownrigg's cottage because she thinks the baby needs sunlight. And she's ordered Bingham to destroy old Sally. She'll make herself unpopular.'

'What do you think of her personally?' Delia Kilwarne

harped on the subject. Madly in love with Archer, she was jealous of this twenty-two-year-old girl who was now his employer, even though she was vain enough to imagine herself more than a match for Miss Rowe. She was quite satisfied when Archer said:

'Oh, she's rather quiet and difficult to talk to – a queer sort of child. I don't know what bowled the old man over, 'pon my word.'

Then Charlie Kilwarne – a ruddy, kind-eyed, cheery-looking man, inclined to be fat – came in and talked golf. The subject of Elizabeth was dropped.

Yet it was curious that once or twice during that evening at the White House, well fed, well amused by Delia's engaging personality and chatter and Charlie Kilwarne's excellent wines, Archer found his thoughts drifting once or twice to Elizabeth. He remembered how she had flushed when he had said he hoped she would not be too lonely. Queer little thing. He'd never met anybody quite like her before. And she wasn't in the least like the Miss Rowe he had pictured. She must be lonely up in that great house – absolutely by herself. He felt quite uncomfortable about it.

'I hope she won't stay on down here,' he thought. 'It'll be much more pleasant for her and for us all if she makes up her mind not to live permanently at "Memories".'

CHAPTER IX

ELIZABETH, however, made up her mind that she *would* live at 'Memories' – for the summer months, anyhow. Sir James had bequeathed this place to her. He had asked her to take an interest in the things he had loved. She was not going to be driven out by the undercurrent of hostility which she felt and encountered on all sides.

She was a strong-minded little person, and opposition was the thing calculated to make her resolve to stay at 'Memories' and hold her own.

The first fortnight in her new home was not in any sense an agreeable one. She told herself wryly that Grock was possibly the only one who enjoyed it. His delight in the country was unlimited. But Elizabeth met with continual reverses in her efforts to establish herself as the mistress of 'Memories'.

Inside the house she had Mrs. Martlet to tackle. Mrs. Martlet refused to be won over by any attempts Elizabeth made to put her in a good humour. She continued to cook and do her usual work as diligently as ever, and with almost irritating precision and excellence. A few muddy paw-marks from the Dalmatian excited her instant wrath and indignation. But she showed plainly that she worked out of duty and for no other reason, and she considered that Miss Rowe insulted the memory of her late master by making drastic alterations in the various rooms of the house.

Elizabeth occupied a small bedroom facing south and with two windows overlooking the rose-garden and the pond. That smooth stretch of shining water, bordered with poplars and slim, silver birches, was a constant delight to her. It was the view which pleased her most, and she could see beyond, over the woods, as far as the dark shadow of Ashdown Forest. She moved one or two charming old pieces of furniture and a small single bed into this room, and in the linen cupboard she found some shiny chintz curtains – a delicious old pattern – rose and green with a cream background. They put the finishing-touch to the sort of bedroom she had long wanted.

Mrs. Martlet thought the result both bare and ugly and shrugged her shoulders over the 'young person's bad taste'. For two days she maintained a sulky silence because Elizabeth ruthlessly stripped the drawing-room; turned out brocade curtains and the whole collection of Victorian rubbish; kept only the good pieces of china and glass and the Queen Anne walnut cabinet and writing bureau. The satin brocade sofa and chairs, which were ornate Louis XVI, she had to keep for the moment, but she wanted, later on, to buy some Chippendale chairs to put in their place.

She knew that the old housekeeper was scandalised by these alterations, but she went doggedly ahead. And because the woman had been such a faithful retainer in the place, Elizabeth bore patiently with her sulks and silences.

Outside the house, she did what she considered right. The miserable, suffering old setter was sent to the vet. and put painlessly out. This caused intense indignation amongst the men. Bingham fostered a spirit of resentment amongst them. There was not one who looked on the right side of Elizabeth's action in having the old dog destroyed. Bingham went about saying that it was a 'blinkin' shame', and his associates agreed. It was a 'blinkin' shame'. The death of Sally – Elizabeth's first humane command – was distorted into an act of heartless cruelty.

Over the question of the fir-trees which darkened Brownrigg's cottage, Elizabeth met with such acute disapproval that she had to capitulate and leave the trees standing. Brownrigg refused to admit that the lodge was too dark to be healthy. Alice, his wife, took up the cudgels on his behalf, and was grossly insulted by Miss Rowe's suggestion that little Gloria might benefit by more sunlight.

'Them trees have stood by the lodge all the twelve years we've been here,' the gardener told Elizabeth, after a short, sharp argument on the subject. 'And a good many score o' years afore we was gardeners here. I don't 'old with cutting 'em down, miss, and nor do Alice.'

Elizabeth, flushed and perturbed, gave way. Let the fir-trees remain. Let the Brownriggs go on living in darkness. She had tried to act in their interest. They didn't want her help and advice. She would leave it. She was soon to find out that most of Sir James's employees had existed in a rut for years, and they were indignant that they should be asked to get out of it.

It was very discouraging. And the attitude of Archer Hewitson was not much more encouraging.

At the end of the first week at 'Memories', Elizabeth called at Quince-Tree Cottage to see her estate-agent. He received her with his usual cold courtesy, which always had the effect of making her draw into her shell of reserve. But she could not help noticing the homely charm of the sunny oak-beamed cottage. She sighed a little. A tiny place like this would really have suited her better than a house like 'Memories'. It was so dreary up there, with only the servants about the place. Never had Elizabeth had such a lonely week. The days had been fairly full; yet she had met with so much opposition, she had not enjoyed them. And the evenings had seemed interminable – terribly boring in spite of all the books.

She had found herself yearning for the little flat in Chelsea; for the old days when she led a care-free, jolly life with her painting, and good-natured, charming Lilian for a companion.

She stood by the open casements in Archer Hewitson's sitting-room and stared out at the garden.

'How nice your tulips are,' she said absently.

'Yes, aren't they?' he said.

She turned back to the room. Her eyes wandered moodily from the oak dresser – so like the one she had had in the flat – to the oak writing-bureau. Typical of the bachelor – an untidy mess of papers; a tobacco jar; an assortment of pipes; a pile of old magazines and books. Not a photograph, not a flower in here. The feminine touch was missing. Yet it was jolly, cosy, so much more friendly than 'Memories'.

'I hope everything is going on as you wish, Miss Rowe.' Archer made this speech somewhat reluctantly, but he felt it was the graceful thing to do.

'Yes – thank you.'

'You've studied the statement of expenditure I've made out for you?'

'Yes. It doesn't seem to me very extravagant for such a big place.'

'I don't think any money is wasted,' he said. Then: 'Won't you sit down?'

It was the first time she had come to his cottage. He had always seen her up at the big house. She sat down on the arm of a chair. He handed her a cigarette. She had come here determined that he should not see that she was discouraged or depressed, so she smiled as he lit a cigarette for her.

'The Brownriggs don't seem inclined to have those firs down,' she said brightly.

'No – I can't say they approve of the suggestion.' Archer smiled a trifle grimly when he remembered the violent denunciations of the little scheme to which the head-gardener had treated him, personally, yesterday.

'The lodge had better stay as it is, then,' said Elizabeth.

'I fancy so,' he said, and reflected: 'She'll find she can't alter everything as soon as she comes.'

He had to admit that she looked a mere child this morning, and quite nice in a yellow jumper suit – the colour of daffodils – with a flowered yellow scarf knotted about her neck. As usual, she wore no hat. How dark her hair was, he thought – almost black. Smooth and straight. She was not bad-looking, really. But very unapproachable.

'Could you make arrangements to sell the grey mare – I think they call her "Tess"?' said Elizabeth. 'And could you find a mount for me?'

'I think so,' said Archer. 'I might go to Tattersall's on Monday.'

'I might go, too – see what's to be bought.'

'Do,' said Archer stiffly.

'Mr. Hewitson,' she said, 'I went over the fields to the gamekeeper's cottage yesterday. You must agree with me that conditions there are impossible. I was horrified. It isn't a small thing like no sunlight – like the lodge. It's a question of public health. I spoke to Mrs. Hawkson, and she didn't agree with me, but the drainage system is prehistoric and the rooms are filthy. It ought to be pulled down. It really isn't sanitary. There might be an outbreak of diphtheria. I can't imagine that if the sanitary inspector came there it would be passed.'

Archer frowned. Here was more criticism, and he felt that it reflected on him personally.

'The Hawksons have occupied that cottage for ten or

'eleven years and have never been ill,' he said.

'Conditions are rapidly becoming worse there. I could see it for myself.'

'Then what do you suggest, Miss Rowe?'

'Pulling it down and building a modern bungalow with a proper septic tank.'

'The Hawksons would be most distressed. That has been their home for years.'

Elizabeth flushed, and tapped her toe on the ground.

'I cannot see that, because these people are content with staying in a rut, they should be permitted to do so. Nobody who goes into that cottage could help seeing that conditions there are impossible . . . ridiculous for the year 1931.'

'They may be out of date, but –'

'They're unhealthy.'

'Sir James –' began Archer.

'Mr. Hewitson,' she broke in, 'I think I must manage my estate now in the way I think best. Dear old Sir James was a very old man when he died, and he did not go into details when he came down here. That is obvious. He hadn't much love for modern improvement of lighting and heating and that sort of thing. But I cannot allow that gamekeeper's cottage to stand as it is.'

Archer's heart beat a trifle faster. Here was open combat. He felt himself criticised and snubbed by this slip of a girl. He found it difficult not to throw down the gauntlet by offering to resign his post at once. Elizabeth added:

'I can't understand that you don't agree with me.'

'I may agree that the cottage is old and badly built and that the drainage system is poor. But these country cottagers haven't ideas like ours, and they object to being turned out of a home which has a certain amount of sentiment attached to it. The Hawksons like that little place, and they'd hate a modern bungalow.'

'Not once they were in it.'

'More than probably Hawson would give notice.'

Elizabeth's colour rose.

'Then we must find a new gamekeeper, Mr Hewitson.'

'After ten years of loyal service? There isn't a finer keeper in Sussex. He's wonderful at rearing young birds and keeping down the vermin.'

'I like Hawson – I think he's an excellent man,' said

84

Elizabeth. 'But unless he consents to that filthy, unhealthy little place being pulled down, he must go. I'll offer him every recompense, and a brand new home into the bargain.'

'I don't think you'll find it will be a popular scheme,' said Archer.

'I'm not trying to be popular,' she said icily. 'I only wish to do what I consider proper and right now that I am living here. And I shall do nothing that I am not sure Sir James, were he alive, would approve.'

She stood up. For an instant a pair of dark, flashing eyes met disapproving hazel ones. Archer clenched a hand behind his back.

'Well, I'm hanged!' he thought furiously. 'Who'd believe this bit of a girl would take the high hand like this?'

And once again there wriggled into his mind the irritating thought that she was right. He had himself noticed many times that the game-keeper's evil-smelling little cottage was a pestilence. But he had let the matter alone. Had he been neglecting his duty on the estate? It seemed that Miss Elizabeth was, in a subtle fashion, pointing out that fact. He had a grudging admiration for her will-power, but he could not bring himself to toady to her.

'You have every right to give whatever orders you think best, Miss Rowe,' he said in his most chilling voice. 'I'll let Hawkson know what you say.'

'And perhaps you'd get an estimate from a builder for a sensible, economical bungalow.'

'I will.'

Archer opened the door for her. The slim figure in yellow passed out. Grock padded after her. Archer stared at the straight young back and thought gloomily:

'My free and easy days are over with a vengeance.'

Elizabeth found herself walking straight into a tall, fair-haired young woman wearing light tweeds and well-polished brogues, who was swinging down the flagged path toward the cottage.

'Oh, I beg your pardon,' said Elizabeth, stepping aside.

Archer came forward hastily.

'Let me introduce you. Mrs. Kilwarne – Miss Rowe.'

Delia Kilwarne looked at Elizabeth. So this was the famous Miss Rowe. What a funny little thing, with her

85

boyish figure and pale face and that straight, dark fringe of hair.

'Nothing much to be jealous of,' thought Delia. Aloud she said:

'Oh, how do you do, Miss Rowe. I've heard about you, of course. You're up at "Memories" now?'

'Yes,' said Elizabeth. She felt and looked shy. She was never very at home with people she met for the first time.

'Lovely day,' murmured Delia. She looked through her long lashes at Archer. 'Got my clubs in the car and wondered if you'd play eighteen holes with me, Archie.'

'Thanks awfully, Delia, but I'm rather busy this morning,' he said, smiling at her.

'Oh, I'm *so* sorry, my dear,' she said. She turned back to Elizabeth. 'Are you making him do a spot of work?' she said gaily.

'I – oh, I – not at all – if Mr. Hewitson wishes to play golf – ' Elizabeth stammered and broke off, not knowing in the least how to respond to this silken attack. But she knew at once that Delia Kilwarne was an enemy and that she would never like her.

Archer looked uncomfortable now and rather cross.

'I can't play this morning – really, I'm busy, Delia,' he said.

'What a shame,' she said. 'Never mind. Another time. Can I come in and have a cigarette before I go on?'

'Do,' he said, not very willingly.

'Goodbye,' said Delia sweetly, holding out a hand to Elizabeth.

'Goodbye,' said Elizabeth.

Grock suddenly emitted a warning growl. A small wheaten-cream body rushed round from the back of Quince-Tree Cottage, barking furiously.

'Oh, don't let there be another fight!' exclaimed Elizabeth.

'Micky! Come here, sir!' said Archer.

He grabbed the Cairn and picked him up in his arms. Micky snapped and struggled; his bright, black eyes glinting at the Dalmatian.

'I don't think they'll ever be friends,' said Elizabeth.

'I don't think they will,' Archer agreed.

'Goodbye,' she said.

'Goodbye, Miss Rowe.'

She moved away. Archer carried Micky into the cottage and set him down. Delia followed.

'And I don't think Miss Rowe and you will ever be friends either, Archie,' said Delia maliciously. 'Isn't she too quaint for words?'

'H'm!' said Archer.

'However did she manage to vamp Sir James? Is she vamping you?'

'Good heavens, no – far from it. But I feel like packing up and going out East again.'

'Making herself unpleasant, is she?'

'Not exactly – but she's throwing her weight about a bit. I suppose she has every right to, Delia. I'm sorry for the Hawksons, though, for instance. She's going to drag their cottage down.'

'Why?'

Archer explained.

'These people are like animals – they don't want to be turned out of their holes and cleansed and modernised. But one can't deny that Miss Rowe is justified.'

'I should think she's very difficult.'

'Well, I must try not to work myself up about it,' said Archer grimly. 'I promised the old man I'd stay, and I will. I do at least control the expenditure honestly. But I don't like all these changes. How's Charlie?'

Delia didn't want to talk about Charlie. But she had to. And she could see that Archer was not in a good mood, so she tactfully departed. But she meant to see him again – quite soon. And the more Miss Rowe annoyed him, the better it would be for her, Delia, and her chances of making him find out that she was the only woman in the world for him.

Elizabeth walked back to 'Memories'. She felt that she was doing the right and proper thing about Hawkson's place, which was no better than an unhealthy hovel. She was no longer smiling as she had been when she left Quince-Tree Cottage. Her face was tired, and she felt very depressed. That hateful, superior young man – Archer Hewitson. He was undoubtedly an honest and conscientious agent – but why couldn't he be more amiable – pull with her – instead of away from her? His animosity was not helpful.

If only Guy would come down – back her up – advise and help her. But best not to think of Guy. Last night she had had a letter from Lilian. Somebody wanted to rent, furnished, the little flat in Elbury Walk. Lilian suggested they should do this. The tenants might eventually buy the contents and take it over unfurnished. Lilian was staying with an aunt in Hampstead, busily buying her trousseau. Guy wanted her to marry him at once.

Elizabeth's heart ached as she thought of the approaching marriage between these two. The loss of Guy as her lover, her future husband, had affected her more than she had dreamed it would do. It was the loneliness that defeated her, broke down her resistance. And now that she was rich, she was lonelier than ever. Funny, that; how little money counted; how being wealthy could, in fact, increase one's loneliness.

Her thoughts turned to the woman she had just met at Quince-Tree Cottage. Who and what was Mrs. Kilwarne? Certainly she was extremely pretty. And obviously an intimate friend of Mr. Hewitson. They called each other 'Archie' and 'Delia'. And she seemed to have the run of his cottage. Was she a widow? Was there an 'affair' in progress there? She couldn't imagine the stiff, cold young man being in love with anyone. She felt mildly curious about Mrs. Kilwarne. She put a question or two to Annie during her solitary lunch.

'Annie, I met a Mrs. Kilwarne this morning. Where does she live, do you know?'

Annie, who, despite Mrs. Martlet's bullying, was disposed to like her young mistress, gave Elizabeth more information than had been required of her.

'Oh, yes, miss, I know Mrs. Kilwarne, miss. Lives up at the White House, on the Crowborough road, and my eldest sister used to be parlourmaid there and left last Christmas because there was too much entertaining. Always giving bridge-parties. And my sister says – '

'Yes, I see,' broke in Elizabeth. 'Thank you, Annie.'

'My sister found her a terror to work for, miss – so complaining – but she liked Mr. Kilwarne. He is a very nice gentleman – but *she* —'

'I'll have some more cheese, Annie,' said Elizabeth, cutting this scandalous little speech short.

88

So Mrs. Kilwarne was not a widow. There was a husband. Elizabeth raised her brows slightly. What was the beautiful married lady doing floating round the estate-agent's cottage at this hour of the day, inviting him to play golf with her? Was Mr. Hewitson a dark horse?

'Appearances are most deceptive – one never knows what anybody else is really like,' she thought. 'But it isn't my business. Mr. Hewitson can have a dozen married ladies pursuing him for all I care.'

She sank back in her chair and waited for Annie to come back. This was the morning-room – a charming, octagonal room with oak panelling and french windows opening on to the front lawn. It was small and sunny, and Elizabeth used it for all meals. The dining-room was so enormous, full of massive furniture. She had dined in there once and felt lost, and had afterwards shut it up.

'Please, miss,' said Annie, 'there's a gentleman just arrived in a car and wants to see you.'

Elizabeth's spirits rose. She stood up and wiped her lips with her napkin.

'Who is it, Annie?'

'He didn't give no name, miss. I showed him into the library.'

Elizabeth felt her heart-beats quicken and her cheeks grow hot. She fancied that she knew who it was. She was thrilled. She oughtn't to be. But she was. She half ran into the library. Yes, it was Guy.

CHAPTER X

SHE gave one look at the tall, handsome figure and the fair, well-shaped head and knew that she was quite shamelessly glad to see him again.

'Guy!' she exclaimed.

'Why, little Lizbeth!' he said, and came across the room to meet her – both hands outstretched, blue eyes eagerly regarding her.

She stood still. Her heart-beats seemed to hurt her. The same charming Guy; the old pet name; and more warmth than he had shown her for some time. How cruel it was . . . and he belonged to another woman now.

Her joyous spirits died. She gave him her right hand and said, quite formally:

'How are you, Guy?'

He did not know that her heart was racing, nor that she longed to fling herself into his arms and feel his lips, just once again, against hers as they had been so many times in the ecstatic past. He thought:

'Funny little girl – just as cool and remote as ever.'

And if she'd shown a half of what she felt, he would have had no compunction in taking her in his arms and kissing her. He was thoroughly fed up with Lilian. She was stupid and she was going to bore him, and he had come to the conclusion that he had been quite mad to let her physical charms so dazzle his senses that he had broken with Elizabeth.

He looked round at the book-bound walls of the library appreciatively. Lots of good stuff here. Rare volumes, too. He had been looking at 'em with the eagle eye of a collector. And the whole place – by gad! What a place! Magnificent old Tudor house – beautiful state of repair – well restored. And what grounds! Superb. Acres of land. And all belonging to 'little Lizbeth'.

'How are you, my dear?' he said heartily. 'I had to come

down and see you. I've been so worried about you.'

'Worried about me? Why?'

'Oh, lots of reasons.'

'Look here – have you had lunch?'

'No, but I don't want to thrust myself on you –'

'Nonsense,' she interrupted. 'Come along at once and have something. There's plenty in the house.'

He followed her into the morning-room. Everywhere he went, in every corner, he saw something of beauty and value. What a house! And if he hadn't been such a colossal idiot – if he hadn't let his feelings run away with him – it might have been his home. Damn it! Well, perhaps it wasn't too late, even now.

'Lil heard from you, yesterday, and said she thought you were depressed and finding things a bit difficult on your own,' he said.

'Oh, no, I'm all right,' said Elizabeth, with her inborn hatred of whining. She had not meant Lilian to show that letter to Guy. 'How is Lil? Why couldn't she come?'

'She's laid up with a chill. That's why I took the opportunity of running down to see you, Elizabeth. My dear, you've got an extremely attractive home here.'

'Yes,' said Elizabeth.

He was sitting opposite her at the table now. How good he was to look at; and how charming he could be. She thought desolately how much more attractive 'Memories' would have seemed to her had he come here, too. That would have been his rightful place – there at this table – opposite her.

Now that he filled the room with his buoyant presence; his appreciation; his *camaraderie*; she realised forcibly how much alone she had been and what a terrific lot she had lost when she lost him.

'Tell me everything,' he said. 'How are you managing? What's the estate-agent like?'

He questioned her until he had the information he desired. He could tell that, behind her brave efforts to assure him she was managing very well, she found the position difficult. And it was obvious she didn't like the estate-agent. So much to the good, so far as Guy was concerned.

'He's a very nice man – I mean awfully well bred and an absolute gentleman – and he doesn't actively refuse to do what I ask, of course,' said Elizabeth. 'But he doesn't agree with me. Now, Guy, I ask you –'

She launched into a graphic account of the game-keeper's cottage and what she wanted to do.

'You're absolutely right!' said Guy. 'No two questions about it. The place ought to come down. Mr. Hewitson's probably lazy – doesn't like too much work.'

'No – in all fairness to him, I don't think he's like that,' she said unwillingly. 'But his ideas are not mine. His sympathies are with these people.'

'He wants a man to speak to him,' said Guy. 'I'll have a word with him for you, Elizabeth.'

Elizabeth bit her lip. She had wanted Guy and his help. Yet, with her inborn sense of justice and her logical reasoning, she could see that it would not be right for Guy, as an outsider, to interfere – to talk to Archer Hewitson.

Guy, however, became inflamed with the desire to take up the cudgels in Elizabeth's behalf.

'You want my help – I know you do, little Lizbeth,' he said.

She winced. If only he'd drop that name; that caressing voice. It only opened up wounds that were still fresh enough to hurt intolerably.

'Tell me your plans – with Lilian,' she said deliberately.

Guy finished his lunch and lit a cigarette.

'Oh, nothing very definite – I mean no definite date,' he said evasively.

'I see. I suppose you are – both – very happy.'

He did not answer this for a moment. Then he gave her a quick, meaning look.

'I can't altogether answer that, my dear.'

'But why?' she asked, astonished.

He made a gesture with his hand.

'Frankly, I've been too unhappy about you.'

'Unhappy – about me! But why?' she flushed scarlet.

'Don't you see' – he frowned and averted his gaze – 'ever since we broke our engagement – it's haunted me – the thought that I'd been a swine – made you unhappy – and incidentally I haven't been able to be really happy myself.'

That was hypocritical, and he knew it. Elizabeth stared. She did not quite gather what he was driving at. She said:

'But, Guy, you ought to be happy. You and Lil are ideally matched. And I – I assure you, I'm all right.'

'But are you?'

He rose and came toward her. In sudden panic, terrified that she would be stirred into showing her feelings, into breaking down, she backed away from him.

'No, no, Guy – don't let's rake up old ghosts. Please. It isn't fair to Lil – to any of us. I'm all right. You're not to worry. Just go on being my pal –'

He bit his lip. He was not sure he wanted to go on being just Elizabeth's pal. He wanted to be more. To have the right to stay here – with her. In the glamour of her new and lovely possessions he was near to falling in love with her all over again.

'Of course I'll always be your pal, my dear – but I don't believe you're as matter-of-fact and unemotional as you pretend to be.'

She looked at him very straight, and she was quite white now.

'Guy – is this – this sort of conversation any good to either of us?'

'But don't you see – I've been driven quite frantic with remorse,' he said extravagantly. 'I don't think I realised how caddishly I behaved.'

'But you didn't,' she said, deeply distressed. 'You had every right to change – to tell me you'd changed. It would have been much worse if you'd married me and found out afterwards that you loved Lilian.'

He pulled at his collar and looked out of the windows at the broad sweep of green lawn sloping to the pond, and the exquisite blue of lobelia fringing the herbaceous border. The very beauty of the garden irritated him. Hang it all, if he'd married Elizabeth and shared all this with her, he wouldn't have found out that he loved Lilian. If only he could see a chance . . . a chance of unravelling this tangle; of getting back on the old footing with Elizabeth: If only he could make sure she was still in love with him! He was a conceited man, and he liked to imagine that she had not stopped caring for him. Whereas, not so long ago, he had accused her of being unsentimental, it pleased him now to imagine that she had plenty of emotion hidden away under a calm exterior. Thus, to satisfy his vanity, he came nearer to real understanding of Elizabeth than he had ever been before.

Elizabeth did not for an instant imagine that he regretted breaking with her. She thought he was 'being sorry for her'. That was intolerable. She tried to look at him calmly, and even to laugh.

'You're being a silly old ass, Guy,' she said. 'Of *course* I'm quite happy and content. I've got a tremendous lot to interest me down here, and I've put the memory of our affair – right out of my mind. Now, have a cigarette and come and look at the grounds.'

He was forced to fall in with her mood. As he followed the slim, yellow-clad figure into the gardens, he chafed at his failure to make this girl wear her heart on her sleeve for him. But he was not going to lose hope. No, not while there was so much at stake. And the more he saw of 'Memories', the more he assured himself that he was in love with 'little Lizbeth' again.

She walked beside him through the rose-garden and down toward the shining pond. Grock followed; keeping a doubtful eye on the man. Here was this objectionable god once more . . . the god his little mistress had once acknowledged; and Grock was jealous. He had hoped they had left him behind when they came down here.

Elizabeth chatted lightly. But there was a strange, hot mist in front of her eyes, blurring the lovely gardens for her. Her heart was beating quickly. She thought:

'Oh, Guy, Guy . . . wasn't it rather cruel to try and break down my defences with your pity? I do love you still. I know it. But I shall never let you know – never, never. . . . '

She cleared her throat, stood still and looked back at the house.

' "Memories" looks so charming from here, doesn't it?' she observed.

'It's a topping old place,' he said warmly. Then he added: 'Hello – who's this?'

Elizabeth turned and saw the tall figure of a man in grey flannels coming toward them. He was striding along, hands in his pockets, bare, brown head bent. He appeared to be lost in thought, so that he did not see the couple standing there until he was within a few yards of them.

'It's my estate-agent – Mr. Hewitson,' Elizabeth murmured to Guy.

Arlingham squared his shoulders.

'Ah! I want to see this fellow.'

Archer stopped dead when he saw Elizabeth and the fair, well-groomed man beside her; a man whose appearance at once suggested London and the West End.

'I beg your pardon, Miss Rowe,' said Archer. 'I wanted to see you for a few minutes – but I didn't know you had a guest.'

'It doesn't matter at all,' said Elizabeth.

'Any time will do,' added Archer.

'No – no – don't go. Let me introduce you,' she said. 'Mr. Hewitson – Mr. Arlingham – a very old friend of mine. Guy, this is Mr. Hewitson, who manages the estate for me.'

'How do?' said Guy, drawling.

'How do you do?' said Archer shortly.

'Fine old place this,' said Guy. 'Keeps you pretty occupied, I expect.'

'Quite,' said Archer.

He gave the other man a quick look and summed him up as a bounder. The conceited type of ass he couldn't stand. And he found his manner rather offensive. He turned to Elizabeth.

'I'll come up another time, Miss Rowe. It was just about Hawkson's place.'

'Oh, do tell me what's been done,' she said. 'Mr. Arlingham won't mind, I know.'

'Is this about the gamekeeper's unhealthy abode?' drawled Guy. 'You were telling me at lunch, Lizbeth.'

Archer thought:

' "Lizbeth," eh? So the difficult Miss Rowe has an admirer. He looks as though he were head-over-heels in love. And she's been discussing the estate with him. "Unhealthy abode" indeed! Blast his impudence!'

'What's Hawkson say, Mr. Hewitson?' asked Elizabeth.

'He won't hear of his home being pulled down,' said Archer. 'He is quite satisfied with it, and he says his wife would break her heart if she were turned into a modern bungalow.'

'That's rather stupid of them, isn't it?' said Elizabeth. 'Of course, I understand their point of view – a sentimental attachment to an old home.'

'I'm sorry about that, but I feel I must have the place down. Tell him I'm sorry, but there it is.'

95

'I think he'll leave, Miss Rowe.'

'Then he must leave,' said Elizabeth, frowning.

'I've never heard of such nonsense,' put in Arlingham. He regarded Hewitson with a supercilious eye. 'You don't, surely, let these labourers ride over you like this, Hewitson?'

The blood crept up under Archer's brown skin. This was not Mr. Arlingham's business, and he was not going to be spoken to in that tone.

'It isn't a question of letting them ride over me, I assure you,' he said. 'Neither is Hawkson a common labourer. He is a very excellent gamekeeper, who has taken care of the game preserves on this estate for twelve years. His feelings about his old home are perfectly comprehensible – to me, anyhow.'

'Oh, they are to me, too,' said Elizabeth, with a little pucker of the brows. 'But we must have sanitary conditions on the estate, mustn't we?'

'I'll tell Hawkson that he must either accept the new house or leave,' said Archer coldly.

'I consider Miss Rowe is absolutely justified in what she says,' put in Guy. 'My advice to her is to have that place down – the sooner the better.'

Archer gave him a quick look; opened his lips as though to retort, then closed them again. Confound the impudence of the fellow – interfering like this! His face was hot and angry when he spoke to Elizabeth again.

'There's a point about some fruit-trees Brownrigg would like to have settled – perhaps I can see you in the morning when you are by yourself again, Miss Rowe.'

He turned on his heel and marched away.

Elizabeth felt her own cheeks grow hot. Guy exclaimed:

'By Jove, that young man wants putting in his place!'

Elizabeth, distressed, looked up at Guy.

'Oh dear, it's all very difficult. Perhaps you oughtn't to have spoken to him like that, Guy. I mean – he probably resents an outsider discussing the estate and – '

'Am I an outsider?' he broke in in an offended tone.

'My dear, you're my best friend – but to him you are a stranger,' she said quickly. 'I'm afraid he's upset.'

'Pooh! What's it matter? You're not going to let a man whom you employ – an estate-agent – order you about, surely?'

'No,' she said, biting her lip. 'But I must remember – Archer Hewitson isn't – an ordinary employee – inasmuch as he was a personal friend and protégé of Sir James's – and he's a Public School and Varsity man.'

'He wants putting in his place,' repeated Guy. 'Let's forget him. Take me round the grounds, Lizbeth. You did absolutely right, my dear, in sticking to your guns about the gamekeeper's cottage.'

He put an arm through hers.

In silence Elizabeth walked beside him through the sun-lit gardens. She felt a little upset about the encounter between the two men. She had an uncomfortable feeling that Archer Hewitson would have every right to say he wouldn't stand interference from strangers. How red and angry he had looked. Yet how well he had stood his ground. He had dignity and poise, had her estate-agent.

'This won't add to *my* success in the place,' she thought grimly. 'And I can't help feeling Guy was at fault. He shouldn't have interfered.'

It was quite on the cards that Archer might chuck up the whole job. Elizabeth contemplated this a trifle uneasily. She had only been at 'Memories' a fortnight, but it was long enough to satisfy her that Archer was a most conscientious and honest guardian of her business affairs. She might find it difficult to find an agent more thrifty about expenditure and with as keen a personal interest in the estate. After all, Sir James had asked her to keep him here. She wondered if she was failing in respect to the old man's memory by allowing this state of animosity with Hewitson to continue?'

'I'd better see him in the morning and smooth his ruffled feathers,' she thought.

Guy stayed on to tea. He was charming and amusing and made the hours fly by. She was genuinely sorry to see him go. Yet in a way she was relieved. It was such a strain, laughing and talking to him in a friendly way, when every nerve in her body ached with memories of him as her lover.

Guy drove away, promising to bring Lilian down as soon as she was well enough to come out in the car. He held Elizabeth's hand a little longer than mere friendship demanded, and said:

'My dear, you must let me help you over the difficulties in such a big estate as this, and don't allow that objectionable young man, Hewitson, to bully you.'

'I don't allow anybody to bully me!' she said, laughing, and drew her fingers quickly away. She felt almost cross with Guy. Why couldn't he realise how he hurt her . . . by the lingering touch of his hand . . . by such tenderness as he instilled into his voice and manner when he said '*Au revoir*, little Lizbeth, till we meet again'? It wasn't fair. It was cowardly. Or perhaps he didn't think that she cared any more . . . and he was trying to be kind.

After he had gone the house seemed very big and empty. But she made up her mind that she would never be able to bear things if he came too often . . . if she saw too much of him. Friendship was impossible where passionate love had flamed so recently. It was all very well for him, she thought bitterly. He had Lilian. But she had nobody . . . nothing to comfort her.

She was in an unhappy, restless state of mind for the rest of the evening . . . worse than she had felt before Guy came. And she was worried by the thought that Guy had offended Archer Hewitson.

The beauty and the warmth of the starlit night increased her restlessness and drove her out of the house. She put a light tweed coat over the green chiffon frock into which she had changed before dinner and took Grock for a walk.

She strolled along the road which was like a broad, white ribbon in the moonlight, passed Archer Hewitson's cottage. She saw a light in one of the lower casements. She stopped, and frowned at the little square of light. Mr. Hewitson was probably in. Should she go in for a second and speak to him? She would like to make sure, before she turned in to-night, that he was not offended. He had been Sir James's friend.

Elizabeth grew desperately shy when faced with the prospect of having to make an apology. And yet she felt, really, that she owed Hewitson one. Guy had meant well – wanted to champion her – but it was not his affair.

She stood a moment by the quince-tree which shadowed the little white gate of Archer's cottage. Then, suddenly, someone pulled aside the curtains of the sitting-room window. Elizabeth moved back so that she was indistinguishable. But she saw, plainly, framed in the lamp-light, the beautiful, blonde head of Delia Kilwarne . . . white arms and a white throat about which big Roman pearls were twisted. She wore a black lace dress. Her voice floated across the still night to Elizabeth:

'I simply had to come, Archie – it's such a heavenly night – and I knew you wouldn't mind –'

Elizabeth did not wait to hear what Archer replied to this. But she whistled softly to Grock and moved away. Her lips were set, and there was some contempt in her heart.

It didn't seem to her that Mr. Hewitson was much of a sportsman. Fooling around with a married woman. And when one talked to him, nobody could appear more reserved, more strait-laced, more conventional.

Elizabeth was a little disappointed. She had thought more highly of Sir James's estate-agent than that. She returned to 'Memories' without seeing him or making that apology for Guy's interference. She told herself that what her agent liked to do in his private life was of no account to her. She was surprised – that was all.

CHAPTER XI

COULD Elizabeth have seen matters as they really were in Archer's cottage that evening she would have known that Mr. Hewitson, far from fooling around with a married woman, was greatly displeased by Delia Kilwarne's nocturnal visit.

She had come surreptitiously. That annoyed him. She had left her car at the bottom of the road so that it should not be seen by passers-by. That savoured of intrigue, and worried him. He was astonished that she should do such a thing. She had said, when she arrived:

'Charlie's gone to a Masonic banquet and won't be back. I've been feeling so depressed and bored all day, I thought I'd come and see you, Archie. Everyone knows my car, and people do talk in a small place like Maplefield, so I've left it just down the road.'

Archer had been forced to ask her into the cottage. But he had said awkwardly:

'Dukes is out – Wednesday is his half-day, you know, Delia. Ought you – '

'Oh, it doesn't matter. Don't let's be Victorian,' she had interrupted easily.

She did not, of course, mention that she had known it was the manservant's half-day and that was why she had come here, instead of asking Archer to go up to the White House. There were too many maids about her home. She yearned for a real *tête-à-tête* with Archer.

She found him what she called 'a bit snotty' and out of humour. Her *tête-à-tête* was not shaping as she had hoped. And she had put on that new black lace from Lanvin, too – such a pet! It showed her beautiful, slim figure to advantage.

She sat down on the sofa where the standard lamp shed a becoming light on her golden head, and smiled at him. He – after she had been in the room ten minutes – felt uneasy and not in the humour to entertain her. He walked restlessly up and down, smoking hard at his pipe.

Then Delia looked out of the window, sighed at the stars, and said:

'I had to come, Archie – I knew you wouldn't mind.'

'I'm delighted, of course,' he said shortly.

'Nobody would think it,' she laughed, turning back to him. 'You are a bear this evening.'

'I'm awfully sorry, Delia. But I – you – we – '

'Are you being old-fashioned enough to object to my coming down to your cottage unchaperoned?' she laughed at him again.

He flushed, and made a gesture with his pipe.

'My dear Delia – we know each other pretty well – but you must admit – people do yap and Charlie's in town – '

'Oh, bother Charlie.'

'Well – he is your husband.'

'That isn't a recommendation!'

Archer frowned. He wasn't sure he liked Delia in this mood, and neither did he understand her. She looked extraordinarily pretty with the lamplight shining on her fair head and pale, powdered throat and arms, and that black lace thing she was wearing suited her. It was very long, but he could see slender ankles in black gossamer stockings and black satin shoes. He liked black silk stockings. He wished women hadn't abandoned them for all these light, coloured ones. He vaguely remembered having made that remark to Charlie in front of Delia one night. But surely she hadn't put black ones on – especially to please *him* –

Archer, for the first time since he had become friends with the Kilwarnes, felt uneasy and unhappy in Delia's company. She was being so different tonight . . . not the jolly friendly woman who played golf and bridge with him. She was ultra-feminine and seductive. There was ardour in her big, blue eyes which he could not fail to see. He was startled and worried by the feeling that she was falling in love with him. Yet he was so lacking in vanity, he told himself this was surely impossible.

'Cheer up,' said Delia. 'Look pleased to have me here, old thing.'

'I'm de-lighted,' he said.

'I shan't eat you – just because Charlie's in town and Dukes is out.'

101

'Of course not. Don't be absurd.'

'Perhaps you'd like me to go, now, before I finish my cigarette,' she said plaintively.

'No – no – please sit down again.'

She balanced herself on the arm of a chair. He could not help seeing plenty of the charming leg in the black silk stockings now. He fingered his tie nervously.

'I – I feel so unkempt – not changed and that sort of thing. Must excuse me, Delia.'

'I don't mind. I like you in flannels. Tell me how you got on with that quaint Miss Rowe today.'

Archer forgot to be afraid of Delia. His blood flared up with indignant memories of his last encounter with Miss Rowe and her friend.

'I very nearly resigned my post, I tell you,' he said hotly. 'Miss Rowe had a man there with her – a most objectionable fellow – absolute bounder – and he started throwing his weight about with me.'

'My dear – how intolerable!'

'Yes, quite. Said he thoroughly advised Miss Rowe to have Hawkson's cottage down. No dam' business of his – forgive me, Delia.'

'But I agree. No dam' business of his at all.' She smiled at him and swung one slim ankle provocatively. 'Poor old Archie – you are having a rough time.'

'I don't know about that, but I'm hanged if I'll take orders from Miss Rowe's gentlemen friends as well as from her.'

'Who was this gentleman friend? An admirer?'

'I really don't know. . . . ' Archer's tone became curt and uneasy again. His anger evaporated. It had stewed most of the evening, and he was tired of the thought of his present position at 'Memories'. 'I really do think I shall chuck in my hand shortly,' he added.

Delia's face grew serious. She bit her lips, which were painted that bright red which Archer disliked. She stood up and came nearer to him.

'You mustn't leave the district, Archie – you really mustn't.'

He gave her a swift look, then averted his gaze and took refuge in his pipe again.

'Oh, I don't know . . . I might. . . . '

'But you mustn't,' she said in a queer, husky voice. 'I –

couldn't bear you to go –'

Archer grew frankly terrified of this new Delia.

'My dear Delia, I – it's very nice of you – but you and Charlie'll soon find another chap for bridge and all that – ' He tried to laugh.

But now she was standing close . . . so close to him that he could see the agitated rise and fall of her breast, and the unmistakable passion that darkened her eyes. She held out both her hands.

'Charlie doesn't come into it,' she said impatiently. 'It's I who would miss you – miss you terribly – don't you understand, Archie?'

He did understand, definitely now. But he tried not to let her see it. He was amazed and distressed. He thought he saw the end of what had been a very pleasant friendship, and his heart sank. He did not want to take her hands.

'Delia, let's walk along to your car, if you don't mind,' he said quietly. 'Come on, I've got a spot of work to do. You'll forgive me, won't you?'

Mrs. Kilwarne clenched a hand against her breast. She tried desperately to regain self-control. She could see that she had made a blunder with Archie. She was madly in love with him, and was distraught at the thought that she might altogether lose him. It was only by a gigantic effort that she managed to laugh the thing lightly aside:

'Of course, I'll forgive you. So sorry I interrupted your work. But I mean it, old thing – Charlie and I would both be horribly dull if you left. So try and stick it. Good night.'

'I'll walk with you,' he said, much relieved.

'Do,' she said casually.

The dangerous moment had passed. Archie left Delia in her car; she was smiling and behaving quite normally, and he had promised to play tennis up at the White House on Sunday, if it were fine.

But he walked back to Quince-Tree Cottage feeling uneasy and distressed. In an uncontrolled moment Delia Kilwarne had revealed the fact that she loved him. He was not thrilled. He was not in love with Delia – nor with any other woman. And Charlie Kilwarne was his friend. The idea of starting an intrigue with Charlie's wife was repugnant to him. All the same, he had liked and admired Delia. He was sorry this had happened. He knew he would never be able to feel the same toward her . . . the memory of that fleeting revelation of her passion would haunt him – come between them in the future. And there was always the fear that it might happen again.

Back in his sitting-room, he thought about Delia in none too happy a state of mind. He seemed to see her standing there before him, lovely, provocative, intimate, with out-stretched hands. And he could hear her passionate voice saying: 'You mustn't go . . . I couldn't bear you to go.'

Damn it all, he was not made of stone, and supposing that sort of thing had happened again? She might catch him in a weak moment. He might so easily, tonight, have taken her in his arms and kissed her. It would have been beastly – rotten to old Charlie – and he'd have regretted it all his life.

'I mustn't see too much of her in future,' he thought.

He looked at the terrier who was lying in a ridiculous attitude on his back, all four paws in the air; tiny white teeth showing in a comic smile, while he slumbered.

'Dear old Mick,' said Archer. 'Women are the devil. We were perfectly happy together before Miss Rowe came and interfered with us, and Mrs. Kilwarne came and scared us out of our wits! Let's bar Quince-Tree Cottage to females in future.'

In the morning Archer saw Hawkson and delivered to the gamekeeper his new employer's message. Hawkson immediately gave a month's notice.

'Jobs may be 'ard to find, but me and Florrie's made up our minds, we're not going to quit our cottage and go into one of them new-fangled bungilows.'

For the sake of the general peace, rather than to support Elizabeth, Archer protested with Hawkson.

'Isn't it rather cutting off your nose to spite your face? After all, Hawkson, if you leave Miss Rowe's service you'll have to quit the cottage, anyhow.'

'That may be,' said the gamekeeper stubbornly. 'But we're leavin' of our own accord, and, anyhow, I don't fancy staying on for this young lady. Things were peaceful enough in Sir James's time, and that I will say, and you've always been very easy to do for, sir, but –'

There Hawkson finished. Archer found it useless to argue. The man was foolish, but he had made up his mind to go rather than consent to Miss Rowe's scheme. Archer went up to 'Memories' secretly echoing the gamekeeper's words, 'Things were peaceful enough in Sir James's time.' Yes, there was going to be little peace now.

Elizabeth received the gamekeeper's notice calmly.

'He's a very stupid man, Mr. Hewitson. But if he feels I'm doing him such a wrong in building him a new, clean house, he must go. Tell him you will give him a first-rate reference when he wants one, and will you please advertise for a new gamekeeper?'

'I will,' said Archer. He added gloomily: 'I'm afraid Hawkson going will have rather an unfortunate effect on the people round about Maplefield. He's a Maplefield man, and very well liked.'

'I'm extremely sorry,' said Elizabeth. 'But really I can't do more than offer him a nice new bungalow, and if he so bitterly resents moving out of his cottage, why doesn't he move into the bungalow instead of giving notice?'

'Funny tempered, I suppose,' said Archer.

'Unreasonable, you must agree.'

Archer did agree, but he said so reluctantly. He was standing in the front drive of 'Memories'. He had found Elizabeth picking daffodils. It was a warm morning. It might have been midsummer. Elizabeth wore a brown linen dress with short sleeves, and was, as always, bareheaded. With a great sheaf of the golden flowers in her arms, she looked like a child. Archer found himself noticing how absolutely natural she was. There was no trace of the 'arty' Chelsea girl about Elizabeth. No make-up on her face. Her skin was pale and pure. Her lips naturally pink. In a vague way he compared her favourably, in this respect, to Mrs. Kilwarne. He thought uneasily of that vivid scarlet mouth upraised to his in Quince-tree Cottage last night.

'I don't suppose Maplefield will approve of anything I do,' Elizabeth ventured to remark with a faint smile. 'Brownrigg met me just now and looked scandalised because I was cutting his daffodils. I suppose he is used to cutting all flowers himself. But I enjoy pottering about in my own garden.'

Archer was entirely in accordance with her there.

'That's quite comprehensible,' he said.

'By the way,' she said, and the fleeting smile vanished.

'I – I want you just to realise, Mr. Hewitson, that my friend – Mr. Arlingham – did not mean to – to offend you yesterday by what he said about Hawkson's cottage.'

Archer stiffened.

'Please don't apologise,' he said coldly. 'And if at any time you come across anybody whom you think would manage the estate better than I do – please don't hesitate to say so.'

'Now I didn't mean you to take it that way,' said Elizabeth, distressed. 'I am sure nobody could manage it better than you do, Mr. Hewitson.'

'Thank you,' said Archer.

An awkward silence followed this. Elizabeth felt nettled. She had tried to be nice to Mr. Hewitson, but he had not met her half way. She bent over the daffodil-bed and cut half a dozen green spikes to put with her blooms.

Grock, who had been wandering round by himself, appeared in the drive; cocked his comic head at the tall young man beside his mistress; decided that he rather liked the look of him, and bounded up to him joyously, wagging a tail.

Archer, despite his dislike of the breed, could never resist the friendly overtures of any animal. He stooped and patted the sleek, spotted body.

'Hello, old fellow,' he murmured.

Elizabeth regarded this sight in astonishment. Grock made friends with so few people. For Guy, for instance, he had never had any liking. He still growled when Guy entered the room. But he looked up at Archer and wrinkled his nose.

'That's his way of smiling,' Elizabeth explained. 'He's honouring you, Mr. Hewitson.'

'He's rather a nice beast,' said Archer.

'How's the little terrier's lip?'

'Oh, all right again.'

They were on common ground now. Some of the stiffness was gone. And Elizabeth had heard a new note in the estate-agent's voice when he had said, 'Hello, old fellow,' to Grock. Quite a warm, deep note in what was usually such a frigid voice.

'I should think he could be nice if he wanted to,' she thought.

'Mr. Hewitson,' she said, 'what about my mount?'

'Oh, yes. I was going to tell you. I was told this morning by my man, who is an amazing chap for information, that Lady Cribbdale has a beautiful little mare for sale, if you'd care to see it.'

'Who is Lady Cribbdale?'

'I don't know her personally, but the Cribbdales live at Dorminster Towers – this side of Tunbridge Wells.'

'I see,' said Elizabeth. 'Well, if the mare would suit me . . .'

'Perhaps you would like to drive over to Tunbridge Wells and see her?'

'Yes, I'll go this afternoon. I'd better phone up and make an appointment.'

'If I can be of any help – ' began Archer politely.

'Perhaps you'd come with me,' she said. 'I do ride. I'm used to horses. But I'd like a second opinion before buying the mare.'

It was agreed that they should take Bingham and the car to Tunbridge Wells after lunch, providing that Elizabeth could make the required appointment.

It chanced, therefore, that Delia Kilwarne, driving back from the golf-links that fine May day, passed the blue Daimler saloon which she recognised as the late Sir James Willington's car. And she also recognised the couple in it.

'Archie and that girl from "Memories",' she said to herself as they went by. 'Well, I'm hanged! Where the dickens are they off to?'

Delia was feeling very sore; annoyed with life in general. Last night's little scene with Archie had humiliated and disappointed her. And she was terrified of losing him altogether. Now, to see him driving toward Tunbridge Wells with Elizabeth Rowe did not improve her temper. From the beginning she had been secretly jealous of the girl . . . envious of the fact that she was constantly in touch with Archie. And, from what Delia had glimpsed as they passed her, Miss Rowe wore riding kit and looked rather well in it.

'Who was it you raised your hat to, Mr. Hewitson?' murmured Elizabeth. 'I didn't notice. . . .'

'Oh, Mrs. Kilwarne,' he said, and he was horrified to find himself flushing.

Elizabeth shut up like a clam. She mistook the flush for

one of guilt, whereas it was really one of embarrassment. She was reminded of what she had seen at Archer Hewitson's cottage last night. She lapsed into disapproving silence.

The afternoon did not prove wasted. Grey Lady – the mount which Lady Cribbdale wished to sell – was a pretty dappled grey, standing about sixteen hands. The owners of Dorminster Towers were out, but the head groom had authority to show off the mare and saddled her for Elizabeth to try. Elizabeth immediately fell in love with Grey Lady, who had a mouth like velvet and charming manners. She nuzzled her lips into Elizabeth's hands, requesting daintily for sugar, and Elizabeth made up her mind to buy Grey Lady at all costs.

'She's a beauty,' she told Archer.

'The groom says Lady Cribbdale is devoted to the mare, but she's going to South Africa for a year and wants her to have a home where she'll be happy and get some hunting.'

'I'd love to have her,' said Elizabeth with enthusiasm. 'I shall just gallop her across the fields.'

Archer and the groom stood watching whilst Elizabeth took Grey Lady for a canter over the fields adjoining the Towers estate. Archer was bound to admit that his new employer knew how to manage a horse. Those square, boyish little hands were very capable with the reins, and she had a straight seat; looked quite attractive in her fawn coat, white silk riding shirt, and a pair of well-cut jodhpurs.

'Young lady do ride well,' the Cribbdale groom ventured to remark.

'Yes, she does,' said Archer, and felt suddenly quite proud that she did.

Elizabeth came back, flushed, panting, smiling. She slid from the saddle and patted Grey Lady's neck.

'I must have her, Mr. Hewitson,' she said.

After that it was simple. Lady Cribbdale wanted 150 guineas for the mare. Archer considered her a good looker, fit and worth the price, and arranged to come over and complete the transaction on the morrow when her ladyship would be at home.

'I'm frightfully pleased about that,' was Elizabeth's comment as they drove back to Maplefield. 'I shall like Grey Lady. And I must teach Grock to run behind me like a proper Dalmatian.'

Archer glanced at her curiously. This Elizabeth Rowe was a transformed being. She was glowing – no longer a sober, matter-of-fact young woman; she looked happy and quite pretty, he thought. Her eyes were very expressive and full of life when they lit up like that.

'She isn't bad, really,' he reflected. 'But I wonder if she's going to marry that frightful bounder who was so damned insolent to me yesterday? If she does, it'll be the last straw and I shall feel like Hawkson ... I shall quit!'

CHAPTER XII

THE ill-feeling caused by Hawkson's retirement from his job as gamekeeper on the 'Memories' estate was manifested to the new owner of 'Memories' in a variety of ways.

By the time Elizabeth had been in her new home a month she had unwittingly made many enemies and few friends. The uneducated are easily influenced, and when poison poured from the tongues of such old retainers of the late Sir James as Mrs. Martlet and Hawkson and Brownrigg, it was bound to do damage. It did a great deal of damage to Elizabeth's good name in the village. Without in the least deserving it, she earned the reputation of being a hard-hearted, disagreeable young woman, bent on making alterations and ignoring all the old traditions of the place.

Elizabeth had, up till now, found it so very easy to get on with her inferiors. She was kind, considerate, and sensitive to their feelings. But in Maplefield she was not given a fair chance. The people of the locality were prejudiced to begin with, and such rancour as the old housekeeper and the gamekeeper spread once Elizabeth came destroyed all her efforts to show Maplefield that she was a friend and not a foe. They refused to accept friendship from her.

Hawkson and his wife left their cottage at the end of their month and put up in the vicinity. They spread an ugly stream of gossip about having been brutally turned out of their old home, and the villagers were intensely sympathetic about this. It was said by Hawkson in the Cap and Bells that Miss Rowe accused all Maplefield folk of being 'lousy', and indignation became rife.

Then Mrs. Martlet added her cup of poison by spreading it through the village that Miss Rowe was disposing of all the late Sir James's treasures; encouraging her ugly, spotted dog to ruin the home and trying to turn Annie Judd's head with her favours. Mrs. Judd immediately removed Annie from 'Memories' and gave no reasons. This distressed

110

Elizabeth, who liked the honest, simple girl and had hoped to make a decent housemaid of her. Mrs. Martlet was maliciously pleased. She hoped that Miss Rowe would find it difficult to get maids, and would then retire from the contest and return to London.

'I'm only staying on because I know poor Sir James would wish me to,' was what Mrs. Martlet said to her cronies, and was looked upon as a heroine.

Brownrigg and his wife added not a little to the general ill-feeling against Elizabeth. They accused her of trying to cut down their favourite trees just to spite them; of saying that their Gloria was rickety, which cast asperions on their care of her; and of ruthlessly cutting all the priceless blooms Brownrigg preserved for his show. All quite untrue, because Elizabeth was careful not to pick any of the head-gardener's show flowers.

The fact that she was unpopular was made quite plain to Elizabeth. The men were surly and uncommunicative, and seemed to do their jobs without enthusiasm. The women were equally sullen, and avoided her when they could. None of them had a welcoming word or smile for her when she visited the cottages. In the shops even the tradesmen were churlish. Those who in their hearts rather liked the young lady who had never really done them any harm, were afraid to show it.

Archer was a silent witness of the growing hostility against Elizabeth. He himself had ceased to feel resentful, and was doing his job much the same as usual. He could not honestly say that Elizabeth often interfered with or annoyed him. And while, at the back of his mind, there was still irritation caused by her arrival here, and a feeling which he could not eradicate that she was an interloper, he was no longer actively her enemy. Neither was he her friend. They had never really broken the ice. When they met it was on formal terms . . . as Miss Rowe and her land-agent.

He wondered how long she would stick it out at 'Memories' in the teeth of so much opposition. He had to admire her for the quiet dignity with which she took the rebuffs . . . and for standing Mrs. Martlet's tantrums just because she knew Sir James had liked the old woman.

'She'll get tired of it here and go,' he thought. 'So much the better. Maplewood will never take kindly to her.'

111

He did not yet know Elizabeth. She was, behind her calm, cool exterior, deeply hurt by her failure with Sir James's people. But she did not intend to let them drive her away. She asked herself sometimes why she did not make use of all her money and go abroad . . . travel . . . wring some colour and amusement out of life. But somehow 'Memories' had got a hold on her . . . the lure of the lovely old Sussex place was strong. She was, also, always hoping to surmount the resentment and animosity of the folk around. Once, after a disagreeable encounter with one of the village women, who was openly rude to her, she felt so incensed that she asked herself whether Archer Hewitson was responsible for some of the ill feeling. He was immensely popular with everybody. Perhaps he set them up against her. Hoped she would go away.

But as a matter of fact Archer was, in a quiet fashion, her champion. Those who in his hearing ran down the present mistress of 'Memories' were called sharply to account by the land-agent. But Maplefield whispered amongst themselves that Mr. Hewitson was in sympathy with them, and only considered it his duty to uphold Miss Rowe.

If Elizabeth was treated to slights, her dog was even more slighted. Mrs. Martlet and Brownrigg spread scandalous stories of his destructive habits and inclination to snap and bite. Poor, gentle Grock was nobody's favourite. The small boys in the village were encouraged to throw stones at him. And one day the head-gardener was heard to say that if the nasty, spotted brute dug up any more of his garden he'd put a bullet through his head.

This was repeated to Elizabeth by one of her few friends in the place – young Dick Sandler, the stable lad, who had an immense admiration for his young mistress and the way she handled the horses.

Elizabeth, ready to put up with unpopularity for herself, was not going to have her beloved pet threatened. She went straight to Brownrigg and tackled him with what he had said. The gardener denied it at first, then sullenly admitted that he had said 'something of the sort.'

'Very well, Brownrigg,' said Elizabeth, white-lipped. 'You can take two months' salary in lieu of notice and leave to-morrow. I shall not have you in the grounds of this place another day . . . making threats of that kind about my dog.'

Brownrigg flushed to the roots of his sandy hair, pulled at his moustache, and stared round-eyed at the girl.

'Me . . . to leave 'ere – to-morrow?' he gasped.

'Yes,' said Elizabeth.

'Me . . . after fifteen years in this place . . . '

'Perhaps you didn't mean it, Brownrigg, but did you ever threaten to murder one of your late master's pets?'

'No . . . and I'd never have done it to him, neither,' said Brownrigg spitefully. He thereby sealed his doom.

There was thunder in the air at 'Memories' that night. Brownrigg appealed to Mr. Hewitson. Archer came up to the house after dinner and discussed the matter with Elizabeth.

'I don't think the man really meant it. It was an idle threat. He's devoted to the place, Miss Rowe.'

'I gave him the benefit of that doubt,' said Elizabeth. 'And all he said was that he wouldn't have threatened one of Sir James's dogs.' She turned and laid a hand on the smooth head of the Dalmatian at her feet. 'He must go, and at once. I will finance his removal from the lodge and give him two months' salary. But I won't even risk my Grock being shot. Grock shot . . . my best friend,' she added with a note of passion in her voice, and then paused and bit hard at her lip.

Archer was silent a moment. In his heart he was in sympathy with Elizabeth. He knew how he'd feel if somebody threatened Micky. Brownrigg had a nasty temper, too. On the other hand, if the Brownriggs departed resentment against Elizabeth in Maplefield would boil up.

He looked at her. He had never seen her in evening dress before. She was sitting on a leather hassock by the open window in the library. That red georgette dress, shorter than the present fashion, suited her. Her bare throat and arms were a faint golden tan from the sun. The small dark head was smooth and like black silk in the light of the lamp on the desk behind her.

He had fancied when he had first came up here, tonight, that she looked very depressed – rather a forlorn little figure. He could not help feeling that she was not having a very gay time here. She entertained very rarely. That fellow Arlingham had been down twice, for the day only, with a very pretty red-haired girl. Mrs. Martlet had told Dukes.

that Mr. Arlingham and the red-haired girl were engaged, so Archer had gathered that Arlingham was not the future master of 'Memories,' for which he was thankful. Beyond those two, Elizabeth had not had many visitors at the house. Several of the local inhabitants had 'called' and left cards, and in each case Elizabeth had been out and had not returned the call. She was not the kind that liked the conventional social round in a country place. So perhaps, Archer thought, it was her own fault if she was lonely. But tonight he was quite sorry for her . . . the queer, solitary little thing.

He found it quite useless to plead Brownrigg's cause. The fellow must go at once. Elizabeth was furiously indignant over the threat to her beloved pet.

'I'm sorry about it,' he told Elizabeth. 'Hawkson, you know, is still in the locality, spreading a lot of nasty talk, and Brownrigg's dismissal won't add to – '

'My popularity,' Elizabeth finished with a wry smile.

'Exactly,' he said, frowning.

She stood up and looked squarely into the hazel eyes of the young man.

'As you know, Mr. Hewitson . . . I'm not out to be popular. Brownrigg must go. Public opinion means nothing to me. I've tried to make friends with these people, and they're quite impossible.'

'They're a bit prejudiced,' he murmured.

'Perhaps everyone wants me to throw in my hand and go,' she said, two small, red flushes on both cheeks. 'But I'm not going. I shall stay here and do as I think best!'

He had never seen her in this mood before. The reticent Elizabeth was off her guard . . . out of her shell for a moment. He felt a grudging admiration for her pluck, her spirit. Then the moment passed. Elizabeth drew back.

'I'm looking forward to hunting Grey Lady this winter,' she added calmly. 'Thanks for coming up about Brownrigg, Mr. Hewitson. Good night.'

He left her. As soon as she was alone, she felt a horrid, sinking feeling of loneliness, of wounded pride. It wasn't very nice to know that all these people were prejudiced against her . . . hated her. Nowadays Archer Hewitson was quite pleasant. They did not openly disagree. But she could not count on him as a friend. Somehow, this evening, she would have liked to have said:

'Sit down . . . have your pipe . . . let's talk about anything but the estate . . . let's forget you're my land-agent and that I'm in Sir James's shoes . . . and be pals!'

But she hadn't been able to say it . . . She couldn't have endured a rebuff. She wouldn't risk one.

Last Sunday, Guy and Lilian had come down to lunch. Elizabeth had not enjoyed a moment of their visit. To see these two as lovers jarred on her at every turn. Guy had been very charming . . . so had Lilian . . . but they were going to be married, and they were out of the circle of her existence now. She had felt so very much the 'third person'. But she had pretended to be in the best of humours; shown off her new home with much pride; sent Lilian back with a great basket of flowers. She was not going to let them see that she was unhappy and that she had been a failure down here in her magnificent domain.

Tonight, after Archer had gone, some of Elizabeth's courage and will-power seemed to evaporate. She felt sick at heart and dispirited. She knelt down on the rug and took one of Grock's big, white paws in her hand.

'Oh, Grocky,' she said, 'nobody understands me but you. Isn't it queer? I've got such a lot to give and nobody but you wants it, Grocky darling. I failed with Guy . . . I've failed down here with everyone . . . and they all think I'm cold and that I don't care!'

The Dalmatian licked her fingers. But she had to withdraw them and let go of his paw because she wanted to find a handkerchief. Rare tears were pouring down her cheeks. That night Elizabeth came very near to giving up the fight and going away from 'Memories'. It was only her pride that stopped her . . . that defiant little feeling that she could not go . . . could not let these people have the laugh on her and feel that they had won. She fancied she could see them, headed by the land-agent, crowing over her departure.

A piece of paper, stirred by the breeze through the open windows, fluttered from the desk on to the floor. Elizabeth picked it up and looked at it through a hot mist of tears. It was a letter from Lilian. She could just see one paragraph.

'I'm so frightfully pleased you are so happy, darling Elizabeth. I told Guy on Sunday I'd never seen you in

115

better spirits, and it does make me feel now that I can marry dear Guy without feeling so guilty of having thieved him from you . . .'

The humour of this suddenly struck Elizabeth. The ironic humour. Just because she didn't wear her heart on her sleeve and show her emotions . . . Lilian was satisfied that she was happy. '*I've never seen you in better spirits,*' Lilian had written. Yes, Elizabeth had laughed and joked with them on Sunday . . . and it seemed that she had played her part well.

And here she was feeling that she was the most miserable person in the world. She still wanted Guy and that happiness, that enchantment, that had been 'thieved' from her.

She brushed her smarting eyes with the back of her hand, like a boy. She swallowed hard.

'I don't believe in broken hearts, Grocky,' she addressed her dog, who looked up at her with his faithful, liquid eyes. 'But things can hurt . . . *damnably* . . . and they do! Come on to bed, old man, and let anyone on earth put a bullet through *you* . . . if they dare!'

CHAPTER XIII

ONE week later, on a fine morning at the end of May, Elizabeth rode Grey Lady through the woods which were part of her estate. Grock followed at the mare's heels, which he had learned to do now, and he seemed to like it. A faint, fresh wind stirred the trees, rustling and shivering the young leaves. Elizabeth rode the grey mare down the beaten track and lifted a contented face to the warm sun. Whatever the difficulties and grievances that beset her at home, here was a place of enchantment and peace. Every morning now she rode Grey Lady over the fields and came back slowly, lazily, through these woods which were an unfailing delight to her.

Every tree and sapling, every bush, wore that bright, brave green of the spring. The primroses were out in gay yellow clumps and clusters. Everywhere there were new shoots and tendrils; even the cut, fallen logs seemed to sprout and deny that there must be an end to living. And on either side of the open track along which Elizabeth's mount so daintily picked her way, bluebells – gloriously purple – lay like a vivid sweep of colour from a painter's brush. The lights and shades were exquisite, changeful, as the sun rose higher in the unclouded sky. There came the continual chirp and twitter of birds; the joyous song of the blackbird and thrush; the low, amorous cooing of wood-pigeons from their nests. Now and then there was a delicious rustle of dry leaves and bracken as the young rabbits scampered to their holes, scared by the dull echo of Grey Lady's hoof-beats along the ride.

Elizabeth pulled in the reins, Grey Lady stood still, her velvet nose twitching and smoking. Elizabeth patted the hot, smooth neck.

'Just one moment, my beauty. It's so lovely out here . . . I don't want to go back . . .'

She took off her hat and let the breeze stir her hair. This

117

was the happiest hour of the day. She almost dreaded going back to the house. There was bound to be trouble there. Brownrigg had gone. There was open indignation in the village, and Tom, the gardener's boy, whose father was related to Brownrigg, had removed him to show his disapproval. Archer Hewitson had been busy replacing the men.

There was now a new head-gardener, who with his wife and family of three small boys had settled in the Lodge and seemed quite capable. Another lad from the locality was working in Tom's place. But Brownrigg and Hawkson remained in Maplefield and were quietly stirring up trouble. Already some damage had been done in the grounds of 'Memories'. Some fencing had been wantonly torn down and damaged. One or two fruit-trees in the orchard were stripped of the budding fruit. A bed of roses had been trampled and destroyed. And a piece of paper with an uncomplimentary allusion to Miss Rowe had been found nailed to a tree outside the house.

Archer had, of course, complained on Elizabeth's behalf to the police, and knew pretty well who had done the damage, and nailed up that paper. It was one of the dismissed men, no doubt. But nothing could definitely be traced to them. It was all undoubtedly cheap revenge on their part – perpetrated perhaps by some village lads under their influence. It was very petty, but sufficient to worry and distress Elizabeth. She fancied that the last time Archer had spoken to her she had seen faint pity in his eyes. That enraged her. She could not tolerate the idea that she was not only the most unpopular amongst these people, but the object of derision and pity from her estate-agent.

She tried, this morning, to concentrate on the beauty of the Maplefield woods, but her brain kept harping back to 'Memories'.

She sighed and rode on. Apart from trouble down here, there was another trial to be faced. The wedding of Guy and Lilian. That was fixed for the first week in June, and she dreaded it. The loss of Guy was still an open wound in her heart. Lately he had been so charming to her, it had made her feel his loss more acutely. He was constantly telephoning; asking what he could do for her; sympathising and counselling her when she told him what was going on at

'Memories'. Once or twice he had brought Lilian down for the day. She felt that she would have nothing – nobody to comfort her when he was Lilian's husband and finally lost to her.

As she neared the fringe of the woods she pulled Grey Lady in again and sat still in the saddle a moment, listening. She fancied she heard the yelping of an animal in pain. Grock seemed to hear it, too, for he stood beside Grey Lady and sniffed the air, growling a little in his throat.

The yelps which came from the thicket just to the right died down to a tired whining.

'There's some creature in there in pain,' Elizabeth told herself. 'I must see what it is. Perhaps it's some dog caught in a trap.'

She knew that there were poacher's gins in this wood. She had found one when she walked through, the other day.

She slid from the saddle, tethered Grey Lady to a tree, and walked with Grock in the direction whence came that piteous whining. She found herself having to scramble through a tangle of birches, sharp thorny bushes and brambles. She scratched her face and hands, but forced her way in, determined to reach the animal whose whining was louder and nearer now. Certainly it was in pain.

Then she came upon the sufferer suddenly, and the indignant blood rushed to her cheeks. She saw a familiar little wheaten-coloured body crouching shivering on the ground. It was Archer Hewitson's cairn – Micky. One of his small paws was caught in a trap.

'Oh, you poor little thing,' exclaimed Elizabeth.

He looked at her with eyes that were suffused and pathetic, and barked wildly for joy. His tail wagged furiously. As Elizabeth knelt beside him he tried to lick her hands. His coat felt damp and lank. Elizabeth imagined he must have been there all night. He was hungry and very frightened. She soothed and patted him as she examined the trap.

'I must get these poachers,' she thought angrily. 'Wretched creatures!'

Gently and carefully she released the trap. Micky found himself free. He hopped about on three legs, then sat down and feverishly licked his injured paw. The Dalmatian kept

119

his distance, growling a little.

'Now, Grock,' said Elizabeth, 'be a sport and leave him alone. He's had a nasty time in that trap, and it might have been you.'

Grock wagged his tail. Elizabeth picked Micky up and carried him back to Grey Lady, scrambling through the bushes and thorns again. The paw which had been in the trap was tender and swollen. Elizabeth could see that he was too lame to walk with any pleasure.

'I wonder how I can get you back to your master, old man,' she said to him.

Then breaking the stillness of the morning came a piercing whistle and a man's voice calling

'Micky . . . Micky . . . Mick . . . here, here, Micky!'

Micky's small black ears shot up. He whined and struggled in Elizabeth's arms.

'Ah,' she nodded. 'Here he is – looking for you!'

She put a hand to her mouth and shouted.

'Mr. Hewitson! Mr. Hewits-on!'

'Hello!' came the answering voice.

'Here!' she called. 'Micky's here!'

Another minute and Archer Hewitson's tall figure appeared, striding along the sunlit ride. Elizabeth went to meet him. He looked worried and depressed, but when he saw the terrier in her arms his face cleared like magic.

'You've got Micky!' he exclaimed.

'Yes, I've just this moment found him.'

'But where? Do you know that I've been hunting Maplefield for him since dawn?'

'You haven't, have you?'

'Yes. I thought I was never going to see him again.'

He took the little Cairn from her and hugged him as though he had been a child.

'Mick!' he said. 'Dear old Mick . . . I say, it's good to see you. Where were you? Where've you been?'

Elizabeth did not know her chilly and superior land agent. His voice was quite husky with emotion, and he caressed his pet and talked to him with the utmost tenderness. Elizabeth found it most touching. She understood this sort of emotion so well. It would be terrible to lose Grock . . . to imagine him lost.

120

When Archer looked up at Elizabeth, his eyes were bright with gratitude.

'I say, I don't know how to thank you, Miss Rowe,' he said. Where did you find him? Hello . . . what's the matter with that left paw?'

'He was in a trap' Elizabeth explained.

'A trap!' repeated Archer. His face grew hard and stern. 'My God . . . if I could lay hands on the fellow that put it down! One of those damned poachers! Forgive me. . . .'

'I agree with you. We must get on to them somehow. I was riding along and I heard an animal yelping and whining. I followed the sound and found him. It was one of those beastly steel gins. I got him out, but his paw must be very painful.'

'Poor old fellow,' said Archer, caressing the terrier. I'll take him home and bind it up. Look here, Miss Rowe, I'm eternally grateful. He might never have been found.'

'I know. It would have been ghastly if he had just lain there and died.'

'Or left his paw in the trap, which was what happened to one dog I knew,' said Archer grimly. 'You know, he didn't come back as usual last night, after I let him out for his last run, and I thought perhaps he'd gone hunting and that he'd get tired of it and come home. I left the door open for him and turned in. To my horror, when I woke up at five I found his basket still empty, so I dressed and made a search for him. I didn't think he'd be in these woods. I've been scouring round those woods at the back of my place.'

'Well, thank goodness he's all right,' said Elizabeth.

Archer looked at her. Their eyes met in a glance of mutual understanding and sympathy. Suddenly it seemed to him that Elizabeth was extraordinarily nice and not at all difficult, and he really didn't know why he'd ever found her disagreeable or unattractive. She stood there beside Grey Lady, slim and young in her riding kit, her dark hair ruffled, flecked with bits of leaf and twig after her scramble through the bushes. And she was actually smiling at him. He found an altogether unexpected charm in Elizabeth's smile and the softness of her wide, brown eyes.

He suddenly held out a hand.

'I'm immensely grateful to you for getting Mick out of that trap. Thanks ever so much,' he said heartily.

Elizabeth took the outstretched hand. His strong, hard fingers gripped hers, then dropped them. All stiffness and hostilility seemed to die between them and she was no longer shy of him.

'That's all right,' she said. 'I'm so glad I found him. Well, I must ride Grey Lady back. Have you noticed how well Grock is following now?'

'Yes, I have,' said Archer. He whistled to Grock, and the Dalmatian immediately went up to him. They were good friends in these days. Archer still preferred the terrier breed, but he had to admit that the black and white spotted dog, running along beside the grey mare, was a goodly sight.

Elizabeth swung herself into the saddle.

'Things going all right?' she asked.

'More or less . . . ' He smiled up at her. 'But the ill feeling is still rife.'

'I'm sorry about it.' She found herself suddenly able to talk to Archer. 'You've no idea how sorry. I didn't want to come to "Memories" and cause all these ructions and upset all the old retainers. But it hasn't been altogether my fault.'

'Far from it,' he said.

'I'd like to have made friends with everyone,' she said, knitting her brows.

He was struck by the sudden feeling that Maplefield had not given this girl much of a reception nor anything of a chance. And she was, at heart, a very friendly little thing. She had sympathy and understanding. She'd just been unfortunate enough to come up against most of the folk. It must have distressed her. He could see that she was upset about it now. He was, in this moment, rather ashamed of himself. For after all, he hadn't helped matters much. He had been against her from the start, and had shown that he wasn't pleased she had come. In other words, he'd behaved badly and he regretted it. Thinking things over, she had always been very decent to him.

He came nearer Grey Lady and raised a face that was puckered and faintly red under the tan.

'Look here, Miss Rowe . . . I'm a bit ashamed of all this business. It's been rotten for you. And it's all got to stop. I shall advise you to make a clean sweep of all these people – including Mrs. Martlet – and start with an entirely new staff, if the mischief goes on. We can't have any more of this.'

She looked down at him and felt curiously touched and pleased. To have Archer Hewitson in sympathy with her — up in arms on her behalf — was an altogether new and most satisfactory feeling. She realised that he was trying to tell her that in future he would work for her and with her if she wanted him to.

'Thanks awfully,' she said. 'And you're quite right. This mustn't go on. It is so disagreeable. I fancy Mrs. Martlet is at the bottom of a lot of the mischief. She can't bear me, and she hates Grock.'

'Well, you've done your best to meet her and she won't be met, so you'll be justified in sacking her,' said Archer. 'Sir James would have been horrified at the way they're all carrying on.'

This from Archer. Elizabeth smiled a little, but she felt a glow of satisfaction.

'We'll see how things go on,' she said. 'Meanwhile, it's a glorious day. How about some tennis this afternoon? The grass court is perfect. Jennings rolled it yesterday afternoon and the boy's marking it this morning. I thought we might get up a four. Do you know anyone you'd care to ask up?'

He thought a moment. Delia Kilwarne leapt to his mind. But he wasn't going to ask Delia. He was afraid of her these days. He had not been up to the White House since that night when she had revealed her feelings for him. She had sent down several messages, but on each occasion he had excused himself, and with each message felt that it would be a very good thing if he saw very little of Delia in the future.

'If there isn't anybody . . . would it bore you to come and play some singles?' she suggested.

'Not at all,' said Archer. 'I'd like it.'

'I don't suppose it'll give you much of a game. I'm rather a rabbit.'

'A confession of that kind generally means you're Wimbledon form,' he laughed. 'But anyhow, I'm bad.'

'Come along about half-past three, then,' she said shyly.

He thanked her. She touched Grey Lady lightly with her crop and moved on. He followed on foot, carrying Micky, who was half asleep in his arms — exhausted after his night of

123

pain and terror.

'Micky,' said his master, 'I'm just beginning to see why Sir James liked Elizabeth Rowe.'

'Grock,' said Elizabeth, looking down at the Dalmatian trotting beside the mare, 'he's really a nice young man, and most good-looking when he smiles. What a pity he's got himself tied up with a married woman. He's too nice for that.'

She found herself looking forward to tennis with Archer that afternoon.

CHAPTER XIV

TENNIS up at 'Memories' that afternoon was surprisingly successful. Archer found that Elizabeth played extremely well. He, himself, was a good average exponent, but the 'slip of a girl' gave him a good game. The ice between them had been broken by the service that Elizabeth had rendered Archie's pet, and it thawed steadily from that hour onward.

Elizabeth for the first time since her arrival at 'Memories' began to see hope – some hope of finding life bearable here, if this young man intended to be her friend and to work with her instead of against her.

Just before Archer returned to his cottage, after tea which was served to them on the lawn under the green shade of the trees, Elizabeth somewhat shyly expressed the wish that he would come and play tennis with her again.

'Thanks, I'd like to,' said Archer. 'Next time I'll try and get hold of Mr. and Mrs. Ascot, who live at the Manor House. They're rather a nice couple – quite young and just back from India. Big-game shooting. Mrs. Ascot intends to call on you, I know. She's very informal, so perhaps she'd waive the rules and come along up to tennis without calling.'

'I hope she will,' said Elizabeth. 'I loathe formal calling.'

'I'll try and fix it up, then,' said Archer. 'Goodbye, and thanks very much.'

She shook hands with him. He took his racquet and turned away. It struck her suddenly that he looked extremely nice in his white flannels, shirt open at the neck, showing a strong, brown column of throat; dark hair inclined to curl because his forehead was damp after the strenuous exercise. Face a good healthy tan. He was altogether a very healthy, masculine person, this Archer Hewitson. She found herself comparing him with Guy. Guy was just a little too effeminate and *soigné*. She called after Hewitson:

'I say – is Micky's paw better?'

Archer turned back.

'Thanks – yes – I've bound it up. I left him in the garden with Dukes, in his basket. He'll be all right in a day or two.'

'Good,' said Elizabeth.

He looked at the slim young figure in the short, green tennis frock, then smiled and lifted a hand in greeting.

'Thanks so much. So long.'

'So long,' she said boyishly.

He strolled over the fields to Quince-Tree Cottage with most of his ideas about Miss Rowe revolutionised.

'I've been a swine,' he thought. 'She's a jolly little thing when you get to know her. I must buck these Maplefield people up and tell them to mind their p's and q's with Miss Rowe.'

But what might have been the commencement of a very pleasant and helpful friendship between Elizabeth and her young estate agent was baulked that very next day by Delia Kilwarne.

Mrs. Kilwarne called at 'Memories'. She had intended to call before, but had put it off – bored by the prospect of tea with Elizabeth. Then something had happened which decided her that the sooner she called on Elizabeth and talked to the girl the better. She had not seen Archer for some time. He avoided her. She knew it, and she was growing desperate. She had called at Quince-Tree Cottage with her husband yesterday. Charlie had been subtly persuaded to go down and make Archie return with them to the White House for dinner. On reaching the cottage they had been told by Dukes that Mr. Hewitson had gone up to 'Memories' for tennis with Miss Rowe.

'We owe it to Miss Rowe that our Micky was saved from death,' Dukes informed the Kilwarnes solemnly and with some pride. 'Rescued him from a trap in the woods early this morning, she did!'

The Kilwarnes drove away. Delia was silently fuming; her cheeks hot with rage. Charlie Kilwarne unconsciously added fuel by saying, in his bantering fashion

'Ho, ho, my dear! What's this? We must rag old Archie. The misogynist is turning his attentions to a woman. Tennis with Miss Elizabeth Rowe, hey? Well, when I saw her out riding I thought she looked a nice little girl – quite pretty. I was surprised.'

Delia could have killed her husband. But she bit hard into her lower lip and controlled the impulse. She only knew one thing. If Archer had started to go up to 'Memories' on friendly visits to that girl, she must put an end to it speedily, and by using what weapons she possessed.

She called upon Elizabeth Rowe that next afternoon. Elizabeth was at home. She was not certain that she wished to see Mrs. Kilwarne. She felt rather uncomfortable about her, remembering the night she had seen her in Archer Hewitson's cottage. And she did not wish to concentrate on her estate agent's private affairs and be forced to lower her opinion of him.

She received Mrs. Kilwarne courteously, however. They had tea together in the library. It was one of those cool, treacherous days the first week in June when the atmosphere was cold and damp out of the sun and had made Elizabeth change from a summer dress into a woolly jumper suit again.

Delia Kilwarne – beautiful, perfectly turned out, with a chic little dark blue hat on her golden head which suited her admirably – sat in an armchair opposite Elizabeth and smoked and chatted with apparent friendliness. But before she had been in the house ten minutes she brought the conversation round to Archer.

'You couldn't have a more wonderful man to manage your estate, could you, Miss Rowe?' she began sweetly.

'No – he is excellent, 'said Elizabeth.

'He and I have known each other for a long time,' continued Delia. She sat back in her chair and looked dreamy and serious. Elizabeth looked at her and – always generous in her praise of other women – admitted that she was lovely. Yet there was something very bold and selfish about her face. Delia in her turn regarded Elizabeth and condemned her as plain and dull. Badly dressed, too, in that ugly tweed skirt and orange jumper. And her hair wanted cutting. Surely she needn't imagine Archer would be attracted by the girl? Still, she had better nip the affair in the bud.

'I wonder how long Archie will be here,' she added, in the same dreamy voice.

'Is there any question of his leaving Maplefield?' asked Elizabeth quickly.

'No, not exactly,' said Delia, in a hesitating way. 'But there are reasons . . . *why* he might go . . . '

Elizabeth stared at her. Delia stubbed her cigarette end in a tray, then sighed deeply.

'It's all very difficult,' she said.

'I don't quite understand –'

'Of course not. My dear, you're unmarried and free. I envy you!' said Delia significantly. She put a hand over her eyes for a moment, which she thought would be effective. 'Ah . . . if one only were free,' she whispered.

Elizabeth went scarlet. There was no mistaking what Delia Kilwarne meant now. Delia gave her no time to say anything. She added;

'But don't let's talk about Archie and me . . . it's too rotten . . . for both of us . . . especially for him. . . .'

Silence. Elizabeth's face remained hot and red. She felt thoroughly embarrassed. She thought it in execrable taste for Mrs. Kilwarne to come here and flaunt her intrigue with Archer. Surely Archer himself wouldn't like it. But it left no room for doubt in her mind that there *was* an affair in progress between this woman and Mr. Hewitson.

It chilled Elizabeth. She had enjoyed her tennis with Archer yesterday. She had hoped to become good friends with him. She had talked to him and he to her and they had found quite a lot to chat about . . . the time had passed very pleasantly. But how could she be friends with a man who was unscrupulous enough to have an affair with a married woman? He himself had told her that Charles Kilwarne was a good fellow. It seemed to Elizabeth low . . . unsporting. It wasn't playing the game.

Archer went down in her estimation . . . and Delia saw to it that he went down still lower before she left 'Memories' that afternoon. Elizabeth did not particularly enjoy the visit from Mrs. Kilwarne. But Delia was sweetness itself, and begged Elizabeth to dine at the White House next week.

After she had gone, Elizabeth felt depressed. She thought of her young estate-agent and was sorry about this business. It seemed beastly. She couldn't be pals with him . . . respect him . . . after this. And Delia Kilwarne was so beastly . . . to boast and brag of her disloyalty to her husband.

She saw Archer that evening. He came up to the big house for dinner with plans which he had just secured from an architect in Crowborough for building a new gamekeeper's bungalow.

128

Archer was in good spirits when he arrived, and much more hopeful and contented about his position as land-agent than he had felt since Miss Rowe's arrival. But he had not been in the study with Elizabeth for ten minutes before he was struck by a coldness and hauteur in her manner which had not been there yesterday during their tennis match. She had no friendly smile for him tonight. She plunged straight into the subject of the gamekeeper's bungalow, and was so persistently cool and business-like that Archer's good humour soon evaporated. He was surprised, but he supposed he had been too previous in making up his mind that Elizabeth was easy to get on with. He was disappointed. He soon lapsed into a business-like manner which matched hers. Then, when they had completed the discussion, she said:

'Mrs. Kilwarne called on me yesterday.'

He looked at her quickly.

'Oh, yes?'

'She asked me to dine at the White House next Tuesday.'

'Oh, yes. Kilwarne's a very nice fellow. You'll like him.'

'I doubt if I shall be able to go. I may have guests here,' said Elizabeth coldly.

And she thought how horrid it was of Archer to make love to the wife of a man whom he considered a 'nice fellow.' She noticed at once that he flushed and avoided her gaze when she mentioned the name of Mrs. Kilwarne. Guilty conscience, of course.

Archer went back to his cottage, baffled. So Delia had called on Elizabeth? Could she have said anything to Elizabeth that would account for the latter's sudden change of manner toward him? Surely Delia wouldn't be so unprincipled as that. Besides, what could she say? He had never made love to her. He had nothing on his conscience. But she was in love with him, and he had snubbed and ignored her. 'A woman scorned . . . ' Archer was most uneasy at the thought. Yet he could not credit that Delia was deliberately making mischief. It was queer, all the same, that Elizabeth should have been so distant, so short with him, this evening.

'Hang these women!' thought Archer angrily. 'How disturbing it all is!'

He found his peace of mind very much disturbed the more he dwelt on the thought of this business. And he was helpless. He couldn't find out what Delia had said. It only made him doubly determined not to see more of her in the future than he could possibly help. But all that evening he thought about Elizabeth. He compared the Elizabeth of tonight with the Elizabeth of yesterday, in the woods, out riding, when Micky had been found . . . at tennis, laughing with him, talking to him. And he felt regretful that she had changed. He had liked that Elizabeth. She had been jolly . . . charming. He had thought the atmosphere would be one of peace and unity in the future.

Still, if she chose to be unfriendly for some inexplicable reason, he was not going to grieve about it. He would take his cue from her. They would drop back on the old, difficult, hostile footing – and there it was.

Elizabeth sent for him that next morning. When he went to her he found her quite unapproachable again, but full of ideas for improvements of the place. She had one project in particular in which she asked him to assist her – a plan for entertaining the tenants of the estate.

'Mrs. Marlet informed me last night,' she said, 'that Sir James, every summer, used to give a garden party here in the grounds for all his tenants and their kiddies. I suggest doing this . . . it may show the people that I am not the disagreeable enemy they imagine, and also keep up old traditions.'

'I agree,' said Archer. 'It would be an excellent thing.'

'Can I rely on you to send invitations to every tenant on the estate . . . all the staff and their family included?'

Archer took his diary from his pocket.

'What day do you suggest, Miss Rowe?'

'The middle of the month?'

'About today fortnight . . . June 15th? That's a Wednesday – early closing day in the village.'

'Yes – that would do. What exactly did Sir James provide in the way of entertainment?'

'Oh, a big spread, you know; a marquee; a band and that sort of thing. Last summer they danced on the lawn, and they had a tent with a fortune-teller and one or two little side-shows for the children. Nothing very complicated, but they all seemed to enjoy it, and they presented Sir James with a token of gratitude. It was all rather nice.'

'Well, let's do it,' said Elizabeth. She looked down at the Dalmatian who lay at her feet. 'You shall have a frill

130

round your neck and be festive – in other words, the clown, Grocky,' she murmured. 'You're such a comic, darling!'

Archer, scribbling in his diary, glanced at her and thought how nice she was when she forgot to be cut and dried. He wondered if those brown eye of hers ever softened for anybody, anything else but her beloved dog. He felt suddenly annoyed, resentful, that she had withdrawn her friendship from him and was treating him with such cold politeness again. But he made no comment. He stayed a moment, fixing up details with her for the intended garden fête for the tenants, then departed, equally cold and polite.

Elizabeth thought about him after he had gone.

'If it hadn't been for his affair with that woman, we might have been pals. It's sickening,' she thought. 'But how can I like him . . . if he's that type of cad?'

Yet he didn't look or seem 'that type of cad.' she was perplexed and quite depressed about him. The old feeling of intolerable loneliness overcame her tonight.

The invitations for the garden fête and tea for June 15th, were duly sent out by Archer to all Elizabeth's tenants. The numbers, including all the staff and their families, were quite considerable, and amounted to close on a hundred.

CHAPTER XV

IN the last few days before June 15th, Elizabeth and Archer had so much to think about and do together that they had no time to nurture grievances and hostilities. They became almost friendly again over their united efforts to produce a really good fête for the tenants.

The great day dawned just as Elizabeth had hoped . . . warm and windless. The sun shone brilliantly from a blue sky, and the gardens of 'Memories' looked their best. The lawns smooth as the pile of green velvet. The beds neat and gay with countless flowers . . . and on the wide lawn in front of the old Tudor house, stretching down to the shining pond, everything 'set' for a really jolly garden-party. A striped marquee, for refreshments; tables spread with good things under the trees. A special fortune-teller from London, waiting in her tent for clients who would seek her mysteries; half a dozen improvised swings for the children; and fireworks for after dark, which Archer had volunteered to manoeuvre.

Elizabeth felt quite excited about her party. She was at heart a very friendly little person, and she wanted to establish the right contact with her people here. She fancied this was her chance.

She stood by the estate-agent surveying the preparations in a satisfied way.

'It's a quarter past three,' she said. 'They've been invited for half-past, haven't they, so they'll start drifting in soon.'

'That's so,' said Archer.

He could not help noticing the fact that Elizabeth looked extraordinarily nice this afternoon. She had been up to London and bought a new dress for the occasion – a fashionably long one of pale yellow chiffon, with a tiny pattern of green flowers on it. It was sleeveless, but had a wide transparent cape which veiled the slim sun-browned arms effectively. Contrary to habit, she wore a hat today – a big yellow crinoline hat through which the dark satin of her hair was visible. She looked altogether softened, feminine, and Archer was quite startled by the difference such clothes made in her. Here was the mistress of 'Memories' indeed, and quite a charming one.

They strolled together over the lawn. Elizabeth stopped to say a few words to the fortune-teller and then to the three musicians whom Archer had engaged from Crowborough . . . a violin, piano, and 'cello.

'You might start playing,' she told them. 'A nice, cheery tune.'

As the music commenced, Elizabeth smiled at Archer. 'I think they'll enjoy it, don't you?'

'They ought to,' he said. 'You've given them a wonderful spread, and taken a lot of trouble over the details. They ought to be grateful.'

All the same, he wasn't sure he liked the expression on the face of Mrs. Martlet, who came out from the house now and then bearing various dishes of sandwiches and cakes. She was smiling, but it was such an unpleasant smile . . . almost a malevolent one, as though some secret, rather nasty joke were amusing her.

'Now I wonder what the old girl's up to,' he thought.

He said nothing to Elizabeth, however. She seemed childishly pleased at the preparations for her garden-party, and not in the mood to notice Mrs. Martlet's expression.

Half an hour later, when Elizabeth looked at her wrist-watch and saw that it was a quarter to four and nobody had come yet, she became a trifle uneasy.

'They're late, aren't they?'

'Oh, they may be busy,' he suggested.

'But it's half day in the village – we particularly made it the early closing day,' she reminded him.

'They'll turn up in a second,' he said.

One hour later . . . a quarter to five . . . Elizabeth was no longer smiling or regarding the festive preparations with any pride and pleasure. She stood beside her estate-agent, listening to the trio who were dutifully playing one dance tune after another, and staring down the drive with eyes that had grown grave and anxious. The invitations were for half-past three. It was nearly five and not a single guest had turned up. The urn of tea was boiling away. The fortune-teller in her tent was solitary and restless. What had happened?

'Mr. Hewitson,' said Elizabeth, 'there isn't any mistake, is there? I mean . . . about the date of this show?'

'None whatever,' he said. 'June 15th, 3.30p.m. was printed . . . I saw it myself.'

'Then where is everybody?'

'I can't think,' he said.

But he had a shrewd idea. He looked across the sunlit garden with stern eyes. His lips were set. He thought he knew what had happened. Elizabeth's tenants were not coming, and did not intend to come. Mrs. Martlet, aided and abetted by Brownrigg and Hawkson, who still hung about the village, had spread their poison and done their dirty work well. They had influenced the villagers not to attend this garden-party. This was open hostility . . . Maplefield's method of revenge . . . of showing Elizabeth Rowe that they hated her and resented her coming.

Archer was not only angry, he was thoroughly ashamed of these people amongst whom he had worked for so many years. As the moments ticked by and the gardens of 'Memories' remained empty, and the people hired for the occasion hung about idle, he grew more and more furious. He gave one look at Elizabeth's face and then dared not look at her again. She was quite white. Her lips were quivering. She looked hurt beyond words. Her pride, her sense of hostess-ship, were hurt. No wonder. She had spent a lot of time and trouble on this party.

Then she said:

'It's half-past five now. I don't think they're coming, Mr. Hewitson. . . . I fancy I understand. This is the work of those vile men . . . Brownrigg and Hawkson . . . and possibly Mrs. Martlet into the bargain.'

'I am terribly afraid it is,' he said.

'I think you might as well tell the trio and these various people they can pack up and go. And send the eatables to some Crowborough charity or something.'

Archer forced himself to look at her. She looked so forlorn, so wounded, standing there in her pretty, festive dress . . . staring at the deserted gardens. He could well understand how humiliating this was for her. . . .

'It's unpardonable . . . damnable!' he said hotly. 'By

134

gad, I'll have something to say about this!'

'Please . . . ' She cut him short. She was smiling now, although her lips trembled and her eyes were full of bitterness. 'It doesn't matter at all. But it's just finished me. I shall not try and make friends with these people again.'

'I'm most awfully sorry,' he said. He came nearer her. She saw that his good-looking face was stern and angry, and that his eyes were full of pity for her. That made her wince horribly. It was all so humiliating, so disappointing . . . and to be the object of *pity* . . . she, Elizabeth Rowe! . . .

Grock came bounding over the lawn . . . ridiculous and comic with a Toby frill round his neck. He reached his mistress, wagged his tail at her. She set her teeth and tore the frill off his collar.

'Will you please . . . get rid of everybody . . . put an end to this,' she said.

'Miss Rowe . . . believe me . . . I'm damned sorry . . . '

'Thanks,' she said, swallowing hard. 'Thanks very much. But I am really only sorry that so much good time has been wasted. That's all, if you'll excuse me. I'm going indoors.'

He looked after her. He wanted to follow her; to try and apologise for Maplefield; comfort her. She looked like a hurt kid. But he could do and say nothing. She wouldn't let anybody pity her.

' 'Pon my soul, she's game,' he thought. 'And this is a *damnable* show.'

He strode across the lawn and came face to face with the old housekeeper, who had been chatting to the woman behind the tea urn.

She gave him a slightly malicious look.

'Doesn't seem to me Miss Rowe's guests are coming, sir,' she said.

Archer narrowed his gaze.

'Mrs. Martlet, who is responsible for this?' he asked sternly. 'I think *you* know something about it – don't you?'

The old woman shook with silent, derisive laughter.

'The young lady isn't so very popular . . . is she? There wasn't many wanted to come here, after Mr. Brownrigg and Mr. Hawkson had told them a few things –'

'And you,' broke in Archer furiously. 'How much harm have *you* done? Yes, Mrs. Martlet. I think you'll find yourself out of a job, and, by heaven, I hope Miss Rowe does tell you to go. You've insulted Sir James's memory by this day's work.'

Mrs. Marlet started to protest, but Archer strode past her toward the trio who still, somewhat dismally, twanged their fox-trots and grew flatter every moment.

Up in her bedroom, Elizabeth stripped off her gala dress and tore the delicate chiffon ruthlessly. Her lips were tight and set. There were unshed tears in her eyes, but she was not going to cry.

'It's the end,' she told herself. 'Absolutely the end. They've beaten me. I'll go. Yes, I'll go away tomorrow and I'll never come back. Mr. Hewitson can reign supreme – do what he likes – so far as I care! I'm through!'

CHAPTER XVI

ELIZABETH sat at the dinner table that night and ate nothing. She tried to eat. But she didn't seem to want her food. She felt too utterly wretched. She kept thinking about the humiliation of that afternoon. All those preparations for the garden fête for her tenants. The wasted tea and amusements. The grim emptiness of the place. Maplefield's last effort to oust her . . . the interloper . . . the girl who had vamped Sir James into leaving her his possessions.

With great bitterness in her heart tonight, Elizabeth regarded the beautiful, luxurious home which had been left to her and hated it. Hated Maplefield, and all these people who had rejected her and regarded her as an enemy instead of a friend.

Florence, the new maid from Tunbridge Wells, brought in soup, a meat course, a savoury. Elizabeth bade her take them away. She had a childish feeling, this evening, that she could not and would not eat a thing that Mrs. Martlet had cooked. That horrible, malicious old woman had had a hand in this afternoon's ugly work, and Elizabeth knew it.

She could have marched downstairs and given her notice – turned her out. But she didn't. She wasn't angry enough to do that. No – let the housekeeper who had been at 'Memories' for so many long years stay here until she died. Elizabeth didn't care. She was going away. She wouldn't come back here, and it wouldn't matter to her if Mrs. Marlet stayed.

Elizabeth sat with her elbows on the table, chin dug in the palms of her hands; brows drawn fiercely together. Intensely lonely and hurt she sat there, brooding over her failures as the mistress of this home.

Where was she going now? What would she do? Money she had, certainly. And Grock . . . her faithful dog. Nothing much else. Every day the wedding of Guy and Lilian drew nearer. They were already lost to her. She had several acquaintances – but nobody with whom she particularly wanted to stay, or with whom she wished to go away. There was an old aunt who lived in Dorset . . . her father's aged sister. But Aunt Constance was more or less bedridden these days, not a possible companion for Elizabeth. There were cousins of hers. But either they were married and leading their own lives, or uncongenial to her. No. There was nobody she cared about or wanted. How frightfully lonely she was. Tonight, following the dismal affair of the garden-party which had been such a fiasco . . . and so terribly wounding . . . she felt like creeping into a corner to weep. But her eyes were dry. She just sat there, a forlorn little figure . . . brooding . . . solitary . . . miserable.

She wandered into the study, lit a cigarette, and then rang the bell for the maid.

'Don't forget Grock's meat and biscuits . . . bring it along to me, Florence.'

'Yes, miss,' said the girl.

Elizabeth looked round and whistled for her pet.

'Grock . . . Grocky . . . where are you?'

'I 'aven't seen 'im since dinner, miss,' said Florence, setting the coffee down on a low stool beside her mistress.

'Neither have I, Florence. I wonder where he is. Just have a look. He's probably wandering round the garden.'

Florence departed. Elizabeth put some sugar in the coffee, which she drank strong and black, and was about to raise the cup to her lips when she saw a tall, familiar figure swinging over the lawn toward the house. Archer Hewitson. What did he want? She winced at the remembrance of the pity in his eyes this afternoon. Heavens, how she hated being pitied . . . by anyone! Yet he had been quite kind.

She stepped through the french windows and went to meet Archer. Not for the first time, she noticed how very good-looking he was, this hazel-eyed, bronzed young man. She liked that grey suit with the herringbone stripe . . . and the tie . . . it was a Marlburian tie, surely. She recognised it. Her father had been at Marlborough. She had an old scarf of his now, and a cricket cap. She told herself that she must ask Archer about it.

He came up to her with a faint, almost anxious smile.

'Good evening. Am I in the way?'

'Not at all. I'm quite alone.'

'I . . . I thought I'd ask myself up for a c-cigarette.'

Archer was stammering. As a matter of fact, he felt extraordinarily embarrassed. Ever since the débâcle of the garden-party he had worried about this girl. It had struck him so forcibly that she had been treated abominably here. He was ashamed of Maplefield. He could not forget the hurt look in Elizabeth's eyes when she had realised that none of her guests was coming. 'And she had been so cheery and happy about the show . . . so decent about it all. Yes, that was what appealed to Archer about this girl . . . she was such a *decent* kid . . . he couldn't have paid her a higher compliment than that. He thought of her as a boy who played the game.

Maplefield had given Elizabeth Rowe a bad deal. She had been extremely nice, and this was her reward. He had pictured her feeling more than usually lonely up here tonight. He had felt he must come along.

He followed her into the library. She rang the bell.

'You'd like a cup of coffee, wouldn't you?' she said.

He had half feared she would not be at home to him, or would be frigid and aloof, as she had been since Delia Kilwarne had called on her. But she was quite nice tonight. She just seemed unutterably weary. Her voice, her manner, her eyes, were tired.

She had discarded the pretty chiffon frock which she had worn this afternoon for the party. But she was not in evening dress. She wore a grey pleated skirt and a soft grey woolly jumper with a square neck, which made her look a mere child. She was paler than usual. Somehow, all that was most kind and understanding in Archer Hewitson rose to the surface at the sight of his young employer tonight. She looked so utterly forlorn and dispirited. Yet she still held that small dark head of hers high. And she wouldn't whine. He admitted that he himself had a somewhat similar nature to hers. He loathed showing that he was hurt. He understood her these days.

'Look here, Miss Rowe,' he said. 'About this afternoon – '

'Oh, don't let's worry about it,' she interrupted quickly. 'Have a cigarette.'

'I'd rather have my pipe, if I may.'

'Do.'

He pulled the pipe from his pocket and blew through the

139

stem. His face was puckered and worried.

'It was such a rotten show. I had to come up and tell you again how I regret it,' he said.

Elizabeth looked at him. Her eyes, which had been hard and bitter, softened a trifle. After all, it was nice of him to worry on her behalf. Nice of him to come. He wasn't a bad sort, this Archer Hewitson. She wished, gloomily, that he were not mixed up with that hateful Mrs. Kilwarne and that she could respect him. They might have been such good friends.

'Thanks very much indeed, Mr. Hewitson,' she said. 'I appreciate what you say. But I'd rather just put it out of my mind. These people here obviously loathe me, and resent my being in Sir James's shoes, so I've made up my mind to quit . . . that's all.'

'You are really going?'

'I am. Aren't you pleased?' That slipped out in the bitterness of the moment.

'No,' said Archer slowly. 'Certainly not. Why should I be?'

She flushed scarlet and turned away.

'I thought . . . everybody would be.'

'Lord, how damnable we've all been!' he thought. Aloud he said: 'Look here, don't go. Stay and give Maplefield another chance.'

'No,' she said. 'I don't want to stay now.'

'I've been making inquiries. I know what happened to-day. It was what we thought . . . Brownrigg and Hawkson made a tour of all the people we invited . . . got up a sort of union . . . and made everybody turn down the party to show their disapproval. But I'm going to get those swine out of this village, and Mrs. Marlet with them, and then . . .'

'No . . . please,' she broke in, turning back to him. 'Leave it now. I've finished with them. I don't want to stay here. I shall go and shut the place up or let you carry out Sir James's original plan – to turn "Memories" into a home for blind children.'

Archer sat on the arm of a chair and filled his pipe. He felt a peculiar lack of enthusiasm for that scheme. Yet, when he had first heard that Miss Rowe had been left Sir James's estate, he had felt furious. He hated the idea. He had wanted 'Memories' to be converted into a charity home.

140

Queer that it didn't appeal to him so vastly now! What was it? Perhaps he had grown used to this queer, solitary little person with her grave, brown eyes and business-like manner and boyish sense of sport. He would miss her when she was gone. He wasn't so keen on running the show alone, without her to talk things over with him.

'How rum life is,' he thought. 'Human nature is so devilish perverse. Somehow I don't particularly want her to go. . . .'

And neither did he relish the thought that she had been literally driven away . . . that he had headed the list of people who resented her presence when she had first come. But he knew her so much better now . . . and liked her so much better.

He blew a cloud of blue smoke into the air and then looked at her almost apologetically.

'Don't leave "Memories" if you could bear to stay and give the folk another chance here,' he said. 'I'll guarantee that such a thing as happened today will never happen again.'

She shook her head.

'I'm sorry. I don't want to stay.'

'It's been wretchedly lonely for you, I'm afraid.'

'I suppose it has.'

'You don't know how sorry I am.'

'Why should you be?'

He shrugged his shoulders and pressed a thumb down in the bowl of the pipe.

'I feel almost responsible.'

'Not for my happiness, surely.' Her lips suddenly trembled into a faint, wry smile. 'You needn't feel that. You've done a lot for me, Mr. Hewitson – managed everything extremely well. By the way, I shan't like leaving Grey Lady. I've got rather fond of her. I hoped to hunt her. But I've always got Grock, which means a lot. My funny old plum-pudding dog.'

'You do love that spotted hound, don't you?'

Their gaze met, and they both smiled. They were friends again. Delia Kilwarne was forgotten.

'Yes, I love my spotted hound dearly,' said Elizabeth.

'You're equally keen on your terrier.'

'Micky's a great pal of mine.'

'Grock's my best pal,' she said gravely.

141

'You've had him long?'

'Five years. I had him when he was a puppy of four months, and he's never left me since.

'Did you always live up in town?'

'No. Only for a year. I shared the flat in Chelsea with my friend, Miss Maxwell . . . I think you saw her down here one Sunday with Mr. Arlingham . . . before that, when my father was alive, we lived in Eastbourne. Then I went to Paris, studied painting for a year . . . not very seriously . . . but it amused me. Oh, by the way, isn't that a Marlborough tie you're wearing?'

He touched the tie and nodded, surprised.

'Yes, it is. You know it?'

'My father was at Marlborough.'

'Really? How interesting.'

'A generation before yourself.'

'My own governor was there, though. They must have been contemporaries.'

'Father was in the cricket eleven in his time.'

'Then undoubtedly they knew each other well. My governor was a bit of a lad at cricket in his day.'

They both had plenty to discuss now. Definite contact was established after that . . . a real tie discovered. Archer's pipe went out. He sat there talking eagerly about Marlborough and his father. And in her turn Elizabeth spoke of hers. They were learning quite a lot about each other. And Archer found himself thinking:

'If she'd been a boy, what a sportsman she'd have made. She wouldn't have disgraced the old school!'

They talked until the clock struck ten. Elizabeth had had no idea how the time was flying. Then Florence came in and informed her that Grock was nowhere to be found.

Archer stood up and put his pipe in his pocket.

'I've stayed much too long,' he said. 'Do forgive me.'

'That's quite all right. It's been most interesting, but I wonder where Grock is,' said Elizabeth.

'Not lost, is he? Are we going to have another dog hunt?'

'I can't understand it. He doesn't go into the woods chasing rabbits, like your terrier.'

'I've been everywhere, miss,' said Florence. 'I did chance to see Bingham at the back door just now, and he said he thought he'd seen him down the front drive somewhere.'

142

'He so rarely leaves me,' Elizabeth said to Archer. 'I let him out before dinner and haven't seen him since.'

'I'll have a look for him for you.'

'I'll come out with you as far as the Lodge,' she said.

They strolled together down the drive. It was dark now. The sky was milky with stars. A full moon flooded the beautiful gardens with white light. It was a perfect June night, but a little damp underfoot. There had been a heavy dew.

'You won't be cold without a coat, will you?' said Archer.

'No. I don't catch cold,' she said, smiling.

She thought it was nice of him to think about that. And he looked down at the small, slender girl with her smooth dark head and face that looked so pale and wistful in the starlight and knew, definitely, that he regretted her going. He liked Elizabeth Rowe. He was just beginning to understand her. They had much in common . . . the certain knowledge that their fathers had been friends at school . . . a mutual love of animals and of country life. What a fool he had been to greet her with such hostility when first she had come; to imagine that he would detest her. He had been rather a fool all the way along. He knew it now, and he was sorry because he was afraid it was too late.

They reached the Lodge. Elizabeth looked anxiously up and down the road.

'Grock . . . Grocky, here, old boy!' she called.

She stood there whistling and calling. As a rule, when Grock heard her voice he came bounding to her side at once. There was no sign of the spotted hound now. Elizabeth looked at Archer Hewitson. There was a horrid niggling of fear in her heart.

'Nothing can have happened to him, can it?'

'No, no, of course not,' he reassured her. 'I know what you feel. I felt it myself, when old Micky stayed out all night. But Grock isn't likely to be caught in a trap.'

'No . . . but if any of those beastly men . . .'

She stopped and bit her lip. She felt positively sick at the idea that anything might have happened to her beloved pet.

'Oh, nobody will have hurt the dog,' said Archer.

Elizabeth whistled again.

There was no sign of Grock on the dark deserted road. She looked up and down and then back at the grounds of the house.

'Grock . . . Gr-ock . . . Gr-ock-y!'

Her voice echoed through the quiet night. Then she looked at Archer. There was real concern in her eyes now.

'I can't think where he is. It's rather worrying. He doesn't go far – ever.'

'Let's make a tour of the gardens,' he suggested.

'Don't you wait, if you want to go home.'

'No. Please let me come with you.'

They turned and walked back, up the drive to the gardens. Elizabeth whistled and called her pet ceaselessly. Archer added an occasional whistle. There was no sign of the dog. They inspected the rose garden; the walk beside the big herbaceous border; the lawns sloping to the pond which was like a round, glittering mirror in the summer moonlight. They walked through the stone archway into the orchard. Elizabeth continued to call, a hand to her lips:

'Grock! Gr-ock! Gr-ock-y!'

Her heart was beating quite fast and her face felt peculiarly damp and hot. It was so strange . . . that he should have wandered so far. Yet she felt it would be absurd to think anything had happened to him.

'He'll turn up in a minute,' said Archer, as they paused in their search to take breath. 'I expect he's found something exciting.'

'But he *always* comes when I call!' exclaimed Elizabeth.

'Well, can he be in the woods – like Mick was?'

'We'll go and call him,' said Elizabeth. 'But I'm absolutely certain Grock wouldn't stray so far as the woods.'

Archer looked round. They were at the end of the orchard. Through the archway they could just see the flagged path which was bordered with old-fashioned, sweet-smelling herbs and dwarf plants. An ancient, chipped bird-bath stood in the middle of the path. Flooded with moonlight, and seen here from the shadows, it looked full of enchantment. He could hear a nightingale singing close by . . . filling the night with enraptured song. But Elizabeth did not hear it – did not notice the magic of the moonlit garden. Her mind was centred on Grock. She would have given quite a lot to see him with his sleek, spotted body, his comic head, come bounding along through that archway toward her, lifting his lips back from his teeth in his funny, affectionate smile.

'Where *can* he be?' she said.

144

Archer put his hands in his pockets and moved to one side of the path. To the left stood a lot of currant bushes and several rows of growing asparagus. He looked casually over the asparagus bed. And then, suddenly, his heart gave a horrible jerk and his muscles tautened. He took his hands out of his pockets. He stared hard . . . at something which showed white on the ground, in the shadows there between the asparagus bed and some gooseberry-bushes. Was that . . . could that be . . . ? He hardly dared let the idea formulate in his mind. He threw a quick glance at Elizabeth. She was not looking his way. She had begun to walk toward the arch-way, still whistling for her pet.

Archer made a dive into the bushes. He reached the object that was gleaming white and had caught his eye. He leaned down. His pulse-rate quickened. He felt positively sick as he looked. It was what he had thought. Elizabeth's dog . . . stretched there. The Dalmatian might have been asleep, but Archer knew that he was dead. He was already growing stiff, and his eyes were wide open . . . a piteous, glassy stare in them. His lips writhed back from his teeth. He looked to Archer as though he had died in agony.

'Poisoned,' was the thought that flashed through Archer's brain. 'My God, what devil's work is this?'

Then he stood up, his heart thudding, the palms of his hands wet. Poor little Elizabeth Rowe! Poor little thing! Her adored Grock . . . how in the name of goodness was he going to tell her? Yet he must.

CHAPTER XVII

ELIZABETH had reached the archway.

'I think we'll go in,' she said. 'He may have gone back to the house – we'll probably find him there by now.'

Archer cleared his throat. Never in his life had he had a more difficult task than this one . . . of telling Elizabeth what he had just found.

'Can you come here a minute?' he stammered.

Elizabeth walked toward him.

'What's the matter?'

He looked at her, then away from her.

'Look here,' he said, still stammering. 'I . . . you . . . you've got to face something rotten . . . something damnable . . . I . . .'

'What's up?' she broke in quickly. She went cold as ice. 'What is it? What have you found?'

'Grock,' he said.

'Grock? Where? How . . . oh, my *God*!'

She broke off on that anguished cry. She had seen now . . . seen the familiar white, spotted body on the ground in the shadow of the gooseberry bushes. She rushed up and flung herself down beside it.

'Grock,' she said in a panic-stricken voice. 'Grocky . . . old boy . . . *Grocky.* . . .'

But Grock remained very still and silent. For the first time since he had belonged to her, his tail did not wag in response to her voice, and the lips, writhing back from his teeth, were ghastly in a mask of death instead of the comic smile with which he had always greeted her.

For a few moments Elizabeth knelt there, patting, shaking him, unable to grasp the fact that he was dead and beyond recall. Then, when she did realise it, she went almost crazy. It was totally beyond her now to control her feelings; to hide them. This dog had been her constant companion and pet for five years, and had worshipped her. She had known that whoever failed her, lover or friend, Grock never would. When she had been unable to bestow open adoration on anybody else, she had bestowed it on him. And now he was dead. He would never answer to her whistle again. Never caper up the path or over the fields toward her. Never curl up in his usual way on the rug beside her bed ... or sit beside her whilst she ate her meals, wagging his tail, appealing for the scraps and bones.

She sprang to her feet. Archer saw that she was livid, white to the lips.

'How did this happen?' she asked, panting. 'Mr. Hewitson ... tell me ... how did it happen? How did he die? Why? Who's done this? Oh, who's done it?'

Archer knelt beside the dog and moved his head gently. He examined the jaws. Then he knew. . . . He stood up, wiping his fingers with his handkerchief.

'Miss Rowe,' he said. 'I'm terribly afraid Grock was poisoned. There's a bit of raw meat in his mouth now ... and he looks like an animal that has died like that.'

'Poisoned,' repeated Elizabeth. 'Poisoned . . . my old Grock . . . yes, that's what it is. One of those *damnable* men in the village . . . or Mrs. Martlet . . . more beastliness and revenge because Brownrigg and Hawkson lost their jobs. They've killed my dog. Murdered the only thing I loved. Oh, Grock . . . Grock!'

She broke down completely . . . went to pieces . . . stood there with her face in her hands and sobbed aloud. Archer's heart was wrung with pity for her. It was awful to see this girl, who bore things so well, who was such a plucky child and habitually so cold and reticent, broken to pieces with grief for her beloved pet. And he did not find her sorrow out of proportion or absurd. He knew that he would have felt it if it had been Micky. And Micky was a much newer pet than Grock, whom Elizabeth had had for five years. He went up to her and put a hand on her shoulder.

'Don't,' he said huskily. 'Don't cry like that, my dear ... but I'm dreadfully sorry ... sorrier than I can say.'

She went on crying desperately. A torrent of passionate denunciation of Grock's murderers broke from her.

'I'll use ... every penny I own ... to get them ... I'll never rest till I find ... who killed him ... who poisoned my Grock ... oh, the beasts ... the *beasts* ... why couldn't they

147

have left *him* alone!'

'Oh, my dear,' said Archer again, unconscious of any undue familiarity in that moment. 'My dear, I'm sorry.'

And then – she never knew how it happened, but in the tempest of her grief she found herself in his arms. He held her tightly with one arm and stroked her hair. He kept on saying: 'Don't cry . . . don't cry . . . poor little thing . . . I'm so damned sorry . . . '

She was broken; utterly feminine and weak in that moment, almost stupefied with grief; with misery at the loss of her beloved dog. She hid her wet face against Archer Hewitson's shoulder and let him hold her and smooth her hair.

'I . . . loved him so much,' she wept passionately. 'All these years . . . he's been my pal . . . oh, why couldn't they have left him alone? . . . Oh, the beasts! The cowards!'

'It may not have been anyone in particular . . . who had ill-feeling against Grock. It may be he picked up rat poison – ' began Archer. Then paused, aware that this was absurd, because the raw meat in Grock's mouth suggested that he had been deliberately given the poison. And he had a horrid suspicion that this was the work of some of the men who had objected to old Sally being destroyed.

'Brownrigg threatened to shoot him if he dug up the garden . . . he loathed him . . . and Mrs. Martlet hated him because he made dirty marks in the house,' Elizabeth sobbed. 'Oh, my poor old Grock, why did I ever come here . . . why, why did either of us come?'

Archer felt himself bitterly reproached . . . and was bitterly remorseful. He tightened his hold of her.

'Don't speak like that,' he said. 'I hate to hear that. My dear, don't cry any more – you'll make yourself ill.'

'I don't care . . . I don't care about anything . . . I want Grock back,' she wept childishly.

He caressed the dark, cropped head gently, his heart aching for her. She no longer seemed the difficult Miss Rowe, his employer. She was just a broken-hearted child, weeping for her dead pet. How small and soft she was to hold, he thought . . . a slip of a thing. He felt suddenly the strangest thrill run through him. His pulse-rate quickened. Before he could restrain the impulse, he had touched her hair with his lips.

148

'Poor little girl,' he said.

Then, through the grief, the pain obliterating her, she realised that she was in this man's arms and that he was kissing the top of her head. She flushed crimson and checked her sobs. She withdrew herself from his arms and moved away a pace. She hid her face in her hands.

'I ... haven't a ... handkerchief.'

'Take mine,' he said.

He handed her a big coloured silk handkerchief. She took it and wiped her eyes. He watched her with extraordinary tenderness. Then he glanced at the pathetic, still body of her pet and his lips tightened.

'By God, I'll get those hounds if they did deliberately poison him,' he thought.

Elizabeth had control of herself once more. But she shivered from head to foot when she gave the handkerchief back to Archer. She could not look at Grock again. She moved on to the path. In the moonlight her face looked white and tragic.

'Can I leave you to ... to ...'

'I'll see about the poor old fellow, yes,' he said as she broke off.

'I'd like him ... buried somewhere ... under the trees.'

'I'll see to it. Come along back to the house. You're all in,' he said kindly.

He moved to her side and took her arm. She swallowed hard.

'You've been – most awfully nice about it. Sorry if I was ...'

'You're not to apologise,' he cut in. 'I understand – absolutely. I know what I'd have felt like it it had been Micky.'

She was silent. But instinctively her thoughts flew to Guy. Guy had never liked Grock; had always been absurdly jealous of her devotion to the dog. If he had been here to-night, he wouldn't have been so sympathetic or so understanding as Archer Hewitson. She felt the friendly pressure of Archer's arm against hers and was amazed to find how it helped ... and how grateful she was to him for his kindness and sympathy. And Grock had liked Archer. Poor old Grock. Even now she could not believe that he was dead.

Florence met them in the doorway.

149

'Please, miss, have you found him?'

'Yes,' said Elizabeth in a dull voice. 'He's dead, Florence.'

'Dead, miss?' The girl was shocked. She had not been at 'Memories' long, but long enough to know how her mistress adored the Dalmatian. It was common talk among the outside staff . . . almost a subject of derision . . . the fact that Miss Rowe was never without her 'spotted hound'. It seemed to her a very grievous thing that the dog should be dead.

'Oh, miss, but how . . .' she began.

Elizabeth cut her short; he eyes narrow, flashing in a white little face.

'He was poisoned, Florence. Tell Mrs. Martlet that he won't make any more marks on her carpets and that I hope she . . . she's satisfied. . . .'

She broke off, choking, pulled her arm away from Archer, and hurried into the library. She was so afraid she was going to break down again. Archer said to the maid:

'Phone up the garage, Florence, and ask Bingham to come up to the house. I want him to bury the dog. We don't want Miss Rowe to see him again.'

'Yes, sir,' said Florence. She departed, quite upset.

Archer followed Elizabeth into the library. She had switched on a table lamp, but stood by the window, where her face was in shadow. She had lit a cigarette and was smoking, but she looked so desolate, he wanted to go up to her, take her in his arms again, and hug her. But instead he took out his pipe and filled it.

'I can't believe it yet,' she whispered. 'That he'll never come again when I whistle for him.'

'Try not to think about it,' he said.

'It's difficult.'

'I know.'

'I loved that dog.'

'I know you did.'

'I wonder why it is . . . everything, everybody I love gets taken from me,' she burst out with an unusual desire to talk . . . to get some of the load off her mind. She turned to Archer with tears in her eyes. 'I seem fated,' she added brokenly. 'Absolutely fated.'

'Is it as bad as that?' he said gently.

'Just before I came here I . . . lost the only man I cared for. . . .'

He looked into the brown wet eyes and felt something keener than pity.

'He died?'

'No . . . he just discovered he – cared for someone else. . . .'

'Rotten,' said Archer.

So that was the history behind this queer, solitary little thing. An unhappy love affair. That fellow Arlingham, perhaps . . . and the red-haded girl. Strange, but Archer felt curiously glad that Elizabeth Rowe had not married Arlingham. He had disliked the fellow on sight.

Elizabeth sat down on a hassock; crouched there, smoking; the tears drying on her lashes.

'I was lonely when he went,' she said. 'But somehow I shall be lonelier . . . without Grock.'

'I understand,' he said. 'One's pet dog is a constant companion. . . .'

'And such a faithful pal. I hate to think of him bounding out there into the garden on a beautiful night like this . . . loving life, and then picking up or being given a bit of meat . . . wolfing it . . . like any dog would do . . . and finding that it was the end of him. It must have hurt him . . . and been. such an astonishment. My poor old Grock. . . .'

'Look here,' said Archer gently, 'Let me mix you a drink . . . it'll do you good.'

'No, thanks. I never drink.'

'Well, I'm afraid I must push off,' he said. 'It's nearly half-past eleven.'

'Is it?' she said dully. 'So late? I suppose we were a long time . . . calling Grock.'

'I've got Bingham coming up . . . I'll just get him to . . . see to things.'

'Thank you.'

'Good night,' he said. 'And, honestly, I'm more sorry than I can possibly express.'

She stood up and held out her hand. He took it and pressed it very hard.

'You've been – awfully decent to me,' she said huskily.

'I've done nothing. There's nothing one can do. But try

151

and forget it now ... try and sleep.'

'Oh, I'll be all right,' she said.

She smiled. But he saw that she was on the point of tears again. He knew, in that minute, that he liked and admired her more than any woman he had ever met in his life. And she looked up at his face, which was so grave, so compassionate, and wondered how she had ever disliked Archer Hewitson ... or what she would have done tonight without him. The unhappy hour marking the death of Grock would be a bond between them always.

'You won't be going away tomorrow, will you?' he said.

'Yes,' she said. 'More than ever.'

'Then may I come up and see you before you go?'

'Please do.'

He said good night and left her. She heard him talking in lowered tones outside the front door to the chauffeur. She thought of her beloved pet lying stiff and stark out there in the bushes and she thought her heart would break. Queer, how much more acutely his death had hurt her than the loss of Guy had done. But then Grock, the dog, had loved her faithfully for five long years, and Guy, the man, had only thought he loved her for a month or two. That made a difference.

How awfully nice Archer Hewitson had been. She remembered the strength of his arms holding her ... and how hot and embarrassed she had felt when she had realised he was kissing her hair. No man except Guy had ever held her in his arms. But she hadn't minded Archer somehow. His embrace had been strangely comforting.

It was horribly lonely and quiet in the house now. If she whistled for Grock he wouldn't hear her – wouldn't come.

She went upstairs to bed. In her room she looked at the old rug beside her bed ... specially placed there on top of a good one, because Grock slept on it. She found it difficult to believe that he wouldn't be sleeping beside her bed tonight, that never again would she wake in the morning, stretch out her hand, and feel his warm tongue caressing it in his friendly, joyous way.

'Oh, Grock,' she said aloud. 'Grocky ... '

Then the relief of tears came again. She lay face downwards on the bed, shaken with sobs.

And out in the moonlight, Archer and the chauffeur

carried the Dalmatian in from the orchard; dug a deep, warm bed for him under the oak-tree on the front lawn and buried him there – covered him in brown earth and moss and leaves . . . and left him to his sleep.

The two men looked at each other over the hastily improvised grave. Archer, feeling curiously upset; the chauffeur with an uneasy look in his eyes.

'Bingham, what do you know about this?' Archer asked the man sternly.

'Me, sir? Why, nothing, sir,' said Bingham.

'That dog was poisoned Bingham.'

'Yes, sir.'

'And a good few in Maplefield threatened him after Miss Rowe had old Sally put painlessly away.'

Bingham made no answer, but he mopped his forehead and averted his gaze. Archer felt suddenly that if he could have proved in this moment that Bingham was one of the gang responsible for Grock's death, he would knock him down gladly . . . smash his face to pulp. But he could prove nothing, and probably never would.

He strode across the fields back to his cottage. He looked back at 'Memories' as he went, and saw a light in one of the upper windows. Elizabeth's room. He visualised her there just as she was – crying her eyes out. He thought with a lump in his throat:

'Poor child . . . she adored that beast. And one can't help her. And now she's going away . . . for good. . . . '

He was suddenly immensely distressed because Elizabeth was going. And not only was he haunted that night by the memory of her passionate grief when she had discovered Grock's dead body . . . but by the memory of the softness of her in his arms. The fragrance of her hair . . . the silkiness of it against his lips.

He decided, definitely, that when tomorrow came she must not go. He must do everything in his power . . . if there was anything he *could* do . . . to make her stay at 'Memories'.

CHAPTER XVIII

ELIZABETH awoke that next morning – gave one look at the rug beside her bed – realised that Grock was not there and that never again would she see him lying there – turned over on her pillows and wept, quite frankly and unashamedly, for her pet.

She had definitely made up her mind to leave 'Memories' and forget all its unpleasant associations, and she was ready dressed for travelling when she went down to breakfast.

She had only just taken her place at the table when Florence told her that she was wanted on the telephone.

'Mr. Arlingham, please, miss, and it's urgent.'

She answered the telephone in the study. She wondered why Guy should want her urgently. Had anything untoward happened?

She was astonished to find that her heart did not beat one whit faster as she took up the receiver. Was it possible that her once intense love for Guy had died? Had time and circumstances destroyed it? Somehow, so much seemed to have happened lately to make her forget it. And today she was quite numb with pain at the loss of Grock. She was indifferent to anything else. Guy could not possibly console her for the loss of her beloved pet, because he had disliked Grock and Grock had disliked him.

'Hello, good morning, Guy,' she said. 'What can I do for you?'

Then she was surprised and dismayed to hear his voice – hoarse – quite frantic – over the wires.

'Elizabeth, my dear, something terrible – something ghastly has happened.'

Her heart missed a beat. She said quickly:

'What is it?'

'Lilian,' he said.

'*Lilian*? What about her? What's happened?'

'I can hardly tell you, Lizbeth. It's too awful.'

Elizabeth gripped the receiver tightly.

'For heaven's sake, tell me. . . . '

'An accident,' came from Guy. He seemed quite broken up. . . . 'A frightful accident.'

'An accident – to Lil? But when – where – what was it? is she –'

'She's dead, Elizabeth.'

Silence. Elizabeth felt cold as ice although the warm June sunshine flooded the little study. She could not credit her ears.

'Guy!' she exclaimed. 'It can't be true.'

'It is, my dear. I can hardly believe it myself. She was . . . going out with me . . . we were dining with Aunt Caroline – you know – my aunt, Lady Weylow . . . '

'Yes, yes. . . . '

'Poor little Lilian took a taxi from her aunt's house in Hampstead, and it rained a bit in town last night – the roads were greasy – beastly. She had a rotten driver, I suppose. Anyhow, they crashed – in Piccadilly. There was a triple smash – they hit a private car – a big Rolls – and a motor-bus skidded into them. Everybody escaped – except poor little Lil. She was hit in the head. She was taken to St. George's Hospital with concussion. I was with her all night – hadn't time to get on to you. She never recovered consciousness. She died – at half-past seven this morning. One can only thank God she didn't suffer at all. I've just got back from the hospital. I feel half off my head. . . . '

He broke off. Elizabeth, her face very white, stared over the telephone at a picture on the wall. She did not see it. She was seeing Lilian – beautiful, sweet-natured Lilian, with her vivid red head and her wonderful white skin – and tried to picture her as dead. The lamp of her youth put utterly out . . . and only a few weeks before her wedding-day. It was too cruel – too dreadful a picture to visualise. Elizabeth felt herself trembling from head to foot with the shock of the news.

'Guy,' she said. 'Guy – I can't believe it!'

'Neither can I, Lizbeth. It's broken me – absolutely shattered me.'

'Of course. I know. I understand,' she said helplessly. She felt helpless – floundering. She wanted to burst out crying – to say a thousand comforting things. And as usual,

155

in the teeth of acute emotion, she was inarticulate.

Lilian was dead. She must try and grasp that. Lil – who had been her companion at Elbury Walk – shared a studio with her – and so many cheery, happy days and nights. Lil, who was so young and lovely – *dead*. It was difficult to believe. She felt stunned. The loss of poor Grock, last night, seemed so little in comparison to this tragedy – this loss of human life. She couldn't even tell Guy about Grock. She could think of nothing but Lilian. The hot tears stung her eyes as she said:

'I was coming up to town this morning, anyhow. I'll come at once – immediately after breakfast.'

'Yes, do, for God's sake,' came from Arlingham. 'I need your support, my dear. I feel all in. You can imagine . . . the dreadful shock . . . and you . . . I . . . both cared for her.'

'Yes, I was awfully fond of Lil.'

Elizabeth said that sincerely. She meant it. The fact that Lilian had taken Guy from her had never altered her feelings toward her friend. She was big-hearted enough – broad-minded enough – to know that one cannot always help these things. Poor, lovely Lilian, whose youth and beauty were at an end . . . and who had been flung so suddenly into Eternity!

'I need you, Elizabeth,' said Guy.

'Of course – I'll come,' she said. 'I'll be at the Park Lane Hotel. Come there – at lunch-time.'

'It will be wonderful to have you,' he said.

'Goodbye – and I can't possibly tell you how shocked – how grieved I am for you, Guy,' she said.

She hung up the receiver. She sat a moment with her face buried in her hands; the tears trickling through her fingers. Her sorrow was mainly for Guy – the man she had once loved. She thought how ghastly it was for him to lose his future wife – a few weeks before their wedding. But the man the other end of the wire was not suffering quite so frantically as she pictured; neither was he quite so inconsolable. Naturally, the dreadful accident to Lilian had unnerved and horrified him. In his fashion, he cared for her. Her beauty had thrilled his senses to the end. But for weeks now he had thought more about Elizabeth than Lilian. For weeks he had fretted at the mistake he had made in giving Elizabeth up. And many were the covetous and regretful

156

thoughts he had given to all that Elizabeth now possessed.

He would have been indignant if anyone had accused him now of being a hypocrite. He told himself he was entirely broken up by Lilian's accident. Yet into his mind wriggled an ugly and insidious little feeling of relief; of hope that this unexpected calamity might be the means of reuniting him with Elizabeth.

Elizabeth, however, not for an instant dreaming that Guy had any such callous or mercenery sentiment, grieved bitterly over the death of her friend – for his sake even more than for her own. Poor old Lil had more or less gone out of her life. But it seemed to her a most dreadful tragedy that this should have happened. It wiped all other thoughts from her mind.

It was not until Florence announced Mr. Hewitson that Elizabeth remembered the present and her own personal trials and tribulations. She saw Archer in the study, and the mere sight of him recalled to her last night – how she had wept in his arms . . . over the dead body of Grock. One shock, one grief after another, she reflected. It was terrible. And this last one so much more serious than the other. Yet there was a corner of her heart still inconsolable for Grock, who had never left her side for five years. And she was unashamed of her sorrow . . . because, in her opinion, a faithful dog was as fine a friend as any human being.

When Archer saw her, he was troubled to see how white and haggard she looked. Her eyes were red-rimmed with weeping. Then she told him the fresh calamity that had befallen her.

'One thing after another . . . now it's my best friend, Lilian Maxwell,' she said huskily. 'She died in a taxi smash in town in the early hours of this morning.'

'Good God! I'm most dreadfully sorry,' said Archer.

She turned and looked out of the window at the gay, flower-filled garden.

'I do seem fated,' she said. 'Those that I love . . . '

'It *is* tough luck,' said Archer. 'I can't tell you how sorry I am. Is there anything I can do?'

'Nothing – thank you.'

'You're going away?'

'Yes – up to town by the nine-thirty. Bingham will be here in a few minutes to take me to the station.'

She turned from the window and looked at him. His face was grave and compassionate. Their eyes met. And suddenly, as Archer looked down into her brown, wet ones, he was filled with an intense desire to comfort her – help her. He was astonished by the intensity of this emotion. He, too, remembered last night . . . the softness, the feminine helplessness of Elizabeth in his arms. The blood leapt up under his tan. His heart beat fast. Then he dropped his gaze and fumbled in his pocket for his pipe.

But he knew, definitely, in that moment, that he loved Elizabeth Rowe. He was in love with her. And he would have given a bit to be able to take her in his arms this minute and tell her so. But he was much too embarrassed, and quite certain that if he did such a thing she'd think he'd gone mad and would turn him out of the house.

She became conscious of the acute embarrassment in the atmosphere. Her own heart beat faster. Uneasily she looked away from him. She lit a cigarette. And then the tense moment passed. But the memory, the significance of it, were to remain with both of them. Archer Hewitson was in love, for the first time in his life, and knew it. Her pulse-beats had quickened at the sight of a man other than Guy . . . and she had told herself, when Guy broke their engagement, that never again would that heart of hers beat faster for any man on earth.

Of course, this was absurd. Archer Hewitson didn't mean anything to her. He was just her estate-agent, and he had been very friendly and charming and kind to her; and last night, when he had held her; kissed her hair, it had been from pure pity – a fleeting thing of the moment. Besides, he was in love with Mrs. Kilwarne.

She smoked hard at her cigarette and pretended to sort some papers on the desk.

'Will you – carry on with the estate as usual?' she said.

'I will – of course. Are you coming back?'

'I don't suppose so.'

He was horrified to find his heart sinking like a stone when he heard that, and looked at her stern young face. Was she going for good and all? Wouldn't he ever see her again? Would they never again come as close as they had been last night? No! Just as well not. He was a fool – a complete fool. What business had he to fall in love with his employer?

The thing was impossible, and besides, this girl would laugh at him – or be furious with him. He was furious with himself. But he could not conquer the feeling of depression and gloom at the thought of her departure.

'I hope you will come back,' he said.

He spoke formally. She answered with equal formality:

'Thanks very much. I'll have to see how I'm placed. But I shall be staying in town – at the Park Lane Hotel – if you want me for business reasons. I shall stay there until my friend's funeral, anyhow.'

She sighed deeply. Lil's funeral. How awful! What a depressing thought! And there'd be Guy who needed her mental support and comfort. Somehow she dreaded going through emotional hours and days with Guy. He would be most trying. He had always been exaggerated and dramatic. Even when she was in love with him she had felt that. She wasn't in love with him any more. How queer – to have discovered suddenly this morning, when she had heard that Lilian was dead and he was free again, that her old passion for him was dead.

Archer watched her gloomily. She was putting some papers into a dispatch-case. And now – with the eyes of a man in love – he noticed a dozen little things about her that had not struck him before. How queer – what a difference it made – being in love. He noticed how slightly built she was; what fine wrists and ankles she had; slight yet strong. The ever capable, practical little Elizabeth, with her small, square hands and determined chin. He noticed that her hair was dark as a raven's wing; and her face and throat tanned to warm gold by the sun; and even this morning, although she looked tired and had been crying violently, her eyes were beautiful. Brown, brave eyes under the thick shadow of their lashes. She was altogether a very brave little person. All his admiration for her culminated into the great driving-force which is love – the passionate love of a man for a woman. The thing that Archer Hewitson had shied at; avoided; laughed at – until now. Today he knew that this girl – whose coming he had dreaded; whose authority he had resented – was the one and only woman he could love, entirely and absolutely.

She looked over the desk at him.

'I shall have to come down again, anyhow, to pack all my

personal things and settle up the maids,' she said.

That gave him hope.

'Yes,' he said.

'Did you – did you do as I asked – about my poor old Grock?'

'I did,' he said gently. 'We buried the poor old fellow under the oak on the front lawn.'

'Thanks,' she said. She bit hard on her lip. She didn't want to cry again. 'It's difficult,' she added, 'for me to realise he's gone. And now . . . so awful . . . to get this frightful news of Miss Maxwell. She was going to be married, you know, to Mr. Arlingham – whom you met.'

'Yes, it's a ghastly show,' he nodded. 'I'm awfully sorry.'

'I was engaged to Mr. Arlingham myself at one time,' she said, without knowing why she confided this to Archer. 'Then he fell in love with Miss Maxwell. She was so beautiful – had the most striking red hair. I often used to try and paint her. Most men admired her immensely. It's a dreadful thing for Guy – Mr. Arlingham.'

Archer nodded. But he was smitten with the most ridiculous jealousy of Arlingham. It annoyed him to think that Elizabeth was ever engaged to him. That conceited, insufferable fellow. He did not want to think of Elizabeth belonging to Arlingham. He looked at her moodily. Was it possible that she had ever loved Arlingham . . . with passion . . . meant to marry him? He supposed so. And he had held her in his arms and kissed her, like a lover.

'Oh, damn!' thought Archer.

And now he was tormented by the fear that Elizabeth would go back to Arlingham – and they would come together again – through the death of that unfortunate girl. He couldn't endure to think of her marrying Guy Arlingham.

'Of course I'm off my head,' Archer told himself. 'What right have I to mind what she does or whom she marries? The sooner I get over this the better.'

But it wasn't going to be very easy to 'get over it'. This wasn't the sentimental fancy of a boy. He was a man who had travelled; seen life; had plenty of chance of looking round; making his choice. And he had remained unattached because he had never found a woman whom he wished to choose. Now that he had found one, it went deep. No, it wouldn't be at all easy for him to forget Elizabeth Rowe –

Elizabeth, who was unique in his estimation, different from any girl he had ever met.

He forced himself to say stiffly:

'You'll be a great help to Arlingham.'

'I shall do my best,' she said.

A gloomy silence. Then Elizabeth looked at her watch.

'I must get on my things. The car will be here.'

In through the french windows, the small figure of Archer's terrier appeared. He was limping on three legs. The injured paw was still bound up, but he was quite sprightly, and he made his way toward Elizabeth, wagging his tail with enthusiasm. She immediately stooped and picked him up in her arms, and the set look on her face relaxed.

'Why, it's dear little Micky,' she said. 'How is the poor bad paw?'

'Oh, practically healed. I shall take the bandage off to-morrow. The vet. had a look at him and said he'd had a very lucky escape – thanks to you,' said Archer.

'I'm so thankful I heard him in the trap that day.'

She stroked Micky's head. He licked her hand. And then, in spite of all her effort to restrain them, the tears rolled down her cheeks. Her thoughts turned to her lost favourite.

'Grock isn't here to growl at you this morning, Mick,' she whispered. 'Poor old Grock.'

Archer watched her and could say nothing. But there was a lump in his throat. Poor little Elizabeth! If only she wouldn't go away! The folk down here had been so beastly to her – driven her away with their hostility. It wasn't a pleasant thought to Archer.

Elizabeth put the Cairn down gently and then stood up and blew her nose violently.

'I must apologise for being so – silly, Mr. Hewitson,' she said.

'You know I understand,' he said, and would like to have said more.

'Yes, you really have been ripping to me,' she said boy-ishly. With a sudden charming smile which transformed her whole face, she held out her hand to him. 'Goodbye – and thank you.'

He gripped the small fingers hard.

'Look here,' he said. 'Come back – do – please.'

'I don't know about that. I don't think I can. But you'll

stay, won't you – look after everything?'

She became conscious of the almost violent pressure of his fingers – they hurt her so – and of the look in his eyes. The colour rushed to her cheeks. She drew away from him and made a hasty exit . . . muttering 'Goodbye, and thanks again.'

A few minutes later she was driving away from 'Memories' to Crowborough station. 'Memories'! Well – there were memories for her there now. Not too happy ones. And she had left poor Grock lying in his earthly grave, there under the oak tree. She had glanced at it through a mist of tears as the car went down the drive.

'Goodbye, Grocky – sleep well, my best, my truest friend,' she whispered.

Then she turned to the tragic thought of Lilian and what was facing her in town. And all through the chaos and sorrow she retained a strangely disturbing memory of Archer Hewitson. Of the intensity of his handclasp; of the look in his eyes; the depression in his voice when he said goodbye and begged her to come back again.

CHAPTER XIX

FOR the next two or three days Elizabeth had not time to dwell on the thought of things down at 'Memories' or her estate-agent. She had little opportunity to grieve over the Dalmatian, which was, perhaps, just as well.

The tragedy of Lilian Maxwell's accident and death occupied her mind entirely – that and the effort to help Guy, who leaned heavily on her. So heavily did he lean that his grief ceased to be as effective as he would have wished. He became the object of Elizabeth's contempt rather than her compassion. She herself had courage, and she disliked cowardice. Guy appeared incapable of shouldering his burden like a man.

'I can't bear to be alone for a moment – don't leave me, Lizbeth – stay with me,' was his constant cry. And she was with him as much as possible. But he was so dramatic, and appealed to her so constantly for pity, that she found she had little to give him.

She was certain that Lilian's sudden death had shocked and distressed Guy beyond words. But she liked reticence in people. Being a person of reserve herself, she shrank from public exhibition of sorrow. The funeral, which took place in Norwood and was attended by Lilian's relations and many of their mutual friends, remained in her mind as a most difficult and trying affair. She followed her friend to her last resting place, deeply depressed; asking herself why these dreadful things should happen. She was filled with melancholy at the thought that she would never see Lil again on this earth. They had been good friends before Guy had come into both their lives and separated them. She remembered some of the old merry evenings in the studios, with their pals. Jolly hours when they had held cocktail parties and dances; shared an enthusiasm for music and books and painting. Those care-free days when they had first set up house-keeping in the little flat in Chelsea.

163

Guy had spoiled it all. First she, Elizabeth, had fallen under the spell of his handsome face and his charming manners; his quick wit. Then Lil. And he had made love to them both. Well, they had both suffered for him. It was strange, reflected Elizabeth, to look back on it all . . . to feel that she no longer loved him. She could never suffer because of him again. And poor Lil would never suffer through him again – nor would she find the happiness she had hoped for as his wife.

Elizabeth's eyes were brimming with tears when she drove with Guy away from the cemetery; leaving her friend out there in the June sunshine under all the beautiful, melancholy flowers which had been sent to her as a final tribute. But she did not break down, and it was just as well. Guy was hysterical. He went white and faint at the graveside. He clung to her hands in the car and sobbed as they drove away.

'You must try and pull yourself together, my dear,' Elizabeth said gently but firmly. 'Come – buck up, Guy – Lil would hate you to feel like this about it.'

'I know – but I feel that my heart is broken,' he said, wiping his eyes. 'Don't leave me, Lizbeth. Nobody but you can help me through this.'

'I won't leave you,' she said.

She held his hand. But as she sat in the back of the car she recalled the days when she had first discovered that Guy and Lilian were in love with each other. She had thought her heart was broken then – because she had lost Guy. Old Sir James had said: 'Hearts do not break . . . they sting and ache. . . .'

How true that was. So rarely – so very rarely does that thing, the human heart, come anywhere near to breaking. Hers had not broken for Guy . . . yet he had seemed as lost to her as though he had died. More so . . . for in losing a loved one by death one still has a right to grieve; to remember. When one lost in life one had not even that right; which made it more bitter, more intolerable.

Only two months ago she had lost her lover. Today she sat beside him, and he clung to her hands and babbled that he needed her in his sorrow . . . and she was cold and untouched . . . even scornful of his lack of manliness.

Instinctively she thought of Archer Hewitson and his

164

strong, quiet presence. She would have liked to have gone to Lilian's funeral with Archer. He would have been such silent but splendid support. Archer was a real man. But Guy Arlingham was a weak, temperamental creature – entirely wrapped up in himself.

Guy dined with her that night at the Park Lane Hotel. He was more controlled, and seemed to enjoy being with her – to appreciate her companionship. He made an attempt to 'buck up', as Elizabeth had asked, and just retained that air of sadness, of touching melancholy, which seemed befitting to the occasion. Elizabeth supposed that he had been sincerely in love with Lilian, and was sincerely mourning her untimely end. Guy even tried to deceive himself into believing this. He was quite well aware that he looked pathetic, with an added pallor and dark shadows under his eyes, and that when he walked into the restaurant with Elizabeth that night – well groomed as usual; his head bright and shining – women looked at him and whispered: 'What an attractive-looking man . . . so handsome . . . and so terribly sad. He has the most *tragic* expression. Who is he?' . . . and, of course, somebody would be bound to say: 'Oh, that's Guy Arlingham, the writer. His fiancée has just been killed in a motor smash. Isn't it *dreadful* for him?'

A little public sympathy and support were awfully satisfying to Guy's intensely vain and egotistical nature. And he was banking on the fact that Elizabeth had not lost her old passion for him, and that she, too, would find him tragic and charming in his grief. Then they would come together again . . . a little later, when propriety permitted.

Elizabeth at dinner ordered champagne in her understanding, generous fashion; thinking it would 'cheer Guy up'. He toasted her, giving her the full benefit of his saddened blue eyes.

'Your health, little Lizbeth. Bless you, my dear. You've been marvellous to me. I'm so ashamed . . . of leaning on you . . . but you've helped me . . . I can't ever tell you how much.'

She raised her glass and drank a little of the champagne quickly, to hide her embarrassment.

'That's all right, Guy. Glad I was able to help.'

'I couldn't have done without you, Lizbeth.'

She lit a cigarette and sat back in her chair, looking over

165

the crowded room with a little frown between her brows. When she had been engaged to this man she would have felt thrilled by such words from him. In her shy, inarticulate way she had adored him . . . and longed to be adored. But he had never said such things . . . never told her he couldn't do without her. She had always felt he was rather like a god . . . condescending to stoop to the lips of a mere mortal like herself. But he was no longer a god to her. Tonight she found him a rather weak, selfish male-being inordinately conceited, and oozing self-satisfaction from every pore. She was rather horrified with herself. What had come over her? Why did she feel that she no longer even liked him? Or that she wished it were Archer Hewitson sitting here opposite her? She found herself thinking about Archer and Mrs. Kilwarne. Unpleasant thoughts. She didn't want to believe that Archer was Delia Kilwarne's lover. Yet Mrs. Kilwarne had given her to understand, very plainly, that he was.

Why had Archer held her hand so tightly when he said goodbye to her on the morning she left 'Memories'? Why had those grave, hazel eyes of his looked at her so queerly? Why had he begged her to come back? Did he really want her down there? Did he *like* her? She was very conscious this evening, as she sat opposite Guy and tried to concentrate on what he was saying, that she liked Archer Hewitson. That she more than liked him. But of course it was ridiculous. It was just that she *liked* him, now they understood each other, and he had been so awfully nice about Grock. There was nothing sentimental attached to it.

'You're very *distraite*, Lizbeth.' Guy's drawling voice interrupted her thoughts.

She stubbed her cigarette end on her plate. A faint colour rose to her cheeks.

'Sorry, Guy. Shall we go into the lounge for coffee?'

As they walked into the lounge, Guy noticed that one or two men looked after Elizabeth. Of course, these days she was very well dressed, he thought. That black lace dress fitted her slim figure charmingly. She was much more attractive than she used to be.

'I'd fall in love with her again if she was just painting in that old studio, without a bean,' he thought. Guy could always make himself believe anything.

Suddenly he said:

'What have you done with Grock? It's just struck me he isn't with you. It's so unusual to see you without him.'

Her lips tightened. She said quietly:

'Grock is dead.'

'Oh, really! When did he die? I'm very sorry . . . my dear.'

'He was poisoned, down at Maplefield, on the night of poor Lil's accident.'

'That's the worst of it – dogs do pick up poison occasionally,' said Guy. 'I expect you miss him, don't you!'

She could see he was trying to be nice but that the subject of Grock bored him. She felt suddenly that nobody in the world except Archer Hewitson understood what it had meant to her to lose her dog. She said:

'Don't let's talk about it. Have a liqueur, will you, Guy?'

'She is peculiar at times,' thought Arlingham. 'I'm not sorry the infernal Dalmatian *is* dead. Always hanging round her – it irritated me.'

'Tell me your plans for the future, my dear,' he said, as they drank their coffee in the lounge. 'You'll be going back to Maplefield, I presume?'

Three days ago, after the fiasco of the garden-party, Elizabeth had decided definitely to leave 'Memories'. To-night, without knowing why, she found herself saying:

'Yes, I think I shall.'

'How's that troublesome fellow, Hewitson, been conducting himself?'

She was surprised to discover that she resented Guy speaking of Archer in this manner. She said stiffly:

'Mr. Hewitson has been very decent – he is not at all troublesome.'

Then Guy put his tongue in his cheek and said to himself:

'The deuce! I thought she loathed him. What's been happening there? I'll have to look out. . . . '

Elizabeth stared round the crowded lounge, which was full of smart people. The atmosphere was hot and thick with cigarette smoke. She felt stifled. She thought of the pure, sweet air down at 'Memories'; of the beauty of her garden on a moonlight night. This was June . . . and down at 'Memories' all the wonderful roses were out. Her roses. Yes, it was *her* place. Was she going to be ousted because a few beastly men and an old brute like Mrs. Martlet had spat their poison on her? Was she going to confess herself beaten . . . a failure on the estate which Sir James had left to her?

The humiliation of the tenants' party, followed by the tragedy of Grock's death, had got her down temporarily. But tonight, in some queer way, she felt that she was up again. She was not going to admit defeat. And she wanted to go back. She wanted to work on that estate, hand in hand with Archer Hewitson again, and make a success of it. He had asked her to; begged her to give Maplefield another chance.

A queer nostalgia for 'Memories' came over her. Some queer force . . . she could not explain it, even to herself . . . was driving her back. She said

'I shall go back to Maplefield tomorrow.'

'Lizbeth,' said Guy, looking at her anxiously, 'I'll be in hell in town without Lil now – without you. Absolute hell. Look here, you told me that at any time I felt like it I could come down there with Lil. Now I've lost my poor darling . . . do you think you could tolerate me with – say a chaperon in the form of Aunt Caroline? She told me at the funeral that she'd come away with me for a bit. I'd rather be with *you* than anywhere in the world.'

Elizabeth bit her lip. She was not at all sure she wanted Guy down at 'Memories'. Nor did she particularly care for Lady Weylow, his aunt. She had met Lady Weylow in the days of her engagement to Guy. She recalled her . . . an ultra-smart Society woman of fifty or so, and a hidden barb in every honeyed speech she made. A type of woman for whom Elizabeth had contempt. Yet she felt it would be so deplorably rude and unkind to refuse to have Guy and his aunt at 'Memories'. Particularly as Guy had suggested it.

'If you and Lady Weylow would like to come down to me for a few days – please do, Guy, by all means,' she said.

He leaned across and touched her hand with his.

'My dear, you don't know what it'll mean to me. I shall be frightfully grateful. It will be marvellous – the peace down there . . . I must try and forget this awful thing . . . and you'll help me. . . . '

'I'll do my best,' she said shortly.

But she was conscious of irritation when he touched her hand. She wondered whether he meant all he said . . . if he were really so knocked up by poor Lilian's death, after all?

It was arranged that Guy and his aunt should motor down to 'Memories' that weekend. Tomorrow, Friday, Elizabeth would go down to prepare things so they could join her on Saturday.

'Perhaps you'd drop a line to Aunt Caroline and ask her personally,' Guy suggested.

'I will,' said Elizabeth.

She did so before she left London that next morning. But she made the invitation with a complete lack of enthusiasm. She sent a wire to Bingham; packed her things, and took a train to Crowborough before lunch.

On that journey down she found that she was eager to see Archer Hewitson again. She knew, definitely, that she didn't want to leave her beautiful country home and go abroad. No. She was going to stay at Maplefield, where she belonged, and this time make a success of things. She would begin by sacking that horrible old housekeeper. For the sake of her long service to the Willingtons, Elizabeth decided to give her an annuity. But she must get her out of the house and have a new cook – and another maid to work with Florence.

She remembered the first journey she had made to Crowborough; of the dread with which she had taken up her position as mistress of 'Memories'. Well, she had not had a very pleasant time. Yet, despite all the unpleasantness, she wanted to go back. She didn't really know what it was that drew her back, until she reached Crowborough and saw Archer Hewitson standing on the platform waiting for her. Then, after one look at the familiar, athletic figure in grey flannels . . . at the thin, brown face with the keen, kind eyes, Elizabeth *did* know. Knew, because the blood rushed to her cheeks and her heart began to thud very quickly. It was because of this man . . . her estate-agent . . . her one-time enemy, now so much her friend . . . that she had come back.

She had not expected him to meet her. But nobody could have guessed how fast her heart was beating when she greeted him. She greeted him casually:

'Hello! Good morning.'

He took her suit-case from her. His own response of 'How are you?' was casual enough. Yet he had been on this platform ten minutes before the train was due to arrive, walking

169

up and down, conscious of the utmost relief and pleasure because she was coming back. He had been so afraid she would not come; that he would never see her again. But here she was; just the same . . . the practical, sensible little person, with her grave smile and dark, expressive eyes. She wore the dark tailor-made and black felt hat in which she had gone away. And he noticed at once that she looked better – less strained – less unhappy.

'I came with the Daimler myself,' he exclaimed, 'because I sacked Bingham yesterday.'

'You did?' she said. 'Well, I'm glad. I can't help feeling he had a hand in my – my poor Grock's death.'

'I'm pretty well sure of it,' said Archer grimly. 'We had a few words yesterday, anyhow, and he was damned insolent, so I shot him out. I'm advertising for a new chauffeur-groom. Sandler and I are managing the stables between us for the time being. As a matter of fact, I've been making a clean sweep – booted out all the old staff. I hope you don't mind but I thought it best.'

Elizabeth gave a sigh of relief.

'Have you really? I can't tell you how glad I am. Has Mrs. Martlet gone too?'

'Yes. I had a row with her about the dog, and she annoyed me so much by the way she spoke, I told her she could quit. She got into a huff, packed her things, and marched out.'

'Heavens!' exclaimed Elizabeth. 'A general clearance all round.'

'We ought to have done it long ago,' said Archer. 'We allowed a nest of hornets to settle round our heads.'

They were driving along the Uckfield road now. The sun shone brilliantly. The gorse was in full bloom – great clumps of living gold all over the common. Elizabeth felt amazingly content, sitting beside Archer, listening to what he said. He had been working hard on her behalf in these few days she had been away. She felt as though it were years rather than days . . . that the tragedy of Lil's death and her funeral and Guy's temperamental sorrow were all contained in a nightmare from which she had awakened. She was amused and quite pleased because Archer spoke in the plural . . . talked of what 'we' should have done.

'He really is a dear,' she thought.

'I've got another woman in Mrs. Martlet's place,' Archer informed her proudly. 'Florence had a widowed sister in Tunbridge Wells who is an excellent cook according to her reference, and wanted a place of cook-housekeeper where she could have a small boy in the school holidays, and I didn't think that mattered. So I engaged her, and you can see what you think of her.'

'It sounds excellent, and I'm sure there'll be a much clearer atmosphere in the house without Mrs. Martlet. But I want you to arrange for her to have an annuity – as she was with Sir James and Lady Willington for so many years.'

'I will, if you wish it,' said Archer.

He thought that was typical of Elizabeth . . . so decent and sporting . . . after all the old woman had done.

Only when they drove past the front lawn and Elizabeth's gaze sped to the oak under which Grock lay buried was her feeling of brightness shadowed, and the tears sprang to her eyes.

'I wish dear old Grocky were here,' she said.

'Yes – that was a foul show,' said Archer. 'I'm extraordinarily sorry about it.'

A few minutes later, in the study, he told her that he had been round the village and made things hum with all the tenants of the estate. He had told them what he thought of them and condemned them wholesale.

'I fancy they're all a bit ashamed,' he said. 'And life should be brighter now, because Brownrigg's got a job in Crowborough and left Maplefield, and Hawkson and his wife are clearing off to some relatives in Yorkshire.'

'I'm glad I've come back,' she said simply.

She stood at the open windows, looking at the flower-filled garden. She had taken off her hat and coat. Archer looked at the straight young back with eyes grown amazingly tender.

'I'm extraordinarily glad you have,' he said. 'You will stay for a bit now?'

She turned to him.

'Yes, I'll stay.'

'I'm most awfully glad,' he said.

She could not fail to see the pleasure written all over his face now. Her pulses stirred. In a sudden panic she walked

171

over to the desk and bent over a bowl that was filled with dark red roses.

'How lovely these are,' she murmured.

'Yes, they are. . . . '

He wanted to ask about Lilian Maxwell's funeral and what was happening to Arlingham. All the time she had been in town he had thought of Arlingham, who had once been her lover. He had suffered for the first time in his life from the pangs of jealousy. Was that fellow coming back into her scheme of things?

She unconsciously satisfied his curiosity.

'By the way,' she said, 'I shall have guests here for the weekend. Guy – Mr. Arlingham – has been pretty upset by the death of his fiancée. He is coming down here to stay for a bit with his aunt, Lady Weylow.'

Archer's face fell. He stared at her gloomily.

'That will be nice for you,' he said.

'You must come up and dine on Saturday night,' she said. 'Make a fourth – do– if you will.'

'It's very kind of you,' said Archer. 'But I've promised to dine at the White House with the Kilwarnes.'

Elizabeth stiffened. So he was going to the Kilwarnes'? Going to dine with that woman . . . that blonde beauty, her flagrant disloyalty. How *could* he? How could he carry on an affair with a married woman . . . how could he even *like* Delia Kilwarne?

She was amazed to find that the thought of Archer dining with Mrs. Kilwarne on Saturday night plunged her into gloom. All the pleasure of coming back to 'Memories' evaporated.

'Perhaps you'll come along on Sunday, then, and lunch with us,' she said coldly.

'Thanks – it is nice of you – I'd like to,' he said.

He felt that for some reason she was annoyed with him. But why? Surely she didn't mind him dining at the White House? If she only knew it, he dreaded going. He had only seen Delia to speak to once in long weeks. And that was yesterday at the Golf Club, when she had pinned him for this dinner. He was afraid of Delia these days. But not of himself. There was only one woman on earth who could ever make his heart beat faster . . . and that was this cool, practical little person who stood before him, frowning her disapproval at him this very minute. Elizabeth Rowe. Oh, Lord, how he loved her. Yes . . . more than loved her. The knowledge was as bitter as it was splendid, because it seemed to him that never would he have the smallest right to tell her that he cared. He was only her estate-agent. He lived on the salary she paid him; in the cottage she allowed him. Except for a small private income derived from his savings, which were invested in gilt-edged securities, he had nothing. He had longed for her to come back to 'Memories', and now she had come. But he walked over the fields back to Quince-Tree Cottage feeling strangely depressed. He found her sudden coolness over the Kilwarne dinner inexplicable. It would never have entered Archer's head in a thousand years that Elizabeth was *jealous*.

But she was. She was jealous of the very thought of Delia Kilwarne and Archer.

She had come back to 'Memories' determined not to make a failure of things this time. But she felt very lonely at the big house that night. She missed Grock so badly. And she really hadn't the slightest desire to entertain Guy and Lady Weylow tomorrow when they came down to stay with her.

CHAPTER XX

GUY ARLINGHAM and his aunt arrived at 'Memories' and Elizabeth duly entertained them. Guy seemed to have recovered from his hysterical grief over the loss of Lilian with a rapidity which surprised Elizabeth. He was in one of his brightest moods, and bubbling over with wit and charm.

Lady Weylow – a stupid, over-dressed woman – was also in a good humour, and made herself extremely agreeable to Elizabeth. She understood her nephew. Her mind ran in a similar channel to his. Elizabeth Rowe had £10,000 a year and this estate, and, if she and Guy slipped back into their former state as an engaged couple, Caroline Weylow thought it would be an excellent plan.

She left them together at every possible moment, and when she was alone with Elizabeth, praised her nephew until Elizabeth felt sick of the sound of Guy's name.

The new cook-housekeeper, Mrs. Foster, and Florence were a great success in the house. Conditions were altogether more pleasant at 'Memories' for Elizabeth. But she was not happy. She found her thoughts constantly travelling to Archer, whom she had not seen since the day of her return. On Saturday night, when she dined with Guy and Lady Weylow – both of them making themselves charming to her – her mind would wander to the White House . . . to the thought of Archer and that hateful woman, Delia Kilwarne. Of course, he was up there, basking in her smiles. They would be carrying on their disgraceful intrigue. The picture of it infuriated Elizabeth. She told herself not to be a fool. What right had she got to concentrate on the thought of Mr. Hewitson, anyhow? And what did it matter to her if he were Delia Kilwarne's lover?

Yet she would keep remembering the strong, comforting clasp of his arms that night in the orchard . . . when they had stood by poor old Grock's dead body. And she could not resign herself to the thought that Archer was Mrs. Kilwarne's lover . . . that he held *her* . . . kissed *her* . . . and per-haps one day would run away with her. Let Charlie Kilwarne divorce her . . . marry her, himself.

'My thoughts are running away with me,' Elizabeth told herself grimly. 'I'm off my head . . . Archer Hewitson means nothing to me – except as a first-rate estate-agent – and I'd better pull myself together.'

After dinner, Caroline Weylow – setting herself in an arm-chair with a library book – suggested that the 'young people' should take a walk.

'Such a lovely moonlight night – too beautiful to stay in,' she gushed.

Guy looked at Elizabeth.

'Do come out with me, will you, Lizbeth?' he asked eagerly.

She forced her thoughts away from Archer and Mrs. Kil-warne, and accepted this invitation.

'Yes, I'll come. I don't mind.'

Guy thought she was rather cold and off-hand with him. The sooner he got back to the old, intimate terms the better. With some satisfaction he recalled the fact that once upon a time that straight, slim little body trembled in his arms, and that small, determined mouth had responded passionately to his kisses. Oh, yes, there was hidden fire in Elizabeth. Fool that he had been to ever let it lie down!

He took her arm and strolled with her into the garden. It was warm and windless. She had slipped a short silver coat over her evening dress – a long, graceful dress of orange chiffon.

'You're looking very charming tonight, little Lizbeth,' murmured Guy, pressing her arm.

'Am I?' she said absently.

'I like you in bright colours. This orange thing suits you. Do you remember that red dress of yours which I used to love?'

'M'm,' she said.

She did remember . . . and she remembered the anguished tears she had shed when she had packed it, soon after their broken engagement, how her heart had ached because she would never wear it again especially for him. Heavens, what a lot of water had rolled under the bridge since then! How she had changed! His admiration left her unmoved. She

175

even felt shocked because he flattered her so soon after Lilian's death and burial. And she didn't care in the least whether he thought her orange dress suited her or not.

But she would have liked Archer to see her in this dress. And she wondered what Delia Kilwarne was wearing. She would look beautiful, of course. She, Elizabeth, couldn't begin to vie with Mrs. Kilwarne as a beauty.

'I hate Mrs. Kilwarne,' she thought fiercely.

Somehow, half consciously, she led Guy down the moonlit drive where the great chestnuts proudly bore their white candles in full bloom . . . and along the white road . . . past Quince-Tree Cottage.

'This is a quaint little place,' said Guy, stopping by the gate. 'Look at the quince-tree. A lot of fruit coming. Who lives here? Does it belong to you?'

'It's on my estate, yes. It's Mr. Hewitson's cottage.'

'Oh – that fellow,' said Guy.

Annoyed, Elizabeth drew her arm away from him. Her gaze sped to one of the upper casements. A light was glowing through the drawn chintz curtains. She supposed that was Duke's room. There was a light in the kitchen as well.

Then the front door opened. Micky emerged, scampering to the gate and barking furiously.

Elizabeth's eyes softened. She stooped and held out a hand.

'Hello, little Mick,' she said.

The terrier recognised a friend and stopped barking. He licked her fingers and allowed her to stroke him. Guy stood by with a supercilious expression on his face. He found Elizabeth's passionate love for animals very trying.

Then a man's figure emerged from the hall and came out into the tiny front garden. Dukes – Archer's man – in his green baize apron.

'Micky – come on, old fellow – your dinner –' he began. Then paused as he saw the two figures by the gate. He touched his forehead when he recognised Elizabeth. He liked Miss Rowe. She always had a pleasant word for him when he saw her.

'Good evening, miss,' he said.

'Oh, good evening, Dukes,' said Elizabeth, somewhat embarrassed. 'I – we were just passing – I had to stop to pat Micky. How are you, Dukes?'

176

'I'm very well, thank you, miss. But you know, miss, Mr. Hewitson is laid up.'

'Mr. Hewitson laid up? You mean he's ill?' said Elizabeth quickly.

'Come on, my dear,' murmured Guy, scowling in the darkness.

'Just a moment, Guy,' she said. She looked at Dukes.

'You mean he's in bed?' she added.

'Yes, miss. He was took queer this afternoon.'

'But what with?'

'One of them malaria headaches he used to get when he first come back from West Africa. He hasn't had one for a very long time, but when he do get them he can't do nothing.'

Elizabeth looked up at the light in the upper casements. So that was Archer's bedroom, and he was ill in bed. He wasn't at the White House, basking in Mrs. Kilwarne's smiles, after all. A strange thrill of relief ran through Elizabeth. But she was, incidentally, worried about Archer.

'Is he bad, Dukes?' she inquired.

Guy Arlingham, bored and annoyed that Elizabeth should be showing this interest in her estate-agent, sighed loudly to express his disapproval.

'He's pretty bad, miss. When he gets took like this he has such pains in his head he can't hardly move. He takes half a bottle of aspirin, so far as I can see.'

'Half a bottle of aspirin!' repeated Elizabeth. 'Good heavens – but he mustn't – he'll kill himself!'

'It doesn't seem to hurt him,' said Dukes, his lugubrious face breaking into a smile. 'He generally takes a lot when he gets like this.'

'Well, tell him how sorry I am,' said Elizabeth. 'I'll come along in the morning and see how he is.'

'Thank you, miss. Good night,' said Dukes.

'Good night,' she said.

She walked away with Guy, conscious that she would have liked very much to go up to Archer's room and make sure he was all right – had everything he wanted. Dukes was an excellent servant, but would he make a good sick-nurse? That was the question. And Elizabeth knew – because Archer had once told her – that those terrible headaches which were a legacy from the malaria he had contracted in West

Africa laid him very low for a few days and drove him crazy with pain.

'It seems to me that a great deal of fuss is being made over your estate-agent's headaches,' said Guy in a stuffy voice as they walked back across the fields.

Elizabeth resented his tone.

'Not at all. Mr. Hewitson is ill – he has been out in West Africa, and these bad bouts of fever are the result. They aren't ordinary headaches at all.'

'Oh, well, he can look after himself, surely,' said Guy.

'I daresay,' said Elizabeth coldly.

Guy inwardly cursed. He didn't at all like Elizabeth's tone and manner. For an instant he lost control – forgot that he was supposed to be sorrowing for the unfortunate Lilian whose funeral he had attended a few days ago.

'Lizbeth – don't you care a damn about me any more?' he broke out. 'You're being frightfully stuffy with me.'

She felt her face grow hot, and shot him a quick nervous look. She could see only too plainly in the bright moonlight what lay in his eyes. She was conscious of being suddenly very shocked.

'Guy – really – ' she began.

He caught her hand and carried it to his lips.

'Lizbeth – forgive me – but I can't forget how much we used to mean to each other.'

Then she knew, beyond all doubt, that she no longer loved this man – that she even disliked him. She drew her fingers away.

'Guy – you and I agreed to break our engagement – months ago. There's no question of our – our meaning anything to each other – in that way!'

He saw that he had blundered. His forehead felt wet. He tried to cover up his mistake.

'I – you don't understand – '

'Perhaps I don't,' she broke in coldly. 'Let's talk about something else, anyhow.'

But there was a strained silence between them until they reached the house. And then Elizabeth announced at once that she was tired, said good night to Lady Weylow and Guy, and retired to her room.

Arlingham – in a blazing temper – told his aunt that she could pack her things in the morning.

'My dear Guy – why ever – '

'Because the sooner I get out of this house the better,' he said furiously. 'Elizabeth doesn't care a damn for me any more, and I can't stand it.'

'But surely, dear – '

'My dear Aunt Caroline, take it from me, she's suddenly become sentimental about that prosy, insufferable estate-agent fellow – Archer Hewitson. It's the finish to any hope of my fixing things up with Elizabeth again.'

Lady Weylow removed the horn-rimmed glasses she was wearing, closed her library book with a snap, and snorted at her nephew.

'Then you've been an idiot, my dear Guy.'

'Thanks,' he said, white-lipped. 'You may be right, but telling me so won't help matters. Good night.'

Up in her bedroom, Elizabeth stood at one of the open windows and stared over the starlit garden; over the fields in the direction of Quince-Tree Cottage. Through the trees she could just discern a tiny light glimmering. It was the light from his bedroom. And in that room Archer lay in bed, blind and sick with one of those ghastly headaches which seemed to completely shatter him. She knew that he had come to live down here in the country because he had hoped to cure himself of them. Poor Archer. Somehow she hated to think of him lying there in pain with nobody to look after him except Dukes who would not really be capable of nursing a sick man.

'I must go and see him first thing tomorrow,' she thought.

Then she remembered the amazing behaviour of Guy to-night. She found herself despising him. It *was* despicable . . . to behave like that . . . to try and revive their old intimacy . . . and poor little Lilian had lain in her grave less than a week.

Elizabeth knew that she could never like Guy again. She knew, too, that she had wasted months of passionate devotion upon him during their engagement . . . and afterwards, days and weeks of grief and pain of which he was totally unworthy.

'Dear old Sir James was quite right,' she told herself, looking up at the starry sky. ' "Give crowns and pounds and guineas, but not your heart away." '

But she had a swift mental vision of herself in Archer

Hewitson's arms . . . weeping for poor Grock. She remembered how her pulse-beats had quickened when she saw him waiting for her on Crowborough station yesterday. It struck her suddenly and forcibly that if she were not very careful she would be ignoring Sir James's advice. She would be flinging away her freedom of thought, of body, of action . . . by giving her heart away a second time.

'Idiot, Elizabeth,' she said to herself derisively. 'You're thinking too much about Archer Hewitson. Cut it out, my girl!'

Excellent advice which she found herself quite unable to take. And that was probably because deep down inside her Elizabeth Rowe did not want to take it.

CHAPTER XXI

THAT Sunday morning, Archer Hewitson dragged himself downstairs, despite Dukes's attempt to persuade him to remain in bed.

'I can't stay in bed – I hate it,' he said. 'And it's too hot up there with that low ceiling. I shall feel better with more fresh air.'

He ate no breakfast to speak of. And later he sat in his favourite armchair in the sitting-room, which was cool compared with the upper rooms of the little cottage. It was going to be another hot, summer's day, but the windows of the sitting-room faced west and the sun had not got round to it yet.

Archer still had a bad headache. He felt weak and depressed from too much aspirin. He looked a wreck. He had not bothered to put on a collar. He did not expect visitors. He wore a pair of old flannel bags and an ancient cricket shirt, open at the neck. Then Dukes disconcerted him by announcing that Miss Rowe and a gentleman had called at the cottage last night and Miss Rowe had said she was coming up to see him this morning.

'Oh, Lord,' said Archer. 'Then I'll have to go up and put on a collar.'

Nevertheless, he felt suddenly better. It was nice of Elizabeth to worry about him.

'I told her you was took bad, sir,' said Dukes.

'You say she called here with a gentleman?'

'Well, not exactly called, sir, but I went out to call Micky in to his dinner and they was there outside the gate a-talking to Micky.'

As the manservant departed, Archer rose wearily to his feet, with a hand to his aching head. He must make an effort to dress if Elizabeth was coming. The 'gentleman' was Arlingham, of course. He had forgotten for a moment that

Elizabeth's one-time fiancé was up at 'Memories' being consoled for the death of Lilian Maxwell.

'They're certain to come together again,' Archer reflected. 'Oh, damn!'

Yet what difference could it possibly make to him, argued his inner self. Elizabeth didn't mean so much to him as all that. Did she?

He strolled into the garden for a breath of fresh air. Micky capered round him begging for a walk.

'Not just now, old man,' said Archer. 'I feel too rotten for walks. . . . ' He stooped to pat the terrier, then looked up and saw a two-seater coupé drive up to the gate. His heart sank. Delia Kilwarne. How could he escape? He turned to fly, too late. She had seen him and called:

'Archie!'

He was caught. He stood still, and she switched off the engine and walked quickly down the flagged path toward him. She looked exceedingly attractive in a thin flowered voile dress, with a pale pink linen cap on her fair head, and loose scarf to match knotted about her throat. She was a picture for a summer's morning. But her beauty left Archer unmoved. He felt nothing but irritation when she reached his side and held out her hand.

'Archie – my dear – how are you? When you didn't come up last night, and Dukes said you were ill, I was frightfully worried.'

'Thanks. I'm quite all right this morning,' he said.

'Are you sure? You look awfully pale.'

'No – I'm quite fit again,' he lied.

'I had to see you. May I come in?'

He was forced to be courteous. He said:

'Of course, Delia. Do.'

But his head was splitting and he didn't feel at all like talking to Delia Kilwarne. His dilapidated clothes and lack of a collar worried him a little, but he told himself she would have to put up with it.

Delia would have put up with anything. She was in love – badly in love – and Archer's persistent refusals to go up to her house, and the way in which he had ignored her lately, had been sending her crazy. She had thought he really would dine up at the White House last night, and when he didn't come she had been sure his illness had been only an excuse.

This morning, not caring what Charlie thought, she had put on her newest, prettiest summer clothes and come down to Quince-Tree Cottage, determined to see Archer. When she was standing before him in the sitting-room she saw that he looked ill, and was relieved that he had not deliberately avoided dining with her. She looked hungrily up at the man's thin, brown face and felt a devastating longing to break the ice between them.

She swept off her hat and ran a hand over the fair, shining waves of hair. Then she held out both her hands.

'Archie,' she said huskily, 'why have you been so unkind to me lately? I can't stand it any more. You've hurt me badly – you don't know how badly!'

Archer, rooted to the spot with embarrassment, stared at her. He felt a fool, and was sure he looked it. To have a woman fling herself at him like this was so distasteful – it was so shaming. He was ashamed – for her. And he was quite unstirred by her beauty and the frank passion in her eyes.

'Delia,' he said, 'hadn't we better leave things as they are? I mean – leave it that we *don't* see a lot of each other?'

'But why?' she asked, her face burning. 'Don't you want to see me any more, Archie? We used to be good pals.'

'Pals – yes.'

'But you don't like me – more than that?'

'I'm frightfully sorry, Delia, but I must be frank. I'm afraid I – don't.'

'I see,' she said. She swallowed hard. Her hands clenched and unclenched at her sides. 'Oh, my *God!*' she added, and then sat down and hid her face in her hands.

Archer was horrified and distressed. He really had no idea how to deal with this situation. He only knew that he found it intolerable and wanted to get Delia away – put an immediate end to a scene which could only be humiliating for her and painful to him.

'Delia – look here – ' he began.

'Oh, you don't seem to understand,' she broke in passionately, lifting a face that was flushed and wet with tears. 'I've been in love with you for months – yes, I'm not ashamed to say so, Archie. I have – I am!'

'But, good heavens – you're married!'

'Charlie and I don't get on – he bores me to tears – I bore him.'

'That isn't true – Charlie's devoted to you.'

'Don't let's discuss Charlie. I suppose it's possible for a married woman to realise that she's made a mistake and that she's fallen in love with someone else, isn't it? It's done every day,' said Delia, with an hysterical laugh.

Archer looked away from her.

'Charlie's a good sort, and a pal of mine.'

She put out a hand and caught one of his.

'Do you mean – it's because of him – you don't – you can't – '

'No, no – don't mistake me,' he interrupted, flushing. 'I'm not in love with you, Delia. That's the brutal truth. But I'm not. And I don't want an affair with a married woman, anyhow.'

Crushed and defeated, she sat there, wondering whether she loved or hated him.

'I didn't think you'd be – such a prig.'

'Call it priggish, if you like. But, anyhow, I don't happen to be in love with you,' he said, sick of the whole affair.

Delia stood up. She swallowed hard.

'Perhaps,' she said, with a miserable laugh, 'you're in love with Elizabeth Rowe.'

Archer's face went scarlet. He had never, for a single instant, imagined that any outsider guessed that he was in love with Elizabeth. But this jealous, thwarted woman flung the idea at him and he knew it for the truth. He said coldly:

'I shouldn't say things like that, Delia. They won't help. Do forgive me if I . . .'

'You want me to go. Very well.'

She put on her hat and scarf. He saw that she was trembling. And suddenly, being a kind-hearted man, he was sorry for her humiliation.

'Forget this, Delia,' he said. 'I promise I will. Wipe it right out. I know you didn't mean it.'

But she didn't answer him. She walked past him with a flushed, stormy face, into the garden. He followed awkwardly, conscious that the pain in his head was worse. With eyes half shut he saw Delia climb into her car and drive away. He kicked his toe fiercely against an unoffending stone on the pathway.

'Damn!' he said. 'What a rotten thing to have happened!'

He could hear the echo of Delia's angry, resentful voice: *'Perhaps you're in love with Elizabeth Rowe.'*

His eyes, narrowed with pain, wandered over the fields. And suddenly he saw a small figure in riding-breeches; a very familiar little figure; hatless; coatless; the sleeves of a silk shirt fluttering in the breeze. And his heart missed a beat. That was Elizabeth. What was she doing? Surely, she was walking away from the cottage. Had she come down; seen Delia's car, and gone away again?

Archie never afterwards knew what it was that induced him to race after that small, retreating figure. But he did. Just as he was – in the old flannel bags and cricket shirt – and with an untidy head – he ran across the road – vaulted over the gate and followed Elizabeth. The pain in his head was forgotten. Micky followed, delighted at the unexpected race.

Elizabeth had reached half-way across the meadow when she heard a scampering and rustling behind her, turned and saw Micky. He had reached her first, and stood with his red tongue hanging out, panting joyously. She then saw Archer running toward her.

She stood still. She did not know what she felt about it. She only knew that five minutes ago, when she had arrived at Quince-Tree Cottage to see Delia Kilwarne's car outside the gate and the figure of Delia visible through the open windows of the sitting-room, she had known what it was to be frantically, intensely jealous – for the first time in her life.

She had tried to convince herself that there was not a serious affair between Archer and Mrs. Kilwarne. But now, what could she believe? Archer was ill, and the woman dashed down there to see him – to be with him. Then Elizabeth, realising that she, too, had 'dashed down' to see Archer, had felt furious with herself.

'I don't care whether the man's ill or well,' she told herself angrily. And, without calling at the cottage, she started to walk back over the fields.

Archer reached her. She looked up at him coldly. He was flushed with running. She did not notice how ill he really looked.

'Good morning,' she said in a formal voice.

Now that he had reached her, he did not know what to say or how to explain the crazy fashion in which he had raced over the fields to her. He stammered:

'I – you – Dukes said you were kind enough to say you were coming to see me this morning – surely you –'

'Oh, yes,' she finished for him casually. 'I did intend to look in. I've just been riding, and I strolled over here to look you up and see if you were better. Then I saw you had a visitor.'

'Oh, *blast* Delia Kilwarne!' he thought.

Aloud he said:

'I – Mrs. Kilwarne came to inquire. I – I'm all right again, thanks.'

'Good,' she said.

But now his flush had faded, she saw, with an uneasy feeling, that he was a very bad colour. His eyes looked closed up. Was he still in bad pain? How absurdly young he looked in those old grey bags, with no collar, and his dark, ruffled hair.

'It's a glorious morning, isn't it?' said Archer stupidly.

'Lovely,' she said. 'And oh, by the way – the dinner up at "Memories" tonight – you remember I asked you to come up – is off.'

'My guests are leaving suddenly. Lady Weylow said she had a telephone call from town calling her home. And Guy – Mr. Arlingham is going with her.'

'I see,' said Archer.

He tried to concentrate on what she was saying. But the sunlit fields were spinning round him in a crazy way. The pain in his head was so excruciating that he could not bear it. Elizabeth's severe little face grew hazy. His heart was pounding, pounding. He wondered, in horror, if he were going to faint. He remembered, out in Africa, fainting one morning when he had one of those bad heads and had tried to attend to his job.

What was Elizabeth saying? Something about the hot water system at 'Memories'. She wanted him to order something. He didn't know what. The green fields and blue skies seemed to be turning upside down in the strangest fashion. Then he heard Elizabeth cry out:

'Mr. Hewitson!'

He awoke, quite shortly afterwards, to find himself lying on the grass with his head in her lap. And now she was saying:

'Archer ... '

Yes, he was positive she was calling him Archer. And her voice was full of anxiety. She was saying: 'Archer, oh, oh, Archer, are you all right?'

He closed his eyes and lay still. The world was still dark and strange to him, and it was very pleasant lying there with her lap for a pillow. He could feel soft little fingers stroking his hair, his forehead.

Elizabeth – generally so practical, so calm in an emergency – felt positively frightened when her estate-agent suddenly toppled over and fainted like that in the field. He must be very ill – to faint in this fashion.

Scarcely knowing that she did so, she used his Christian name:

'Archer – Archer – are you all right?'

He opened his eyes.

'Elizabeth,' he whispered.

'Yes, I'm here,' she said, bending over him, and there was a perfect fever of anxiety in the prosaic Elizabeth, who hated any exhibition of emotion or sentiment. 'You're all right, aren't you?'

'All right,' he nodded. 'So – stupid – fainting – like that. It's my damned head – been very bad – oughtn't to have got up really.'

'I'll get some water. Lie still – I'll run back to the cottage – call Dukes.'

'No, don't. I hate a fuss. . . . ' Archer was himself again. 'Look here – if you don't mind – can I take your arm – we'll walk back to the cottage. I'll be all right.'

She stood up and helped him to his feet. She took his arm and slung it around her shoulders.

'Like that. Lean on me,' she said.

'You're a brick,' he said. 'I'm so sorry.'

'You gave me an awful scare,' she said.

'Absurd of me to have done it.'

In silence, then, slowly, they walked across the fields, back to the cottage. He leaned one arm about the slim young shoulders. She had slipped the other hand about his waist. And Archer Hewitson found himself wishing, ridiculously, that they could go on walking like this for miles and miles.

They reached the cottage. In the sitting room, Elizabeth insisted that he lie down on the sofa. She was practical and

187

business-like again. She felt his pulse; found it much too fast; told him that he had a temperature and that he must go to bed at once.

'No – it isn't a temperature,' he said. 'I'm quite normal really. It's my confounded head. I'll take some more aspirin, then I'll be all right.'

'You mustn't take so much aspirin,' she said. 'It isn't good for you.'

'I always do,' he said.

'You musn't,' she admonished.

She had found an overcoat hanging up in the hall, and laid it over him.

'Keep warm,' she said. 'And as soon as you feel fit enough – go back to bed, do.'

He looked up at her. He felt much better. And he liked to lie there with her standing beside him, ordering him about, her grave brown eyes so full of solicitude. He knew that Delia Kilwarne had expressed the truth. He was in love with Elizabeth – completely and hopelessly in love with her.

'I'm all right,' he said. 'I shan't go back to bed.'

'You ought to – really.'

'I get so bored in bed, and it's so hot upstairs.'

'But you'll get better all the sooner,' she argued.

'I shan't go away till I've seen you up. Look here – I'll get Dukes to give you an arm. . . . '

But Archer did not want Dukes to come in and spoil a very precious moment; the memory of one moment, anyhow, when Elizabeth cared whether he lived or died. He pushed the coat off his feet and stood up. He loved her for arguing with him . . . protesting with him. He smiled down at her and said:

'I'll go up – now – if you want me to.'

She could tell that his head still hurt him – from the wry way his lips twisted into that smile. She wanted to help him – look after him. He was a great baby– unable to look after himself – for all his six foot one of height and his broad shoulders.

'You ought to have a doctor,' she said.

'No – I never have one. I know how to cure myself.'

'Well, do take care . . . I'd better go. . . . '

He looked through half-shut eyes at the slim, boyish

figure in the riding-kit; the back of the dark, cropped head which had become so amazingly dear to him. And suddenly he was sunk in the depths of depression. He didn't want her to go. He had no right to ask her to stay. He flopped weakly into a chair and supported his aching head between his hands.

At the door, Elizabeth turned and looked back. At the sight of him sitting there in that dejected way, the queerest sensation shot through her – the feeling that she could not leave him now that he was sick; hadn't the slightest desire to go back to 'Memories' and, once Guy and his aunt departed, spend the rest of the day alone.

She suddenly walked to Archer's side and put a hand on his shoulder.

'I'll stay,' she said, 'if you'd like me to.'

Then he looked up at her, and forgot everything except that he loved her and couldn't bear her to go.

'Yes, do stay,' he said. 'Do . . . oh, *Elizabeth!*'

And after that she found herself kneeling in front of the chair and his arms went round her and held her as though he could, in truth, never let her go again. He kissed the top of the small, dark head passionately; covered it with kisses. He kept murmuring:

'Elizabeth . . . oh, Elizabeth!'

She said nothing, but reached up an arm, shyly, and put it round his neck. Her heart was galloping at the maddest rate, and she was saying to herself: 'Idiot . . . you've done just what Sir James warned you against – just what you said you'd never do again. You're in love . . . you're going to give your heart away for somebody to break all over again. . . . '

Yet it seemed to her in that moment that her heart would have broken if she hadn't felt Archer's arms around her and known the heavenly intimacy of that embrace.

'I love you,' he said over and over again. 'I love you. I love you!'

She leaned against him with a great sigh.

'I may be crazy, but I'm afraid I love you, Archer,' she said in a small voice.

He looked at her upraised face and thought he had never seen anything so beautiful as Elizabeth's eyes, shining up at him.

'Oh, my dear!' he said. 'I have no right . . . '

189

'Her expression changed. She stiffened in his arms.

'You mean – Mrs. Kilwarne –'

'*God,* no!' he broke in, shocked. 'Mrs. Kilwarne doesn't come into it.'

'You don't care for her? I thought –'

'I've never cared for her. There's nothing between Delia Kilwarne and me, Elizabeth.'

'Then why – ?'

'Oh, my dear, she's been a little foolish, but I'm sure she doesn't mean it and I've been spending my days trying to avoid her.'

Elizabeth felt absurdly thankful for those few words.

'I'm glad,' she said.

He looked down at her and then hugged her close.

'You haven't been worrying about Mrs. Kilwarne and me. . . .'

'Certainly not,' said Elizabeth, with crimson cheeks, and tried to get up from that position on her knees before him. But Archer held her down.

'Elizabeth,' he said in a hushed voice, 'do you like me a little bit?'

'A little!' Her voice broke. 'Much too much.'

'Oh, my dear,' he said. 'How wonderful! It's the most wonderful thing that's ever happened to me. I adore you, Elizabeth. I want more than anything else on earth to kiss you. But I've only kissed the top of your head so far, and I don't think I ought to do anything else.'

'Why?'

'My dear – you're the mistress of "Memories" and I'm your estate-agent, and –'

'What's that got to do with it?'

'Everything.'

'But what?'

'You must realise – everything. How can I, without a bean, possibly ask you to marry? If you were me and I were you – I'd do it.'

Elizabeth looked up at him – her heart-beats almost hurting her – conscious that she was thrilled through and through. She loved this man, and wanted him more than she had ever begun to love or want Guy Arlingham.

'Archer,' she said sternly, 'if you love me and I love you, the question of my position and money isn't going to come

190

into it. Sir James was devoted to you. There is nothing he would have liked better than to see you managing this estate hand in hand with me. And if you don't propose to me this minute, I shall be very insulted, and I shall walk out of Quince-Tree Cottage and never see you again.'

'Don't do that,' he said. 'Don't do that.'

'I shall – if you don't ask me to marry you, Archer Hewitson. And for the second time I shall feel that Maplefield has driven me away.'

'Oh, my darling,' he groaned, and he pulled her close to him and kissed her hair again.

'Perhaps,' said Elizabeth with a wildly racing heart, 'this isn't at all good for you – you're ill.'

'I'm well. My headache has gone. I'm absolutely well again.'

'Then kiss me,' said Elizabeth brazenly, and lifted her lips and closed her eyes.

Against all his scruples, he couldn't do anything but kiss that sweet, brave mouth which was offered to him. And during that kiss, which made her so completely his, he knew that life would never be the same again – without Elizabeth.

'Darling,' he said later, when they were calmer, and she sat with her arms about his waist and his about her, 'darling, why on earth do you like me?'

'Heaven knows,' she said, laughing. 'You're a most unattractive man, Archer Hewitson, and with my beauty and fascination I might have done so much better, mightn't I?'

'Mick! did you hear that?' said Archer. He turned to his Cairn, who lay on the hearthrug, licking his paws and regarding with some curiosity the strange sight of his master with a woman in his arms. However, Micky liked this particular woman, so he didn't object.

'Micky knows how horrid you are,' continued Elizabeth, and suddenly lifted one of Archer's hands and put her warm lips against it, which was a thing she had never before done with any man in her life – even Guy. So she knew that what she had never been able to give to Guy she could give to Archer. She could break through all reserves for this, the man of her heart. She could tell him in a thousand different ways that she loved him, and how much, and was no longer inarticulate.

'Sweetheart,' said Archer gravely, 'how can I marry you

– what right have I got to take you and all that you have?'

'Begin that again and it will annoy me.'

'But can't you see – '

'I do see. But if you don't marry me, Archer Hewitson, I shall merely sell "Memories" to the highest bidder – make all my money over to charities – and then sit down and die.'

'Oh, my darling,' he said, and caught her close to his heart. 'My darling, you mustn't do that.'

'Quite so,' said Elizabeth contentedly, her cheek against his. 'Sir James would hate that to happen. So we shall manage the estate together – really together – my funny old agent.'

'Yes,' he said. 'A million times yes, if you really want me to. I adore you.'

'And when I first came here, you hated me.'

'No, I didn't, but I was afraid – '

'Of what?'

'Well – worried – because I thought Sir James had got into the hands of a vamp.'

'H'm,' said Elisabeth, her eyes twinkling. 'And you were terrified you'd get into the hands of the vamp too. Poor dear – your worst fears have been realised. That's exactly what has happened.'

'Praise the Lord,' said Archer piously.

For a moment, in silence, they clung to one another. Over Archer's shoulder Elizabeth looked out of the casements, over the sunlit fields toward 'Memories'. A sudden overwhelming joy of life, of love for her possessions, flooded her being. She had Archer now . . . Archer and this marvellous, satisfying love . . . to make her home a heaven . . . a place which she would never want to leave.

Her thoughts turned, inevitably, to Grock . . . the beloved pet whom she had lost so tragically and who lay out there under the oak-tree in his quiet grave. It was Grock's death which had first brought her close to Archer. The tears suddenly filled her eyes.

'Dear old Grock,' she thought. 'You'd be glad . . . . if you could see how happy I am now. You liked him. You never liked Guy – but you liked Archer. And oh, Grocky, so do I, old man – so do I!'

THE END